To Find Him
and Love Him Again

(Volume One)

Also by this author
Scrap Metal
Brothers Of The Wild North Sea
The Salisbury Key
and many more

To Find Him and Love Him Again

(Volume One)

Harper Fox

FoxTales

Author's Note:

*This book was first published in serial form
via the author's Patreon. She is, and will always remain,
deeply grateful for the support she received there,
and to all her readers wherever they are
who have loved Tyack & Frayne.*

FoxTales Publications
www.harperfox.net

To Find Him and Love Him Again
(Volume One)
Copyright © 2020 by Harper Fox
ISBN 978-1-910224-34-2

Cover art by Harper Fox

Chapter One
Launceston—Just Another Gig

The ghosts of Beaumont Hall were playful, cooperative as if paid per apparition by the Cornish tourist board. Lee's team had caught shadows in the cellar, uncanny laughter bouncing off the old kitchen walls. Privately, Lee had sat down with the lovelorn maid in the attic, and agreed with her that two hundred years were long enough to stare out to sea after faithless Johnny's mast. *Did he die*, she'd asked him, in wingbeat flutters inside his head, the pomander scent of her muslins poignant in the air.

Well, yes, Peg. It's been two hundred years.

No, stoopid. On that voyage?

Oh. No, he never got his sea legs, and he skipped overboard at Falmouth when the captain put in for supplies. If it helps, he wasn't faithless after all. He was making his way home across Wheal Plenty moors when he fell down a mineshaft in the dark.

That would be just his rotten luck, then. Yes, it helps.

Scrambling out of the mineshaft, where he'd allowed himself—stoopid indeed—to tumble to the depths with luckless

Johnny, having to confirm that the lad had broken his neck and died straight away, in case Peg wanted to know, in case any one of the thousands of mums, friends, siblings and kids wanted to know—*did he die easy, Mr Tyack? Did he suffer, was he scared, was he all alone*—Lee had blinked at her. At the empty, sunny space she'd occupied. "What helps?"

Knowing he loved me, of course.

A pomander-scented handkerchief had drifted down out of nowhere into his lap, and Lee had gone back to work. There was a particular Beaumont tale about a grumpy old colonel who'd passed his final years carving out walking sticks in a parlour room overlooking the gardens. Very fussy, the old man had become, insisting that his canes be set in a rack in strict order of size. After his death, if anyone moved them, he'd rattle them in his wrath, loud enough to wake the entire house.

If Lee let himself follow the colonel, as he'd followed poor Johnny Tremaine, he'd have to know that a soldier's brave soul had soured in this room, eaten up with loneliness and pain. Lee would have to know that leaving a few sticks in the right place was a damn small kindness to bestow, and then he would have to march out of Beaumont, overturning camera props and lighting frames with a biblical fervour more suited to his dog-collared brother-in-law. Then his series finale would never get made, and the hard work of all the brave souls around him in this time and place would go to waste. He didn't *have* to know anything at all. His control was good, his home life with his husband and his little girl such a sanctuary, that he could choose what he saw. It was just that lately, over and over again, he'd been choosing wrong.

The parlour was full of movement and life. Gratefully Lee stepped into it. Anna and Jack, once his whole crew, now proudly headed up a dozen production staff. Cables snaked across the Turkish carpets. The curtains had been artfully drawn to minimise glare whilst keeping the lovely effects of sunlight on oil paintings and the colonel's hand-carved oakwood rack. *Spirits of Cornwall* was a hit. Lee had received an offer to lift the whole series from the uncertain internet world and into the hallowed realms of the BBC. A set piece about the colonel and his canes would round out the series nicely, especially if Lee could persuade the old chap to a broad-daylight rattle or two. *What about it, Colonel Henry*, he asked the bright air unhappily, as certain of the name as of his own. *I'm sorry. We'll clear off after this and leave you in peace, I swear.*

Well, since it's you. Since you cleared out that wretched girl from my garret at long last.

I didn't... evict her, sir. She wanted to go.

I'm not complaining, lad. Just be careful what you wish for, that's all.

The usual warning. Lee would have loved to take it. He was tired, despite Chy Lowen and his life there, despite Tamsyn and Gid. He felt sick. Would it be possible, just this once, to switch off the lights, stand down the dozen and go home?

Anna whipped round from a final adjustment of the roses in their great marble vase. She strode across the room to meet him. As far as the lights went, Jack could've turned off his ten-K LEDs in favour of her smile. "Isn't this great?" she demanded, gesturing around the room. "Look how the pillars frame that alcove. We'll have you standing there while you tell the story about the colonel and his sticks, I think. There's something poetic about the space—not exactly solemn, but not light-hearted either. Just right for your piece." She fell silent, focussing upon him as if for a close-up shot. Her smile faded out. She'd worked with Lee for years, and had quietly worshipped the ground he trod since the now-famous footage he'd got for her in the fogou beneath Drift church. "What's up, love? Have we worked your whammy too hard?"

"Not likely. You've only got to look at a wall in here for something to walk through it. You hardly need me at all."

"The owner said the place was quiet as the grave until you got here. The ghosts couldn't wait to meet you." Something in her own choice of words made her expression shadow. "Have you got a vision coming on? Do you want me to call Gid?"

Yes. Call him. Let him come blazing up in the patrol truck, sweep me off my feet and carry me home. Sternly he pushed the fantasy aside. "I'm fine. I like your pillars and the poetic alcove. We'll do the back story there. Did Jack get his exterior shots?"

"Well, yes and no. The gardens are perfect for the era, but none of our ghosts had to cope with Lee Tyack-Frayne fans popping out of the bushes to get a glimpse of their hero."

"Don't be daft. They're here for the show, not me."

"Right. That's why they're carrying *I heart Lee* placards. If you go to the window right now you can see for yourself."

Lee did as she suggested. He hardly knew why: had no desire to see his name up in marker-pen lights. But Launceston was lovely at this time of year, the hawthorn snowdrifts of May giving way to deep green summer, mantling oaks in full leaf-burst all the way from the hilltop mansion to the river and over the border into Devon, just visible from this breathtaking vantage point. The famous Beaumont roses filled the air with citrus, spice and musk, old-breed blossoms drooping sleepily under their own weight. He leaned his elbows on the open frame.

Yes, there was one beanie-clad head peering over the garden wall. Crowded into the gateway behind a wrought-iron door, a clutch of eager faces. They brightened as Lee offered a diffident wave, and some clown wolf-whistled. One placard was visible, though Lee couldn't make out the lettering from here. "See?" Anna said, proudly as if she'd invented him. "You're a star."

10

Shaking his head, Lee began to duck back in. Then he froze, one hand on the sill. There in the gateway—half-hidden behind the placard, serious as an undertaker—was Sergeant Rufus Pendower.

Not for the first time, either. Lee retreated back into the room, dismay chilling him. This was the downside of working locations this deep into eastern Cornwall. Rufus, on secondment to the Devon squad, had found his way to the previous three. Always in uniform, so he must be finding a way to extend his lunch breaks or make business for himself nearby. He'd never tried to speak to Lee, and never hung around. A backward glance showed only the cluster of fans: already he was gone. "Shit," Lee whispered, and followed Anna's beckoning gesture back across the room, glad of the distraction. "Much more of this and I'll need my own bouncer. Okay, are we ready to shoot?"

"Just about. There's one more thing about these canes the colonel made, Lee. This is the best part of all—really creepy. It seems one of them's a flute, or at least he carved a flute and fitted it into the end of one of the sticks. Nobody wants to find out which one it is, because the family legend is that if anyone hears it, somebody who loves them will die."

"Oh, that's just great."

She glanced at him in concern. "But... it *is* great, isn't it? Just the kind of thing our viewers like."

It was. Just the kind of thing Lee liked too, generally speaking—a banshee wail or the howl of a local Black Dog, all good audio backdrop for his tales of the haunted West. He made a strong effort and pulled himself together. "It's perfect. We'll have post-production fill in something suitably eerie on a synth."

"Cool. We'll get going. Oh, one more thing—I thought about laying on a special lunch for the owners today, after we wrap up.

We're maxing out on finance, though, so I wanted to check with you first."

"They've put up with us for a week. Can't think of a better way to spend our last few quid."

"I knew you'd say that." She rested her hands on her hips and gave him a speculative glance. "Of course, if we took up the offer from Auntie Beeb, a tray of fancy sarnies and a bottle of screw-top Riesling wouldn't break us. We might lose a bit of independence, but..."

Lee scratched thoughtfully at the back of his neck, where his silver chain was for once chafing him. Normally he scarcely noticed it was there: perhaps the catch was misaligned. "Honestly? That's a chance I'd be prepared to take, if it meant a bit more security for the show and our motley crew. I've thought it over a lot, but..."

"It's the licence fee, isn't it? The BBC deciding to make pensioners pay for it again, I mean. You don't like that. The bigger they come, the more they should be generous and kind."

She was nodding in satisfaction, as if she'd picked up the credo from him. But Lee had learned it from his big, endlessly generous and gentle other half, who was moving every day further into his maturity of power, and had learned—strongly now, purely, after a halting first couple of steps—to adapt his behaviour accordingly. Lee wanted him, with pained and prickling urgency. "Yeah," he said shakily, trying to hide the sudden rush of need. "Old Colonel Henry could never have paid that. They'd barely invented the box in his day, but he didn't half take to it. Everyone thought he was rich, but he'd spent everything to keep hold of this place. The television was his one companion in the end."

"Lee? Did the owners tell you that?"

"Tell me what?"

"About the colonel and the TV. Did they tell you his name?"

"No, of course not. Why should they? Everyone in Launceston knew old Colonel Henry."

Blindly she reached one hand towards the camera crew. "Jack," she whispered, snapping her fingers to get his attention. "Jack, we're in business. Roll."

She didn't have to tell him twice. Three years on the job with Lee had primed him to drop everything, from his lunch to a chat-up of the latest production assistant, and dive into action. He abandoned his trainee and the Arri on its Steadicam, swinging a portable Sony onto his shoulder instead. Anna stepped out of shot to give Lee room. The background chatter from the crew sank to a pindrop silence. "Everyone in Launceston knew old Colonel Henry," Lee said again, conversationally, making his way to the alcove where Anna had said he and his story would be nicely framed. He pushed his hands into his pockets and turned to find the camera. "He got a bit of a rep for being grumpy in his later years, but really he's a nice old chap. Sense of humour, too. He made these canes in his spare time—the ones in the rack here, you see?"

The light was falling poetically on the oakwood, not too solemnly, just as Anna had wished. He loved Anna in a way, and Jack too. They'd both hung their careers off *Spirits of Cornwall*, taken a punt on a series anchored by a relative unknown. He'd gladly do anything for them. "Colonel Henry," he said, distantly noting in the feedback monitor that his eyes had turned to the sightless-looking silver that spooked the hell out of new friends and guilty strangers alike. "They say you can't abide your sticks left untidy and disordered. They say it makes you angry, so you bang them around at night and wake people up. I don't think that's true. I think you're just sorry about the flute you carved, the one you put a curse on to scare your rotten nephew who tried to make you sell up, and you rattle the sticks these days to make your great-grandchildren steer clear of them. You don't want any of the family living now to hear the sound of that flute. You love them."

The sunlight became crystalline. A coppery tang filled the air, like the warning of a storm. Anna stepped back into shot as she'd been trained to do, a state-of-the-art barometric sensor held out to the camera's lens. "Atmospheric pressure drop," she said levelly. "Five millibars. Six. My ears just popped. Room temp is diving too, fifteen degrees C. Ten. Eight. Lee, what would you like me to do?"

"Put the unit on the table so everyone can see it. Then would you mind... going and rearranging the colonel's sticks? He won't hurt you. Camera, please note that I can see my breath. Anna's too. It's a bright and sunny afternoon, no weather change outside. Air-pressure drops and plummeting temperatures are common phenomena before apparitions. No-one knows why, but there's an interesting line of research connecting the sudden cold to superconductivity... Toby, will you just step up and confirm there are no physical means of communication between me and that wooden rack over there?"

Toby came forward. He was white-faced and looked ready to die of fright, and Lee made a swift mental note to talk to him about presentation: *Spirits* audiences liked to see calm onscreen staff, no matter how wild the action. Nevertheless the boy managed to walk a circle around him, to pass a hand over his head and then beneath each foot as Lee lifted them. That would do. Lee flashed him a smile and let him scuttle away. Over by the rack, Anna had finished disarraying the canes and was standing back, dubiously scanning her work.

"All right," Lee continued, quiet tone unaltered. "Colonel Henry? It looks as though some careless house wench has untidied your rack of hand-carved sticks. Will you show us how you fix that? Will you honour us with your presence, sir?"

Briefly he thought the old man would renege on their deal. He was in violation of his own rules concerning the summoning of spirits, but in this house where things went bump at all hours, what could he do? Henry didn't want to go into the light. He didn't want to surrender his essence to the quantum magic of the universe for renewal and return. He liked it here, watching his grandkids grow up and scaring the pants off visitors. There he stood on the hearthrug, large as life, thumbs hooked into his blue tweed waistcoat.

Nobody else could see him. Anna and the rest of the crew were watching the canes, Jack panning slowly between the rack and the monitor. Temperature and pressure were returning to normal, as if, having thinned and cooled the air for his arrival, Henry could dispense with the special effects. As visions went, he was a benign one, but still pain sliced through Lee's head, new to him in its intensity and depth. *Why* could no-one else see?

Fiercely he controlled himself. He shoved the ache and the sense of weary unfairness into a box in his mind; slammed down the lid. A perfectly good manifestation was in progress. Henry's shoulder passed straight through Anna's, making her frown and twitch. He couldn't interact directly with material objects, but he'd found a way around that. Standing in front of the rack, he ran his fingers across the upright sticks as if they'd been harp strings.

They jumped and rattled in their stand. Anna jolted back, and a shriek or two rang out from the production crew. Then came nervous laughter, and a patter of applause. Lee let the reactions run. Feedback from behind the camera added to the realism of his shows. Maybe that would be all, he thought. Not much, but at some sites they might film for a week and get less. He waited, offering Jack a smile when he panned back to him and zoomed in. "Well," he said after a moment, "I think we'll call a halt there. We've had a wild few days here at Beaumont, and I for one would like to thank the inhabitants of this place, the living ones and... the rest of 'em, too. I'd like to offer our blessing, and..." He paused. The colonel was watching him, hands on his hips, showing no signs of fadeout, but that was just too bad. Whatever was going on here, Lee was too tired to channel it further. "And as our friends the witches say, merry have we met. Merry will we part, and merry may we meet again."

The old man shrugged. He popped out of existence as neatly as he'd appeared, leaving a trace of ozone and plum-cake tobacco on the air. Lee drew a breath of relief, and reached to remember the piece he'd written to wrap up the series and share his plans for the next, which could remain his own now that he'd decided to rebuff the advances of the noble Broadcasting Corporation, whose armour would shine again in easier times, he was sure...

The canes leapt into the air. No rattling this time: just a single, synchronised hop. They hovered. Then, one by one, in an impossibly dextrous movement, they whipped into a row, descending order of size, right to left, just as Anna had found them.

The colonel would have needed five hands to pull the manoeuvre off. Toby began to sob in outright terror, and that wasn't such good ambience: Lee nodded gratefully to the sound engineer, an unimpressionable woman in her fifties, who took hold of the boy and steered him towards the door. "All right," he said, "looks like we're still in business. Anna, how are the readings?"

"Normal. Everything's normal, except..." She pointed at the canes, still poised above their rack. "Except that. Is the colonel still here, Lee?"

"I don't think this is him."

"Oh, shit. Who?"

"I don't know. Come away from there, will you, just in case?"

"Of what? Getting brained by a poltergeist?"

Lee grinned. Anna shied away from onscreen work, but once out in front of the cams she was a natural comic, wide-eyed and entertaining. He waited until she had backed up, then went on, as calmly as he could, "Would the disincarnate entity present in this room like to let me know its purpose? I mean no harm. I'll help if I can."

The smallest cane flipped from its vertical alignment to a flat, steady plane. Something nudged it towards him, intent unmistakeable. "Oh, okay," he said, putting out a hand. "If you must."

He snatched it deftly as it shot by him at waist height, suddenly anxious that no-one else be forced to touch or come near it. This was a message for him alone, whether he wanted it or not. As soon as the cane was in his hand, it lost all weird kinetic power and was nothing but a stick, a cool dead weight.

Masterfully carved, though. Reluctantly he examined the head. Blackthorn, he thought—traditional choice of the pellar witches for their fearsome blasting-rod staves. This was too little and slender to blast anyone. But the top had been fashioned into the head of a man with a wolf's snarl and furred, pointed ears—or, if you preferred, a wolf's head with traces of humanity upon it, a were-beast caught in a moment of change.

Anna broke the silence, just as it had begun to settle like frost around Lee's heart. "Look," she said wonderingly, coming to stand in front of him. She'd forgotten her fright, and, Lee thought, the presence of the camera. She was the same shocked girl who'd come to find him in the Drift farmhouse kitchen, her sturdy disbelief in tatters. She stretched out one fingertip and brushed it across the wolf-man's neck. "There's a little join in the wood here, Lee. I reckon this one's the flute."

The wolf-whistle. Lee let his gaze settle somewhere beyond Jack's lens, deep into the strange space where his visions bred. "You know," he said softly, "whoever you are, you're really not bloody funny."

"Aren't you going to open it?"

"I believe that today—just for once—I'll decline the pleasure."

"Be good for the ratings, boss."

"Bugger the ratings," he told her. "If I hear the flute, someone who loves me dies, right? How can I risk that in a place like this, universally adored as I am? There'll be a massacre."

She stared at him in disbelief for a moment. Then she groaned, and the whole room dropped from tight-wired tension to an ordinary summer's afternoon. The canes rattled down into the rack. Lee opened up his hand and the blackthorn staff shot neatly sideways to rejoin its companions. And that was that: show over, fireworks of unnerved laughter shooting up from the crew and the couple of family members who'd come to watch the proceedings. Someone began a ragged cheer, which they all picked up. Lee stepped into the noise and chatter with relief, Jack swinging the camera to follow him. He supposed it had been a good day's work, an indisputable poltergeist display for the *Spirits of Cornwall* records. As for the wolf's-head cane, the flute and the curse—absurd, only wanting Lon Chaney Junior to stumble in roaring. He'd work out what it all meant when he was less blisteringly tired. Automatically he took up position for his close-out piece. He thought he had that much left in him, at any rate. There was only one way to find out.

To his astonishment, Anna bombed the shot. She strode in to seize him around the waist. She was vivid and bright in the monitor screen, her summer tan a contrast to his own pallor. His eyes had lost their silver and without it he was washed out, ordinary, at a loss to see why people carried placards with his

18

name on them. After a startled moment he returned her embrace, glad of her warm intervention. "And with that final contribution to a record-ratings series of *Spirits of Cornwall*," she said, giving him a squeeze, "talented clairvoyant Lee Tyack-Frayne is signing off for a good long holiday with his handsome beast of a husband. I would too, if I got the chance."

"Me too," Jack added surprisingly from behind the Sony: then, while Lee and Anna gaped, continued, "What—I can't come out?"

"Sure you can," Anna said, bewildered. "Er—*are* you?"

"Actually, I'm not sure. I might just fancy Gid."

"Cut, cut, cut," Lee said, breaking into laughter. But he could relate to Jack's problem. "Well, don't we all?"

"Yeah. What is he on at the moment, anyway, Lee? Vitamins, Viagra, raw steak? He's bloody irresistible."

"Thank God I don't have to resist him." Lee shook his head, smiled at each of his rogue staff in turn. "We won't be using that last part—any of it. Come on, the pair of you. I think I'll record my outtro in the garden."

Anna looked at him anxiously. "What? No, you're done for the day. You don't have to venture out among the masses."

"I think I do, or they're gonna venture in here. Somebody got that gate open. I promised the Beaumonts there'd be no home invasions." He set off towards the hallway that led to the front door, wide open in the fragrant summer heat. The garden path was crowded, a tentative queue from the lane outside making their way towards the house. Lee didn't employ security staff. He'd never needed them. "Hoi," he called amiably, emerging onto the steps. "You lot do realise you're in someone else's garden, don't you?"

The ringleader—who was indeed, to Lee's amused mortification, carrying an *I heart* placard—crunched to a halt on the gravel. "Oh," he said, delighted. "It's you."

In his mid-sixties, crew-cut, resplendently tattooed. Well, it took all sorts. Solemnly Lee shook his hand: found out that his name was Dan, then where he'd come from to see the show being filmed today. Signed the book the beaming guy had thrust out at him. Cheaper than a bouncer by a long chalk: his new friend, something quite different from a fan, turned to the group bottlenecking behind him and announced without a trace of shame, "Hoi, you lot! You're in somebody's garden here, you know. Lee wants you all back in the lane, right now."

Lee followed them. He wasn't quite sure why. He wanted to give them something for their journey, for supporting his show. He hated the idea of sending anyone home empty-handed. Peripherally he noticed Anna, gesturing to Jack to come out too and keep rolling. Once the last straggler was safely off the manicured Beaumont lawns and flowerbeds, he drew the gate closed and joined them in the oak-shaded lane. "Look up there," he said, pointing to a window on the second floor. "That room's been shut up for about a hundred years, the family here told me. Nobody knows why. But one early morning in 1974, a milkman on his rounds looked up and saw a man standing there, wearing nothing but a long powdered wig."

His little audience gave an obliging gasp. Unable to resist, he went on, "Still, it was the seventies. Maybe a naked guy in a wig wasn't all that unusual." They gawped at him, then broke into snorts of laughter. This was good. Lee didn't get to joke around much for the purposes of the show. Most of the stories they covered were by their very nature too poignant for comedy, events that had turned the living souls of Cornwall into spirits. His own lifted, the oppression he'd felt inside the house clearing off like fog in the sun. He wondered if he could ask the Beaumont ghosts for one last favour. "There's another tale you might like, too. A servant girl called Peggy used to haunt that attic room up there. The love of her life, a boy called Johnny, had to leave her to try and make his fortune at sea, but he never came back, and poor Peg eventually died of a broken heart. It does happen, you know."

He glanced around. Several of the group were nodding vigorously. "Well, I'm not so sure we'll be seeing Peggy at her window anymore. But if you just take a quick glance up there right now…"

A big punt, for sure. At worst they might take his suggestion, his bit of harmless flim-flam, and *think* they saw something up there amongst the cobwebs and torn curtains. In the right kind of group like this one, with everyone primed…

"Bloody hell," tattooed Dan whispered. "Look!"

Goddess bless Peggy and the wild, weird ways of the quantum universe, its ripples and eddies and tides. Up in the window, she and a shocked-looking lad in ragged sailor's uniform were clutching each other, waving down at the lane. "Are they actors?" someone rasped, fear and delight cracking together in the question, and Dan spared a moment for a withering look. "Of course not, ya great tuss! You can see right through 'em!"

You could, too. They were fading by the second. Smiling, letting his attention drift, Lee eased back a little way from the wondering, chattering group, half of them missing the thing they wanted to see in their struggle to pull out cameras and phones in time. Movement in the living-room window was snagging at his attention. One of the crew, probably, unhitching the lighting frame and setting the curtains straight to leave the place as they'd found it, minus a disembodied maidservant at any rate…

No. It was the colonel. He was as solid as the window frame around him, and he was gesticulating frantically at Lee. *Go! Get away from here!* Not a hostile motion but the action of a military man, trying desperately to signal across distance to a friend. Danger. A warning. *Go!*

Too late. Music drifted into the lane. No-one reacted to it or looked around. Jack had the Sony trained on the attic window. Anna was gazing upward too, her expression unreadable, as if, despite everything, her grief-filled agnosticism had been easier to bear than the things she saw while working with Lee. Nobody else was hearing the long, low notes of flute music, shimmering like silks in the hot air.

Someone who loves you will die. In one way and another, making a sobering truth out of his clowning back in the house, Lee was surrounded by people who loved him today. Anna and Jack had walked through paranormal fires with him. He looked after his crew, and they repaid him with a loyalty and affection he couldn't have foreseen. Dan, six and a half foot tall and built like the end of a barn, had written *I heart Lee* on a piece of card for all the world to see.

And those people—his crew and his fans—were the very least of Lee's problems, the smallest of the privileges in a life so rich in love he could hardly breathe when he thought about it, thought about his home and his daily world. *Your handsome beast of a husband.*

A police Rover was parked at the end of the lane. Gideon had said he'd be busy today, but it would be just like him to have blown off his last task of the day and come roaring out here to collect him, knowing how tired he got towards the end of a series run. Lee stared at the ground. He wouldn't look at anyone. Wouldn't think of anyone if he could possibly help it. "Hey," he said, in a last-ditch effort of distraction, "the ground sounds a bit hollow here. There's a story of a tunnel running from the mansion house right down to the church. Could be a smuggler's tale, but some geomantic experts say that tunnel legends like that are race memories of ley lines, energetic connections between one ancient site and..."

"And another. Of course. *Marvellous!*"

Lee jerked his head up as if yanked by a cold grasp in his hair. Helplessly he stared into the face of Rufus Pendower, the copper he and Gid had laughingly called Sergeant Weird-Shit until each had realised the depth and pain of Pendower's crush on Lee. After that, they'd spoken of him with wary gentleness, only allowing Gid's feigned jealousy to flare up in the bedroom. *Could Rufus do this for you, then, my 'andsome? How about this? And this?* Pendower's secondment to the Devon squad had come to both of them as a relief. But here he was, smiling into Lee's face, his own lit up with delight. "How are you, Locryn? I was on my way through Launceston, and I thought I'd just pop in and see how the filming was going at Beaumont Hall. It's the most marvellous location, you know—all kinds of stories. And the name itself, the *beautiful hill...*"

Lee tuned him out. Bloody Rufus and his names! Even Lee's old Cornish one became a weapon, a little piece of his identity Rufus could insist upon and keep. *No-one else calls you by your proper Kernowek title, but I'll call you Locryn on every possible occasion, caressing you with it, so gently and invisibly that no-one but you and I will know.* Lee was too weary to deal with the unwanted secret today. The flute music had stopped, possibly only the wind in the trees to begin with. "It's *Lee*," he said, a touch of desperation in his voice. "I'm fine, Rufus, thank you. I'm just trying to wrap up my show here."

"Oh. Oh, yes, of course. I'll stand back. You, er... You don't look terribly well, I'm sorry to say. Do you know that your nose is bleeding?"

It wasn't. At least, one red drop only had hit the front of Lee's shirt. Nothing to speak of, and maybe he'd just chosen the wrong tree to stand under, a cherry, perhaps, filled with greedy, incontinent birds. "Listen, everyone," he said, gesturing to the little group to gather round. "There's a tunnel beneath our feet here. A dowser could locate it, and its old energy line. The colonel's in the window and he says I have to go. The monster's in the schoolyard. I see a little boy with his proud father, and the father's just a pair of initials, a big M and an R." He chuckled, and blood ran down his throat and down his nose, laying a second big splash to his shirt and then a third. "That's stupid, isn't it? But Gideon taught me how to work out stuff like this, so don't worry. M, R, a kind of wheat or grain... Yes, Emmer. And the child... Emmerson. Emmerson primary school, three and a half miles northeast of here, just off the Churchwood road. There's still time. The monster's found a way inside, the window to the canteen. The monster's climbing in."

"Lee?!"

He'd crashed to his knees on the track. Anna was crouching in front of him. She was holding his face between her hands. "Cut, Jack! Cut! What did you say it was called—this school? With the monster in the yard?"

"Emmerson. Emmerson." Lee couldn't stop saying it. He twisted away from her and threw up, distantly grateful that she got behind him and shielded him from the group, and still he couldn't stop. "Emmerson. Send someone. Send police. Emmerson."

"Police are right here." She spared a hand from him to jab a finger at Pendower. "Hoi, you! Sergeant whoever-you-are. He's having a flash. You'd better get someone to this school he's talking about, pronto. Don't just bloody stand there."

"I... I know about his flashes," Pendower said. "I know *him*. I have to look after him."

"Mate, he'll be looked after, I promise. If you know him, you'll know he's never wrong. Get back to your car, and get on your bloody radio and get police to that school, or you'll answer for it. Right now, for godsakes! Go!"

Chapter Two
And Damned If You Don't

The police Rover was a new one. Gideon had finally written off the old girl in which he'd tanked around the moorland lanes for years, driving her roof-deep into floodwater to rescue Roger Quentin's Saluki hound, then Roger himself, who'd fecklessly dived in after the dog. Detective Inspector Lawrence hadn't been pleased, but the *local-hero sergeant* headlines hadn't hurt her department any, and she'd come out in person to Dark to hand over the keys to the sleek new truck.

Surely Gideon had got more speed out of the old one! He'd been working in Bodmin Town when Anna had called, closing off paperwork in the Tollgate Road HQ. He'd surfed the leading edge of the school-run traffic, just in time before the roads congealed, and hit the A30 at a satisfying top-gear seventy. Lee had been taken ill after a long day's shooting at the old Beaumont mansion. Anna and Jack had taken him to Launceston Community Hospital, a tiny place but equipped with a decent minor-injuries unit. Fine. Well, acceptable: Lee was in good hands until Gideon could get to him, and the symptoms Anna described were familiar.

A full-on, overwhelming vision, sharp enough to make him sick and give him a pouring nosebleed. He'd raised the alarm on something happening at a Launceston primary school. Police had been called. At a long stretch, all in the course of a day's work for Gideon's poor beleaguered lad, whose talents could cost him so dear.

But Anna had called again, this time patched through to him from Tollgate over the Rover's radio. Lee, desperately anxious, had refused to be admitted at Launceston, convinced that some aspect of his vision had yet to be played out. He'd tried to leave. Two officers had turned up from the police station down the road, and he'd been arrested.

Gideon could run faster than this damn truck was going. The hot thought flickered past him faster still. Like a half-remembered dream, he saw the moorland surging by, the gorse-patched flanks of the hills. This fantasy had plagued him in boyhood trips in the back of Pastor Frayne's Volvo, grinding lugubriously through fields where he longed to leap and dash, tor to tor, encompassing great stretches of country with each stride. In the outer edges of his mind, the primal places not occupied with fear for his husband and questions as to what the bloody hell the Launceston constabulary thought they were playing at, he was convinced he could do it still, and if each pouncing leap brought him four-furfooted from crest to crest, it didn't bother him. His child-self had run the moors in the form of a dinosaur, a flying horse and Simba from *The Lion King*, as each of these creatures had caught his imagination. He'd liked wolves, too, and those dreams had stuck, that was all.

His speedometer was hovering at eighty five. First rule of police driving: no point at all in dashing to the rescue if you added to the damage en route. Still, the road ahead was clear, the A30 at this stretch a newly widened sweep between Temple and Hawk's

Tor. The dispatch officer hadn't exactly clapped him on the back and wished him godspeed, but she'd been the one to process Anna's frantic call through the system. All Gideon's colleagues knew Lee. The sternest and most sceptical amongst them had learned to respect what he could do, and in the wake of respect came affection, for the diffident, quiet way he did it. In the last couple months alone, he'd been deeply involved with three police investigations, at DI Lawrence's request.

And that was too much. Why was Gideon only realising now? Too much, for a man with a kid, a husband and a successful TV show already demanding his attention. He reached for blue lights and siren, swore softly as the unfamiliar dash squirted his windscreen and flipped the wipers instead. A second attempt got the truck lit up and wailing, and the tailback from the Launceston exit half a mile ahead began to manoeuvre out of his way.

Let this be a wakeup call. Everything in Gideon's world had dropped into place this last year. Tamsyn had started kindergarten and ceased all poltergeist activity as her days filled up with new scenes, new friends and the prosaic fun of an ordinary childhood. Gid's superiors had stopped leaning on him to chase promotion, but nor was he simply the Dark village bobby these days. Tollgate Road was Gideon's kindergarten, the place where he added daily to his policing skills, and used the experience of his injuries and phenomenal recovery to help other officers find their way. He spent two full days a week in the bungalow station at Dark, listening to gossip and keeping his finger on the pulse of his neighbours' lives, and he valued those times just as much as the drug busts and car chases of his broader terrain. Yes, a packed, rich life, made perfect by Lee, who set a daily cherry of joy on the top of it all with his love, his attentiveness, his unflagging care for his husband, home and little girl.

So quietly. That was the problem. Lee just kept handing it all on in. The thing people loved him for most—his laidback modesty about his gifts—was a trap, and Gideon had fallen into it. Something had happened today, something bad enough to cross the wires and land Lee first in hospital and then the hands of the law. Gideon couldn't begin to imagine the sequence of events, but he didn't have to. At last the Launceston exit was there on his left. He laid his foot carefully to the gas and shot up the cleared outside lane of the slip. A brief wait at the junction onto Western Road, where he schooled himself not to honk and rev: if his blues and twos weren't shifting the traffic, boy-racer tactics wouldn't do it either. Then the lights changed, the last bus and white transit van got out of his way, and he blazed into the outskirts of the town.

The station was tucked right into the depths of a housing estate. A nice place, community-oriented, modern and open, but once off the main road, Gideon had to crawl there at twenty miles an hour. No emergency short of life-and-death could justify anything else, not with toddlers fresh out of nursery school tumbling around on the kerbs, parents and guardians nosing buggies across the winding roads. He switched off his siren and lights. A beautiful, sunny, ordinary Cornish afternoon after school: there they all were, the lives he was sworn to protect, gossiping on corners, idly rocking prams back and forth off the edge of bloody pavements. Hands clenched on the wheel, grimly performing each mirror, signal, manoeuvre routine like a teenager out on his test, he pulled into the car park.

The Highway Code need not apply to his personal actions. He sprang out of the truck. The doors to the station were being blocked by a social worker reading the riot act to a sullen, hoodie-clad kid: he got hold of the man by his rotund little midriff and hoisted him bodily out of the way, ignoring his squawk and the kid's hoot of laughter. Inside, the reception was spacious and cool. Also empty, and that was no good at all. Gideon banged one hand down on the desk buzzer, hard enough to make the domestic-abuse leaflets bounce in their racks. Appreciating the irony, he drew one deep breath then another, got hold of himself and began to guide the tooth-and-claw forces of his nature through the proper channels. "Afternoon," he barked, and then, when the buzzer's clatter had died and nothing happened, pressed it again, with a fingertip this time. The soul of patience, for ten seconds anyway... "Hoi! *Shop!*"

A door flew open at the far end of the room. Of all the faces Gideon might have expected to see, Sergeant Rufus Pendower's was among the last, but he threw the oddness out. Pendower was working just over the border in Devon. Not beyond the bounds of probability that he'd found his way to whatever fuck-up might be unfolding here. Anyway, Gideon didn't care. Didn't care that Rufus was flushed and unkempt, shadows beneath his eyes. Definitely didn't give a shit about his own painful flicker of resentment that, when Lee was in trouble and needed him, the weird-shit sergeant had got there first. "Rufus," he said, planting both hands on the surface of the desk, allowing its smooth surface to take the growl out of his throat, the incipient roar. "Where is he?"

"Gideon, I want you to keep calm. Everybody knows what Lee can do, but it seems there's a new sergeant here, a Karen Lennox, and she hasn't encountered anything like this before. You know how unsettling it can be, when—"

Gideon was very calm. He showed it in the absolute gentleness with which he shouldered Pendower aside. "Is he through here?"

"Yes, in the holding cell at the end of the corridor."

"In a *cell?*"

"I couldn't stop them. Gideon! He said some kind of assailant had got into a local primary school, a place called Emmerson. I alerted the officers here—immediately, of course—and they got there in time to see this person climbing in through the refectory window. He was armed—knife or gun, they didn't have time to see, and by the time they'd got inside themselves, he'd vanished. The school was evacuated, but all the kids are accounted for, and no-one's hurt."

"That's nice." Gideon bit his lip for one last effort. He rounded on Pendower. "For the life of me I can't see why my poor bloody husband's been arrested for it."

"Because he couldn't have known. He couldn't have known there was anyone entering the school then, unless... unless he was involved. That's how Lennox saw it. Gideon, I'm sorry. His assistants from the film unit tried to persuade him to stay at the hospital, and so did I. They couldn't have touched him if he'd been admitted. But he tried to leave, and Sergeant Lennox interpreted that as—"

"As his fucking attempt to abscond!"

Gideon turned. A sturdy woman in a sergeant's uniform had emerged into the corridor. She was neatly kitted out, the set of her head businesslike. Nothing about her suggested that she made a habit of storming through the halls of her local station, eyes blank with terror, a rasp of outright hysteria in her tone. "Sergeant Lennox?" he said, advancing to meet her. "I'm Gideon Tyack-Frayne, from over at Bodmin. I'm—"

"I know who you are," she snapped, avoiding his outstretched hand. "You're Lee Tyack-Frayne's husband, and you've come here to tell me he somehow magically fucking well saw a man climbing into a primary school on my turf—a *primary* school, fifty little kiddies from three to five years old—with a weapon in his hand.

But he has nothing to do with it, right? He just fucking magically *sees*."

Lee had warned Gideon this could happen. Right at the very beginning, when he'd made sure Gid knew he had an alibi before beginning to share his insights into the Lorna Kemp case. It hadn't been necessary then—Gid's trust in him had blossomed like a frost-delayed rose, after a bumpy start—and ever since, he'd only seemed to garner respect and desperate gratitude from the people he'd helped. Gideon had let himself wonder if his fears had been a touch of paranoia.

He owed respect to a fellow officer. Her gender made a difference, too, although he tried never to let it. He therefore did not grab her by her epaulettes and swing her out of his way. "That's right," he said dryly. "I tell you what, Sergeant—rather than argue, I'd like to make one phone call to my HQ at Tollgate Road. I'd like you to speak to my DI there."

"Your DI... What does she have to do with this?"

"She's Lee's friend, and can vouch for him, I hope beyond all possibility of doubt." He didn't wait for Lennox's reply. She didn't look capable of making one. Cognitive dissonance, that was what this was called, when the whole damn world a person thought they knew turned out to be weirder than their wildest dreams. Gideon wasn't without sympathy, but he had to get to Lee. He pulled out his phone, hit the speed-dial to his boss's desk at Tollgate.

Someone must have primed her: she picked up on the first ring. "Hello, ma'am," he said, keeping his voice low and level with a larynx-cracking effort. "I'm at Launceston police station, where the local sergeant's taken it into her head to arrest Lee in connection with a crime he predicted, and... You'll speak to her? Thank you. Yes, she's right here." Gideon proffered the phone politely to Lennox. "Sorry for the abrupt introduction, Sergeant. Detective Inspector Christine Lawrence on the line for you."

He left her standing in the corridor. The cell door at the end of it was open, or he'd have had to start ripping out throats then and there. He could hear a voice, just as low and tightly controlled as his own. The only voice that mattered. He set off towards it, Rufus trotting in his wake. "Another thing I don't bloody understand," he rumbled, fear and frustration getting the better of him at last, "was why in God's name *you* didn't do that, Rufus! One bloody phone call to sort all this out."

"I would have. I was going to. I just had to take care of him, Gideon, and I didn't want to leave him alone until..."

He faded out into the blood-rush in Gideon's ears. Lee was sitting bolt upright on the bunk in the cell. He didn't look up at Gideon's approach. His attention was focussed on, or at some point slightly behind Anna Briggs, who was kneeling at his feet. She was trying to hold his wrists, to slow down the frantic movements of his hands. "Oh! Gid," she cried when she saw him. "Thank God you're here. He won't stop."

Gideon leaned down. Gently he helped her onto her feet and into the solitary chair. She looked exhausted, as if she'd been trying to catch the reins of this runaway nightmare for some time. He knelt in her place. "It's all right, Anna. Stop what?"

"He's counting. Like, one to five, over and over again on his fingers. He won't stop."

Gideon captured one sweat-damped fist in his own. "Sweetheart," he said, and Lee sucked in a noisy breath and stopped his whispered chant. Blindly he shoved his fingers through Gideon's, a tight-bound, shuddering mesh. "Good," Gideon told him. "Hold on to me like that. Now the other. Push in. Push through. Hold tight."

Lee obeyed him. His eyes closed, and a wash of exhausted tears tracked pale streaks down the blood and dust on his face. His grasp closed ferociously, a palm-to-palm push against his husband's strength. "One," he choked out wearily. "One, Gid. One, two, three, four, five."

"Too much *Sesame Street* with Tamsyn, this is, my handsome. You're all right. I've got you." Holding him still, Gideon looked him over. His shirt was splattered with blood, his jeans stained. "Christ almighty, Anna. Did no-one take care of him?"

"We tried. He told us about the guy breaking in at the school, and his nose began to bleed so much that Jack and I took him straight over to casualty. They were trying to treat him when he said he had to leave, and he walked straight out, and then two coppers from this station arrived. Someone at Beaumont must have told them where he'd gone. One of them was that... that mad bitch you met in the corridor. It was like she was terrified of him, or she hated him, or..."

"It's okay. Thank you for sticking with him. Where's Jack?"

"They'd only let one of us come. That other fella—oh, this one here, your friend from Liskeard—he was at Beaumont Hall anyway, and they let him come because he's a copper too, but Jack went back to collect our gear and help get everyone out of the house. We'd just dropped everything."

"All right." Gently, powerfully, Gideon returned the push of Lee's hands against his own. "How did the vision come on, Anna? Was he talking about a monster?"

"Yeah. It came out of nowhere. He was showing us the line of an old tunnel outside the house, then he just said... Christ, it was scary, Gid!"

"I know. But tell me if you can."

"He didn't change the way he was talking. He hardly drew a breath. He just said a monster was in the schoolyard, and he worked out it was Emmerson from the letters M and R, and the idea of a little boy—a son, I guess."

"Right. Yeah, he often gets it through kind of puns like that, like charades. I think if he saw it directly, he just couldn't cope. Is that right, Lee? You got Emmerson, and now you're getting something else—another monster?"

Lee didn't answer. His head dipped once in a taut affirmative movement, and his eyes flew open, every trace of their sweet human colour burned out by silver light. "The monster. One, two, three, four, five."

Lennox had quietly re-entered the cell. Whatever wind she'd been sailing on, Lawrence had knocked it out of her. She came to stand beside Rufus, and like him stared down at Lee in bewilderment. "I'm sorry," she said, her voice returning to what Gideon guessed was its normal, kindly tone. "I... I gather Mr Tyack-Frayne works with the police a lot. I didn't know."

"Well, don't sweat it now." Gideon spared her a glance. "This is hard on him, though. I'd like to get it over for him and take him home. Does a count of five mean anything to you?"

"What, like he's been saying over and over again?"

"Yes. It could be something symbolic, like a pub sign or a family's coat-of-arms, or even something that seems stupid at first, like a joke. Local landmarks? Anything in a group of five there?"

"Not that I can think of. I really am sorry. This looks like it's shaking him to bits."

"I wish you'd left him at the hospital. But the best way to stop it is to help him work it out."

"Well—is it ever really basic? Obvious?"

"Sometimes, yeah. Why?"

"Because apart from Emmerson, there's exactly four other primary schools in the Launceston area. Greenfields, Princess Mary, Godolphin Road and Dovecotes."

Lee snapped his head up. "Emmerson, one! One, two, three, four, five!"

"Jesus, that's it." Gideon restrained him as a shock like electricity heaved through his frame. "Five schools. You didn't catch the guy at Emmerson, did you?"

"No, he got away. We closed all the schools, though—the primaries and all the others, too. They've been evacuated, shut down. Everyone's accounted for. Tell him that, will you? Tell him everyone's all right."

But Gideon didn't have to. Lee's hands went slack in his. For once he saw the transition in his eyes from the vision-racked silver to tired, lost green-grey. He let his fingers slide free of Gideon's and looked around him. "Oh," he said faintly. "Oh, shit."

He was back. Relief flooded Gideon at the absolute return. He reached up and grabbed him as he folded forward. "Got you," he said, firmly enough that Lee could have no doubts, no fears. "I've got you. You're gonna be all right."

"Oh, Gid. There was a monster. I couldn't get its mask off."

"I know. But you still gave the warning. Let the Launceston bobbies do the unmasking when they catch this guy, okay? Don't put all us poor coppers out of work."

A chuckle shook Lee's ribs, rusty and uncertain, as if he'd half-forgotten how. "They can't... *keep* the schools shut, though, not on the strength of a half-arsed tip-off like that."

Lennox took a step towards Lee, who sat up at the sound. "It wasn't half-arsed, Mr Tyack-Frayne. It was the eeriest thing I've ever seen in my life. We got a call from Sergeant Pendower here to say an intruder was in the Emmerson Primary schoolyard. Pendower was halfway across town, and so was his informant, whose name he seemed to expect me to recognise. We happened to have a unit close at hand to the school. They attended within two minutes, and there was this guy exactly as Pendower told us

35

you had described, climbing in through the canteen window at the back. I can't keep the schools closed indefinitely, no. But it's Thursday, and I can close the primaries at least for tomorrow, which gives us the weekend to investigate. I can put security staff in the schools, have the gateways and access points watched until this bastard's caught."

Lee watched her uncertainly. "That's good," he said. "Er... am I free to go?"

"Yes. Yes, of course, but... do you have anything more for us? DI Lawrence tore a layer of skin off me, and I'm sure you think it's deserved, but I gather that your gifts are extraordinary. Can you tell me what the intruder looked like, what he was wearing?"

"No. Sometimes my monsters wear masks, and I can't see their faces. I'll work on it for you, but... at the moment, no."

She read Gideon's warning glance and eased back. She still had traces of fear-sweat on her brow, damp patches in the armpits of her uniform shirt. But she was clambering back into her skin, and Gideon watched the process apprehensively. What would her upshot be? "Well," she said, "it seems to me a strange thing. You have these insights, these flashes, this... this *gift*, as Lawrence calls it. You can see a bad thing happening, and I'm bloody grateful to you for helping us protect the kids at Emmerson today. But what use is it, really, if you can't control it enough to stop the same bad thing from happening again?"

What the fuck use are you, if you can't help stop something like this?

The words whipped a silent bloodstained trail through Gideon's mind. Christ, where had that come from? Who would ever dare say such a thing to Lee? For the first time in many, many months—over a year, if he thought about it—he felt ill.

But Lee was smiling faintly. He put a hand to Gideon's face with an unhidden tenderness that forgave all, mended all, set the world to rights. He tried to stand up, and Gideon helped him.

"There you have it," Lee said hoarsely, hitching a wry grin at Sergeant Lennox. "The whole fucking gamut. Arrest you for knowing, then call you worthless for not. Damned if you do, and..."

Gideon held his shoulders, steadying him in the wild white waters that could run beneath the surface of the most peaceable Cornish afternoon. "Right," he finished for him. "And damned if you don't."

***

Rufus Pendower had vanished as inexplicably as he'd first appeared. Before Gideon could begin to worry about him, a flurried clerk stuck her head around the door of the cell, bobbing about to catch Lennox's eye. "Ma'am! I'm sorry, ma'am, I need a bit of help out here. There's a very upset person called Dan in reception, with an awful lot of tattoos and a placard. There's half a dozen others with him, and they all want to see... Oh. Yes. Mr Tyack-Frayne here. If he isn't being detained, do you think he could just come and..."

Gideon inhaled deeply. Perhaps it was the kind of breath the wolf in the story had drawn, before he huffed and puffed and blew the whole fucking town away, pigs and all. Lee, who could read him down to the last pulse and twitch, swivelled to face him, planting a hand on his chest. "No," he warned softly. "Fans and followers not on the menu. Just let them see I'm okay."

Reluctantly Gideon let it go. "Why can't they see you're bloody not?"

"Not on the itinerary. Not on their list of things to do on a tour of haunted Launceston."

"They must be bloody blind, then." Giving it up, he followed Lee into the corridor, stayed at his shoulder as he emerged into the small, agitated crowd disturbing the station's business. There *was* an odd blindness about them, except for tattooed Dan, who seemed to have taken an informal leadership role and was permitting each of his companions twenty seconds or so with Lee, long enough for an autograph and their assurances that they were his biggest fan, even if they couldn't see he was bloodstained and just about ready to drop. "Sorry," Dan declared, once this process was complete. "I'd never have bothered you, Lee, only we thought we'd check in at the hospital, and someone told us there you'd been *arrested*."

"Occupational hazard," Lee said distractedly scrawling his name on the last guidebook. "If you ever take up the trade, Dan, make sure you've got alibis, even if it's just a missing cat."

"What, me? Do what you do?" Dan gave him a look of pure love. "Nobody's like you. The police ought to leave you alone. I call it a disgrace that they messed you around like this today."

Gideon, in uniform and an obvious target, was getting the brunt of this. But Lee had said to hold his tongue and so he did, gazing expressionlessly into the middle distance as he'd been trained to do when only present in his bodyguard capacity. *Still, Lee, for godsakes. I take your point about the menu, but not even a snack?*

Lee snorted as if he'd heard him. "Don't worry, Dan. This is my husband, not my arresting officer."

Dan blushed up to the hairline. He opened his mouth, and Gideon braced: but all that came out was, startlingly, after a moment—"Lucky bastard!"

"I'm sure he thinks so too. I tell you what—if everyone's happy now, you wouldn't half be doing me a favour if you'd round them all up into your minivan and get them out of here."

"Oh! Yeah. Yeah, I will. Honest, it's been a pleasure and an honour... Here, your shirt's a mess. Would you like mine?"

He was starting to unbutton. Lee raised his hands. "Whoa. You hang on to that, man. That's the one you're wearing when your missus finally stops putting you off and says yes."

Dan's jaw dropped. "Oh, my God. It is? She *does?*"

Gideon closed a grip on the back of Lee's belt. It was light and invisible, but said more plainly than a shouted command that enough was enough, that for today at least Lee should retract his crystal ball. Glancing devotedly over his shoulder, Dan returned to the group. "Come on, all of you lot! Back into the bus. He just did one for me, one of his flashes! Wait till I tell you!"

Once the minibus was disappearing down Moorland Road, Gideon pulled Lee into his arms. It was hard to give a comforting hug from inside a stab vest, but Lee was used to all his scratchy accoutrements and grabbed him fiercely. Beneath Gideon's hands he felt rawly, painfully open, as if he were covered in pricked-up ears or satellite dishes set to high-power receive. Only Anna was left in the car park now, and she looked on in concern. "He's lost control of it," she said. "This used to happen to him in London sometimes, when he'd been working too hard and the signals would just fly in at him from everywhere. It's like he loses his filters."

Gideon had seen it too, the worst time in Kelyndar village when Gwylim Kitto had pulled Lee halfway through death's door to find him. But Anna had known him for years before the Lorna Kemp case had brought him to Dark, and Gideon listened to her carefully, anxious for every scrap of backstory that could help him make the world bearable to his husband. "Is that what happened today?"

"Yes, although there was something in the Beaumont house he couldn't identify. Lots of little friendly ghosts, and then one big... thing, very powerful. He shrugged it off, but I think it opened him up to signals from whatever was happening at that school."

"And to everything else." Gideon caressed the tired head on his shoulder. "Is that right, love?"

"Mm. Yeah. But the thing is, Hayley's been turning Dan down for months. Then on Sunday night, she's sitting with him in a restaurant and she just thinks how daft he is, how he doesn't give a shit what anybody thinks and how much he makes her laugh, with his bald head and his tatts and his great big Hawaiian shirt, and she changes her mind."

"Oh, my God. I'm pleased for Dan, but we have to get you unplugged, sunbeam. Anna, any suggestions?"

"Well, there was this woman he used to go to in London. Did he tell you about her?"

"Yeah. Siobhan Reeves, a kind of a counsellor?"

"That's right, only all she seemed to do was yank him out at the mains. He'd come back looking like she'd hit him with a bag of wet sand. Look, Gid, he doesn't need anyone but you. I know it must be a headfuck sometimes, but you turned his life around. He was always a great guy, but it was like we only ever saw a quarter of him. After he met you, he just... shone out."

Gideon took this in. Lee had transformed *his* life, he knew, from the ground beneath his feet to the meaning and colour of sunlight. He'd seldom thought about his own effects upon Lee: had been too busy making sure they were good ones, recovering from his occasional horrible fuckups and redressing the balance. "Thanks," he said, careful to keep his tone level. "I'll just take him home. Chuck him in the freezer and lock it up until he cools down."

Lee gave a rasping laugh and got his head up. "That actually sounds quite good." He detached himself a little way from Gideon's embrace, not letting him go. "Jesus, Anna. I didn't mean to ruin our last shoot."

"What? You gave us a beautiful last shoot, especially the part where you threw up on the colonel's rhododendrons." She grinned, taking pity on his dismay. "The floating walking sticks were spectacular. We'll close with those, and the crew going nuts in the background. You get yourself home with the big man now, and have a good rest."

"What about our wrap-up?"

"Dial us in something local when you feel better." Thoughtfully she surveyed Gideon, then went on as if scarcely meaning to, "Jack's right, you know. If I had what you have waiting for me indoors, I'd never leave the house."

She clapped a hand to her mouth. Lee stared, a grin starting. It took Gideon a moment to realise what she meant, and he gave a bark of laughter. He was dusty and sweaty, a hardworking copper at the end of a long week. Still, there was no accounting for tastes, and he dropped her a small, gallant bow. "Why, thank you, kind lady."

"I am so sorry, Gid. I had no idea I was gonna say that out loud."

It really was unlike her. Lee broke the awkward moment, taking Gideon by the arm. "Oh, my God. Let's get you out of here before you cause any *more* havoc."

"Me? I'm not the one who got nicked this afternoon."

"Lucky I'm in police custody, then. You'd better escort me home."

***

"Things are happening in threes, you know, Gid. Three, two, one."

Uneasily Gideon glanced into the passenger seat. Lee had climbed into the truck gratefully. He'd stripped off his bloodstained shirt and huddled into a spare T of Gideon's. Then he'd kicked off his boots and curled up as far as he could, one foot wedged against the dash, toes placed carefully so as not to hit any buttons or lights.

He was more than half asleep, by Gideon's reckoning, and otherworldly forces were sweeping through the Rover's cabin in spite of the sunlight and the scents of fresh new vinyl. Gideon missed the way the old truck smelled, which was stupid of him. Well, a few long rides with Isolde would soon set that to rights. "You're still counting, love," he observed, laying a hand to his thigh.

"I know, but this is different. Anna deciding you're hotter than Jason Momoa, and telling you so. Me and Dan the fan, who was gonna give me his shirt—literally the shirt off his *back*. But I score two out of three this time, because..." His voice scraped, losing its dreamy cadence. "Because I've got Rufus too. I need to keep away from him."

Gideon considered this, alarm bells beginning to ring. "I know we've joked around about him and his crush. He hasn't... done anything, has he?"

Lee chuckled, rubbing his eyes. "What, you think I couldn't handle him?" He pushed up a little way and went on more alertly, "There's just this stupid legend at Beaumont Hall about a flute, and if you hear it, someone who loves you will die."

Gideon shivered. "Don't tell me. You heard the fucking flute."

"I don't know. I had this bloody vision coming on, and I might have been hearing anything. I thought I did, though, and when I looked up, there was Rufus. I'm scared for him. He looks awful."

Gideon gave him a pat and tugged out another tissue from the box wedged on top of the dash. "Whereas you're the picture of health yourself. Here, your nose is still bleeding a bit. Don't you worry about him."

"No, really. Did you see? He was in uniform, but I don't think he'd shaved, and he's lost a lot of weight."

"He's got a new baby, hasn't he?" Gideon rubbed his own unshaven jaw. He was going to have to start carrying a kit around with him to sort himself out during the day, or he'd start to look disreputable. What sort of early mid-life hormone change was causing his beard to grow in faster, he had no idea, but by the end of a weekend these days he'd have grown a sleek dark coat, causing Tamsyn to stroke it admiringly and Lee to watch him with piratical Cornish lust in his eyes. "That'll do it for the personal hygiene, as I remember. But I'll call in on him shortly, make sure he's okay."

"Okay. Yeah, I'm still counting. Back to five now, and backwards—five, four, three, two, one. What the hell does that mean, do you suppose?"

Gideon didn't know. He waited for a couple of minutes, letting the A30's tarmac whisper hotly beneath the Rover's tyres. As long as Lee wasn't at the wheel and having to listen to the rage and malice of fellow drivers, he found car journeys soothing. He was dropping back into half-sleep now, eyelids flickering.

And he was wide open. Shamelessly Gideon took advantage. "If I asked you something now," he said gently, slowing down through the gears to make the turn off the dual carriageway and into the long green lane to Dark, "you'd tell me the truth. Wouldn't you?"

"Yeah. So be careful what you ask, copper."

"Why are you working so hard at the moment, taking so much on? We're doing fine financially. You don't have to help every waif, stray and basket case who tugs on your psychic sleeves."

"Oh, that's easy. You won't like it, though."

"Better tell me quick, then. Before I change my mind about wanting to know."

"I'm doing it for Tamsyn, of course. To tire myself out, drain my psychic batteries, so when I come home she can't tap into me to boost her whammy."

Oh, shit. Gideon had thought that ghost long since laid. David Rawle, a friend from so deep in Lee's childhood that he'd been *Uncle Dave* for the first half hour of his reappearance last year, had quickly run through his store of credit. His suggestion that Tamsyn used Lee to amplify her psychokinetic powers had gone down like a granite pasty with Gideon. They'd both thrown him out, but not before the bastard had sunk the fear into Lee's heart, a barbed hook. Rawle had vanished, and after one painful clash, they'd left him and his dumb ideas behind. Gideon had thought so, anyway. "You do know that's a terrible pile of old bollocks, don't you?"

"I know with my brain. Guts are taking a while to catch up."

"Well, tell 'em to get with the programme. If Tamsie takes it into her head to float rocks or levitate Truro cathedral, she won't need help from either of us. Can you forget about *that* reason for killing yourself with work?"

"I will try. If I remember this conversation, I will. But I'm counting, counting. Counting down from five."

"You were counting up before. That was the schools, we thought."

"No. Lennox thought that. I was just getting it backwards. Five, four, three, two, one," he said reasonably, as if that ought to have made everything clear. "It never was wonderland, Gid, but take five from these words—she certainly gave it her all. Not quite five, maybe. Four and a half. And three quarters, maybe. She certainly gave it her all."

"Sweetheart?"

"Mmm?"

"Should I dash you straight back to Launceston hospital?"

"No, no. I'm dreaming. I'll be fine."

Chapter Three
Badgers, Bleujyow, Buster

Sarah Kemp had a permanent duty of stand-by, to pick Tamsyn up from school on the rare days when neither Gideon nor Lee could make it. She'd stepped unasked into this role, and many other tasks of care, as the years unfolded and she'd almost ceased—as she'd once confessed, a bit shamefaced but smiling—to be able to distinguish their kid from her brood and her husband Wilf's. They were all just a mass of chattering brats. She had to collect her own lot, steer them through the lanes and home for their tea and allotted screen time, so why not Tamsie too?

Lee and Gideon had been too grateful to question the arrangement. Their girl wasn't lacking a mother figure—Elowen made regular, thoroughly scheduled visits from France, always welcomed by Tamsyn, never missed when she left—but Sarah was a fixture and foundation. And although they'd sworn to do better in time for their daughter's adolescence, Elowen had hit a target when she'd laughed at their blushing incompetence around the word *period*. Lee at any rate hoped that Sarah would always be there, helping Tamsie navigate the waters with the same calm, no-nonsense tenderness she displayed to Lorna, now twelve years old and emerging from childhood in unpredictable fits and starts. She'd been fine about stepping in today, Gid had said, offering not just to escort the little girl home but to babysit for the evening.

Something must have changed. She and Tamsyn were sitting on the garden bench outside Chy Lowen. This bench, unlike the cast iron one at the back of the house, was a place of summer waiting. If either dad was later home than expected, Tamsyn would clamber up, sit cross-legged on a cushion and keep watch.

Her vigils never seemed to be anxious ones. The bench commanded a view down the track into the village. Sometimes she would still give way to her toddler's habit of waddling as fast as she could to meet the oncoming headlights, her other parent hot in pursuit to grab her before she could manage the catch on the gate. More often these days she would remain in dignified stillness until the car was parked, then get down and come running, delight blazing off her in such waves that neither Gideon nor Lee could ever quite think what they'd done to deserve it.

Tonight Sarah was flanked on her right by Mrs Coulter, a neat little lady in her eighties who'd befriended Elowen during her stay in Dark, and become a huge favourite of Tamsyn's since. Bizarrely, both Gideon and Lee had mistaken her for Granny Ragwen at first. But the evening when they'd first seen her had been dreamlike, ambiguous in the wake of Lee's encounter with Clem Atherton at the Lamorna farm. Mrs C bore a strong resemblance, and claimed distant cousinhood to the wily old lady who'd vanished at the Penzance Montol three years before. She was ordinary, though, a retired social worker whose credentials Gid had thoroughly checked before letting her have unaccompanied access to his child. She knew a lot about plants and herbs from her days as a Girl Guide leader, that was all.

On reflection, the whole Jana Ragwen thing had been a crazy stretch of belief, but he and Gid had had a day of it, Lee's discovery of human sacrifice at Lamorna topped by the revelation that Gid's shy, buttoned-up, reactionary inspector was a lesbian. The old lady smiled and waved as the police Rover bumped up the last few yards of the track. Quite a picture, the three of them made, arrayed in a row on the bench. *Maid, mother, crone, though not with quite the right personnel*, Lee's tired brain said to him, but he was done with psychic visions for the day. He just wanted to be home. He wound down the passenger window. "Hi," he called out over the crunch of gravel while Gideon parked on the drive. "Is everything all right?"

"Fine," Sarah shouted back to him, waving. She assisted Tamsyn's wriggling dismount from the bench and followed her over the lawn to the truck. "Right as rain, but we suddenly decided, midway through our tea and our CBeebies, that we wanted to come home. A bit emphatic, we were, so..." She paused for long enough to hoist the little girl up by the armpits and into Lee's embrace as he got out. "So I was a bit concerned that things might not be all right with *you*."

"Oh, no. We're both okay." He swung Tamsyn round in his arms then settled her in her accustomed place on his hip, heavy as she was getting these days, beginning to outgrow her perch. "What's up, my merry morgawr? Why did you want to come home?"

"For Lee," she said simply, as often addressing him as if he wasn't there or was somebody else, a habit he found oddly soothing. "Lee was poorly. Got plants for you," she added, suddenly switching to forceful direct contact. She planted a noisy kiss on his cheek. "Lemme down, please. Got to go and see Dada."

Gideon came round the bonnet of the truck to intercept her. To Lee there was no finer sight than his strong, graceful move to scoop her up, all remaining fears about his injury long departed. "When you say *emphatic*," he asked Sarah apprehensively, rumpling Tamsyn's curls, "did she..."

"What, float me out of the window and down the lane? Not a bit of it, and you two gents can stop fretting yourselves about that, I reckon. She just... explained, like a proper little grown-up. I wish my lot would use their fists less and their words more."

"What on earth did she say?"

"Pretty much what she just told you. Lee was poorly, and she had to go home to get his plants for him. She's a convincing little beggar when she talks like that, so I brought her along. And we happened to meet Mrs Coulter on the way up, who was kind enough to sit with us and wait. She's brought Tamsyn some new books—hasn't she, Tamsie?"

Tamsyn left off trying to pull Gid's radio out of its holster. Always a desirable toy, that had been, and once she'd raised a station-wide alert by hitting its mayday switch. She sat up and surveyed her father as if seeing him in a new light. Then she beamed. "Mr Policeman Badger!"

"Leave that alone, you terror. You know we talked about the improper use of police resources. Who the hell is Mr Policeman Badger?"

"Swear box," Lee said promptly, holding out his hand. "Honestly, Dada."

"Yeah. Sh-... I mean, oh dear. Sorry. How much is a *hell* these days?"

"50p, and another quid for reoffending." Lee turned to look at the old lady, who was nodding benignly at this family scene from her place on the bench. "Thank you for bringing more books, Mrs

Coulter, but you shouldn't, you know. She's already got hundreds, and hundreds again on her iPad."

Mrs Coulter gave a kind of sneezing snort that flashed Lee back through four years to Granny Ragwen's living room, and Rufus Pendower falling helplessly prey to the old pellar sorceress and her sympathetic magic. A little figure fashioned from blue-tack, trailed through the ashes, tormented by a feather-tip to the nose... "Her iPad?" she echoed. "That's an outlandish device for such little hands."

"She has to have one. They all do. The school sends out part of her homework that way." Shaking his head, Lee wondered why he was justifying himself to her. "I'm not poorly, though, Tamsie." It was always best to tell her the truth, so he added, "I was a few hours ago, and you're a clever girl to know that, but I'm fine now. Will you show me your new books?"

"Show in a minute, Lee. Got to get bleujyow. Down, please, Dada."

Obediently Gideon released her. He watched her patter off into the verdant jungle behind the house. "She's gone to get her what?"

"Her bleujyow," Lee said wonderingly. "Old Cornish word for flowers. Did you teach her that?"

"Not me. I just keep inadvertently teaching her to swear. Little imp, to know you weren't well!" Gideon turned to meet Sarah's concerned frown. "He's better now, Sarah, but I'd just as soon get him indoors and—"

"No, no. I'm okay." Lee went to sit on the bench, his eye caught by the bright front cover of the top book on the pile set up there, a vividly painted little squirrel holding hands with a long-necked weasel and a rabbit. "Look at this. *The Tufty Club!* I remember seeing one of these in my gran's attic. They were meant to help teach road safety to little kids. This feckless weasel was my favourite. He keeps getting into trouble, but the others always forgive him."

"Huh. A bit like Daz Prowse, eh?" Taking the book from Lee's outstretched hand, Gideon leafed through it. "This is quite old, Mrs Coulter. Vintage. You don't have to give her things like that."

"Oh, I don't mind, dear. Not having grandchildren of my own, it's a pleasure to hand books on to such a careful little soul as Tamsyn."

"All these cute bunnies and squirrels, though... They finish up here at the end saying their prayers to Jesus around the manger. Setting aside the outdated road-safety information, I'm not sure I want—"

"It's a child of its time, dear, like the rest of us, and I don't see what's outdated about teaching a child not to run under a car. We have some other books, too." She began to turn them over so Gideon could see. *Musa Goes to the Masjid. K'tonton and the Gefilte Fish, Room on the Broom. Humanism—What's That?* "We're interested," she said tranquilly, watching Gideon adjust his ideas. "We're finding out."

Lee recaptured the book. The squirrel and his mates were endearing, brightly depicted in their post-war jackets and shorts. The prayers at the end seemed tacked on, as if the author had been reminded of her duties. For a shilling and a postcard, the back cover promised, you could get a Tufty badge and lifelong membership of the club. A shilling didn't seem bad for lifelong anything. "If the Christian influence is limited to these little guys," he said musingly, "I don't think we need worry. Ezekiel had to learn a Bible verse a day at Tamsyn's age, or the pastor would hit him across the palm with a ruler."

Gideon flinched. The reaction was briefly delayed, as if having to cross the decades to reach him. "What? No. He was a grim old sod, but he never raised his hand to us."

"That's a family legend. Zeke let it go on to shield you and Ma, and the old man's memory. The ruler never left a mark, but it stung, and the humiliation was the thing that really hurt."

"Lee, can we... Can we talk about this some other time?"

Lee raised a horrified hand to his mouth. Gid had gone pale as ash beneath his summer tan. Sarah Kemp was staring, Mrs C nodding with a sympathy he desperately did not deserve.

Tamsyn shattered the moment, a stocky little saving grace. "Lee!" she declared, bursting like a tank through the barricade of adult legs. Her arms were full of stems almost as tall as she was, her fists clenched around bundles of leaves. She tumbled them into his lap and stood panting. "Dreams-of-mice, Murphy's ears, bind-me-round-tightly. There."

"Now, miss," Mrs Coulter said, with the gentlest reproof. "Only the pellar-kind understand those funny old names. You know their proper ones."

"Valerian. Wild lettuce, ivy." She paused for a moment, ordering her thoughts, a little gleam of mischief brightening her face. "*Valeriana officinalis, Lactuca virosa, Hedera helix*. There!"

The old lady broke into a cackle. "There," she crowed, hoisting Tamsyn up to sit between her and Lee on the bench. "There indeed! *What* a clever girl."

"That's Uncle Zeke's work, that is," Gideon said, finding and kindly holding Lee's gaze. Lee knew what he was doing: getting Zeke's name back into the air between them, as calmly and prosaically as he could. "He's taken her round the lanes and taught her the Latin names since before she could walk. Hasn't he, sweetheart?"

The endearment wasn't aimed at Tamsyn. Lee nodded gratefully. "According to this, she thinks I need sedation, a good night's sleep, and to be tied down to heart and home. Can't argue with the first two, but..." He inhaled the valerian's mousy scent, the sticky white sap of the wild lettuce, then put the whole lot aside in favour of her warm little body in his lap. She was small for her age but compact with health and moorland muscle. "I don't need ivy to tie me down here with you and Dada, do I?"

"Don't go."

"Poppet, I'm not." Anxiously he wound one dark curl around his finger. "I just had a bad day at work. And I came back all stupid and saying stupid things. I just need a night in front of the telly with Dada and my spooky little mawgawr, that's all. It was clever of you to know."

"Clever," she agreed, nestling against him. Her plants delivered and her object achieved, she was losing interest, watching down the track as if in anticipation of another visitor. "Zeke's coming now. Zeke and Zold."

Ezekiel had borrowed the dog for a week. Eleanor was convinced that children who grew up with a pet turned out to be kinder and more responsible adults, and she and Zeke had been experimenting to see if they could fit care, feeding and walks around the demands of three-year-old twins. Lee didn't have to be psychic to know that battle was lost before it had begun: Toby and Mikey once having set their hearts on a pup, the creature would be waiting with a bow around its fluffy little neck on the morning of their birthday. "Not yet," he said. "Zeke's bringing Isolde back tomorrow. I know you've missed her, but you've been a good girl to share her..."

Promptly tyres began to crunch in the lane beyond the hawthorns. Lee and Gideon exchanged a look. "Do you ever feel like telling us," Gid asked gently, "how you know this stuff, miss? About Zeke, and... about Lee feeling bad today?"

She wasn't one to waste words. "Clever," she said again, with a perfect blend of mischief and pity for her parents' mental darkness. "Clever, Dada. That's all."

Zeke rolled his ministerial Volvo up the last few yards of the track and parked neatly behind the police truck. He got out, and held the back door open as if he'd been a chauffeur and the shaggy mutt inside a visiting peer of the realm. Isolde heaved herself off her travelling rug and out onto the lawn. Catching sight of Tamsyn, she launched an overjoyed charge. Tamsyn, all concerns with the adult world instantly forgotten, met her halfway, and the two collided in a noisy heap in the wildflower patch, petals and dislodged bees flying up around them. "Afternoon," Zeke said, watching this reunion indulgently. "Sorry to return her a day early. Eleanor and I have been called to a conference in Sussex, and our sitter has an allergy to dogs."

Gideon grinned. "So, you'll be getting a new sitter, then?"

"What? No, Jennifer is very good."

"Not when there's a pup in the house. And I'm guessing there will be."

Zeke glanced skyward. "We'll *see*," he declared, for what was clearly the thousandth time that week. "Is everything all right here? Lee doesn't look very well. And Tamsyn's given him herbs."

"I'm fine," Lee told him reassuringly. Gideon looked as though he could use to hear it too. "Rough day, and I came home with a headache. She knew about it, like she sometimes does, so I'm about to go push all this lot through the blender for a kill-or-cure smoothie, and—"

"No, Lee!" Tamsyn's head popped briefly up over the chamomile daisies. "*Tisane.*"

She vanished before he could ask. "A *tisane*," he echoed, turning to old Mrs C. "You'll have taught her that, then?"

"Must have done, dear. I'm getting on, though, and I don't always remember who I've been and who I haven't. What I've *said* and what I haven't, I mean, of course. She's a very bright little girl."

"She is that. Well, if everyone would like to come in and share my tisane, or just a pot of PG Tips, you're very welcome—aren't they, Gid?"

Sarah Kemp took an accurate read of Gideon's expression. She got to her feet. "Oh, no. Time I got back to my bunch of savages. Wait, though—isn't this f-... Er, the weekend Tamsie usually spends with me and Wilf?"

She'd almost choked on the effort not to say *fuckfest*. Lee carefully straightened his face. "It is. But I think we'll hang on to her, now she's home. How did you, er... know we call it that?"

"I might've heard Gideon strolling away from our house after dropping her off one Friday night, singing it to the tune of *Surf's Up*. Meatloaf," she added for Zeke's benefit, nodding in his direction. "Oh, bloody hell—*you* didn't know they called it that either, did you?"

"Can you imagine me telling him?" Gideon asked. "Honestly, Sarah!"

"Sorry. Sorry. Definitely my cue to be off, then. Sorry, Zeke."

But Ezekiel, for once, didn't seem to have picked up on his brother's impropriety. He'd sat down in the space Sarah had vacated on the bench and was leafing through Tamsyn's new books. "I like this one," he said. "Sound road-safety advice, and..." He turned the last page and glanced up slyly at Gid. "Spiritually improving, too."

"You *would* like it. It's from the bloody fifties, just like your moral outlook."

But Zeke seemed beyond provocation tonight. Maybe a week of negotiations with Toby and Mike had worn him down. He began to laugh helplessly. "Oh, good Lord. Look at this!"

He was pointing to one of the illustrations. A stout badger in 1950s police uniform, complete with helmet, was carrying a wounded bunny away from the scene of a road-traffic accident. His expression was severe, his grip on the little creature tender. The artist had depicted him mid-stride, one big foot poised. The resemblance was irresistible. Lee too began to laugh. Zeke pointed to Gideon and declared, just as Tamsyn had done, "Mr Policeman Badger!"

One huge sob cut Lee's laughter. It felt like the edge of a shovel. He clapped a hand to his mouth, but too late—Sarah was staring at him in dismay: the dog too, frozen between one rollicking leap and the next. Tamsyn and Mrs Coulter seemed less concerned, as if this might be a natural development at the end of Lee's kind of long hard day. But he had the full and overwhelming attention of both Frayne brothers. Zeke, for once, was closest. He put an arm around Lee's shoulders, paling with shock. "Lee, my friend. What on earth's wrong?"

Nothing, Lee wanted to tell him. Or perhaps to tell him the truth: *monsters. A monster who gave it her all, lost and far away from Wonderland as she was. Count down from five, or four and three quarters... And here am I in the House of Love and Wolves, of loving wolves, where I have everything, husband, child, friends, family, an undreamed-of richness of life.* If he moved his hand, would all this come tumbling out—or, worse, another racking sob? He took his chance. "Nothing. I'm fine."

Gideon crouched in front of him. "And I'm a giant badger with powers of arrest, apparently. So if you don't want to get carted into the house like..." He paused, took an upside-down look at the book still open on Zeke's lap. "Like Harry the Hare, you'd better cooperate."

***

Not quite asleep, Lee lay watching the Bodmin sunset, a gilded projection on the bedroom wall. The show could last for hours at this time of year. First the plaster cornicing would begin to shine. Then a vast rectangle of light would start its long journey from ceiling to carpet, holding between the shadows of the window frames bright blocks of gold, crimson, and finally the eerie bronze that presaged the dark.

To watch the whole process meant privilege. Meant life in a house so safe that evening hours could pass undisturbed, meant loving human presences close at hand, guardians of his peace. Tamsyn hadn't let him out of her sight. She'd turned down teatime, TV and a final romp with Isolde, and was curled up tight by his side.

He'd tried to send her away but surrendered. She was exactly what he needed. She knew that as surely as she'd known what herbs to pick for his tisane, and she'd sat on the end of the bed, a small stern monitor, while he'd knocked it back, not omitting to stick out his tongue and make poison-victim faces for her amusement. Isolde had come thumping onto the quilt, completing his captivity. Zeke and Gid had made half-hearted efforts to dislodge child and dog, then given up in their turn.

It was infinitely reassuring to Lee to hear the brothers banging around downstairs. Probably they thought they were being quiet. Pans clattered in the kitchen. A door slammed, and elaborate shushing noises found their way into the gilded light, warm as the brush of a hand to Lee's skin. Drifting, he caught snatches of their arguments, conducted in stage whispers whenever they met in the hallway. Did Lee need a doctor or not? Was what ailed him physical or spiritual? *Once more,* Zeke rumbled, *he has exposed himself, without the least protection, to God only knows what evil.* And Gideon's countering growl: *He's got his own protections. And what if it's just flu, an upset stomach?*

The sunset flowed on. When Lee was next aware, the haunting bronze had filled the room, veils and wings of it, the very last trace of the day. The sounds were closer to him, as if the brothers had settled on the ottoman on the half-landing to talk. "Keep your *voice* down," Zeke was saying, though the deep timbre of his own was making the crystals stir faintly in the old chandelier above the bed. "You may look like a moose, but there's no need to bellow like one. You'll wake him up."

"I won't. He's out cold."

Lee wanted to say that he wasn't, to warn him, but it wasn't quite true. Some part of his brain was blissfully asleep. "Here," Gideon went on, "you're the one who takes the kid botanising around the lanes. I know most of the plants Tamsyn brought him tonight, but what the devil are Murphy's ears?"

"Murphy's... Good grief, I haven't heard them called that since I was a kid, and Granny Ragwen used to come pulling them out of the graveyard by the chapel. They're a kind of wild-growing ancestor of the lettuce."

"The pastor must've loved that."

"Oh, he never knew. I'd give the old girl the heads-up if I found her at it when he was on his way. She would chant the names of the plants as she picked them, and she told me the Murphy part was a corruption of Morpheus, the god of sleep. The leaves have a sedative effect."

"Bloody hell. Are you saying my four-year-old slipped her dad a mickey?"

"Well, a Murphy at any rate. It won't do him any harm."

Lee tried to imagine Zeke in the graveyard. Then he didn't have to: the place and the actions unspooled for him. The lanky teenage boy slipped out of the chapel's rear door and picked his way through the headstones, leaving a trail in the long wet grass. The replay was panoramic. There on the path was Ma Frayne, also looking ready to head the pastor off. By her side, a sturdy, handsome lad of five or six years old alertly watched the scene. Zeke approached the old woman plucking seed heads from a plant like a straggling buttercup. *Herb bennet,* she said, as if to an old friend. *The clue's in the name. They say it's for Saint Benedict, but that's all nonsense of course. Herb benefit's the truth of it.*

All right, but you'd better go. The pastor's coming.

You should learn these things. Beasts and priests, your family are, right back to Lyonesse, and those old drewydhyow weren't ashamed to use the power of the green.

Those old what?

Druids, foolish boy. Learn the Latin names for the plants, if you're too good and holy for the old ones. Start with the bennet here—Geum urbanum.

I can't. He doesn't let me. I don't have time, and anyway...

He stopped. A dazed wonder touched his expression, lifting away the harsh mask his father had begun to fasten there. *Granny? Where did you go?*

The churchyard was empty. Zeke thought so anyway, though a less-brainwashed lad might have seen the old woman's lightning movement, the flip of a hood, the whisk of a moss-brown cloak around incongruous crimplene trousers and flowered blouse. Her seamless drop to her knees amid the foliage. She was right there, and heaving with held-back laughter, the old devil...

Lee began to laugh too. He grabbed a corner of the pillow and pressed it to his mouth. Some aspects of poor Zeke's upbringing were funny, his legacy of easily-cracked ice, the pompousness that melted at the antics of his twin boys. Others were grim. Gideon's mind had been running along the same lines. The churchyard vanished and Lee tuned in easily to his husband's thoughts. "I'm not sure I want Tamsie learning knockout potions," Gid said uneasily, "but I'm glad he's getting some rest. He's a bit out of control today, and he... told me something about you, Zeke."

"Uh-oh."

"Yeah. I didn't know whether to mention it or not. Maybe I should let the dead lie. But—look, I know our dad was very strict with you. I didn't think he'd ever hurt you physically."

"What? He never did."

"He did, though. When you didn't learn your Bible verse. Here."

Lee's control slipped further still, and he experienced both Gideon's sorrow and Zeke's astonished flinch, the way Zeke's hand felt in Gid's when he picked it up, Zeke's hard-repressed pleasure at being touched by the brother he'd adored despite all the world's efforts to blast that affection to death in the bud. "Nonsense, Gideon," he rasped. "It was nothing. And I *did* learn my Bible verse, ninety nine times out of a hundred, so there was no need. I didn't spend *my* adolescence watching *Stargate* and scrumping apples."

"Well. The hundredth time, then."

"It was nothing at all. Our grandfather used to whale the life out of the pastor with the end of his leather belt."

"Much good it did his personality."

"Fair point, but—"

"Look, my own feelings on when to hit children are *never*. But I've come across a few households where the kids take a walloping in good part, and the parents give it that way—lovingly, if love can come on the underside of a slipper. At least they're *being* parents. Not you, though, Zeke. It never should've been done to you."

At length—unhurriedly, as if Gid's recognition had taken the sting from the long-ago punishment—Zeke withdrew his hand. "I think," he said gently, "your focus is on the wrong part of this. Yes, the pastor hit me. I did hate it, and the humiliation made me a far worse person than nature intended in later years. But I'm more concerned about Lee. He'd normally rather have died than probe into memories I'd hidden so deeply away. Wouldn't he?"

"Yes. I... I'll talk to him. But—Christ, I'm sorry for what happened to you."

"It was long ago." Zeke let a beat or two of silence pass, and Lee felt the firework brush of his indestructible straight-faced mischief. A ripple of melody from the same artist who'd inspired Gid's fuckfest theme... "And it was far away. Of course if I said it was so much better than it is today, that would be an outrageous bloody lie. My life today is better than anything I could ever have dreamed of in the pastor's house. A lot of that's down to Lee, and maybe a tiny bit to you too, so... both of you, let that sad old memory go, all right? *I* have."

A stir in the air as Zeke got to his feet. Gideon's sorrow wreathed upward with him, only partly assuaged. "All right, I guess. Will you stay to supper?"

"Perhaps Lee should reveal some dreadful secret from my past more often. I like you like this—all stricken and trying to make things up to me. No, I can't stay for supper, thank you. I have to pick up Buster on my way home."

"Buster, the... pup, I presume?"

"That's right. Six months old, heart of gold and guaranteed childproof. Bought him last Sunday."

"But you'd only had Isolde for a day or so then."

"Yes. She helped me pick him out."

A pause, and then the muffled, rhythmical thump which was Ezekiel's effort to start to creep down the stairs. Gideon must have stayed in place, staring at him. Lee rocked with his amusement. "Zeke," Gid said after a moment, and the thumping ceased: Zeke coming to a halt, looking enquiringly back over his shoulder. "Zeke, you *shmoop*!"

Chapter Four
Depends Who's
in the Changing Room

The child and the dog had left Gideon the narrowest strip on the outside edge of the bed. Manoeuvring into place, he checked that Tamsyn was deeply asleep. He folded Isolde's ears down, and addressed himself in a whisper to the half-awake gleam visible through Lee's eyelashes. "Some fuckfest this is."

The glimmer increased. Lee extracted one hand from the bedclothes and gave him a clumsy pat. "Make it up to you tomorrow."

"How you feeling, sweetheart?"

"Undone."

"Well, your kid drugged you."

The hand made its way from Gideon's hip to their daughter's curls. "Murphy's ears?"

"Yeah. Zeke told me what they were."

"You should probably arrest her."

"I will in the morning. Then, while she's cooling her heels in the Bodmin nick, I'll come back here, and..."

"We can let the festivities commence. Mmm. You will take this stinking lump of dog off me first, won't you?"

Gideon chuckled. "I promise. Speaking of dogs, Zeke's bought one. I reckon he did it as soon as the kids asked, then borrowed Isolde to try and save face and pretend to be thinking about it."

"Shmoop." Lee shifted to face him, as best he could beneath the little girl and the mutt. "I'm sorry I freaked out today, Gid. Sorry I dragged you away from work."

"It was nothing. Lawrence practically threw me out when she heard her favourite clairvoyant was in trouble. Made mincemeat out of Sergeant Lennox, too."

"Lennox is a good copper. She was just scared."

"So was I. You had a bad time of it, love."

"I know. The full bleeding, puking, fugued-out performance."

"When's our next appointment at Trelowarren?"

"End of this month." Lee rubbed his brow against the pillow. "I love how you say *our* appointment, when it's my scrambled mess of a brain that causes all these problems."

"Your brains are my brains. That's how this marriage thing works."

"Ugh."

"Make sure the date's on the calendar. Mustn't miss this one." Edging carefully around Tamsyn, Gideon leaned in and made a softly-growling play of biting the back of Lee's skull. "Attack of the zombie werewolf! Imagine the doctors' horror, when the scan showed... *no brains at all!*"

"Pack it in, you clown. You'll wake the kid."

"I should probably take her through to bed anyway."

"Don't bother. It's four in the morning. She might as well stay where she is. And I feel like... everybody's where they should be tonight. It's fine."

Gideon considered this, listening to Lee's breathing settle back into sleep. If the ship had gone down and the bed were a lifeboat, he had everyone he needed on board. He'd stop to pick up Ma and Zeke, of course. Toby and Mike and their mother, whose quiet administration of her preacher husband and twin boys had endeared her to him greatly. He'd better hoist Buster aboard too, hypothetical dog as he was at the moment, a dog in the bush.

And what about Elowen? Beginning to drift with his bed-boat into deep waters, Gideon shivered. His mind provided a scene half-pinched from *Titanic*, half his own work. Elowen, clinging to a spar of wreckage, cried out piteously to him to save baby Cadan, wrapped up cosily on the wooden board. The boat—pretty full now—wallowed and rocked on the tide. Still, he had to do what he could, and he steered towards her. He reached out and picked up the baby. This was a wish-fulfilment dream, apparently: Lee, stark naked and smiling, intercepted his next move. *Ah, leave her to drown, Gid. Then you'll never have to think again about how a nine-stone girl with no combat skills beat you hollow and stole your little girl.*

Gideon liked that idea. And so, with Elowen falling away to the bottom of the sea, and everyone he loved gathered safe aboard his sacred vessel, he painlessly dissolved into sleep.

***

Alice Rawle had combat skills. She would weigh less than Elowen, dried out and drained by her gift, but she was fair game. Gideon's mind solved its puzzle and dream-dumped him a year into the past, back into the road outside Dark primary school. Alice got out of the car. Gideon tried to approach her, and she held up her hand. And Gideon's nose began to bleed, not Lee's, and something inside him ached with a terrible hunger for change—a held-back sneeze magnified a thousand times over, an interrupted come.

He had no words for the feeling. And then it didn't matter, because Tamsyn, held in Lee's arms, raised her hand too. Pointed one casual finger... Alice folded like matchwood back into the car. The cessation of her pushing, pressing field of influence freed Gideon like a bird from a net. Gave him back command of limbs and action, even of his thoughts. In the dream he began to run.

His husband, kid and dog had manoeuvred him even closer to the edge of the bed, and he flipped overboard with a crash. "Fuck," Lee said, waking up. Isolde began to bark, and Tamsyn, wide-eyed, raised her head. "Lee," she whispered, small voice hoarse with sympathy, as if she'd have let him off if she could. "Swear box!"

"Sorry! Gid, what the f-... Are you all right?"

"Just barely." He levered himself off the floor. "I was dreaming. I've unmasked your Launceston monster."

"What?"

"Yeah. I think it's Alice Rawle."

Immediately Gideon wished the words unsaid. Monsters were best kept out of the bedroom. Daylight and a cup of tea in their cheerful kitchen would have been a better backdrop. But Lee, tough Falmouth deckhand as well as gentle seer, stretched out a hand to him. "Come here. What put her into your head?"

Gratefully he took the offered grasp and let Lee haul him back into the warm, rumpled safety of their lifeboat bed. There was just about room for him now that the dog had shifted her fat backside. "*You* did, on our way home. The counting and the wonderland thing."

"I'm sorry?"

"You might not remember." He put an arm around Lee's shoulders. "I'm sure you were counting from one to five in

Launceston because all five schools there were under threat, yeah. But in the car, you started counting *down* from five, and you said... it never was wonderland, but she certainly gave it her all."

"I did?"

"Yeah, several times. Then you told me you were asleep. Look, sweetheart, this can wait till morning."

"No. I'd best put this kid to bed, though. Come here, you."

Tamsyn sat up and looked at him serenely. "It's okay. Can do it myself."

"Er... you can?"

"Yes, Lee. Take Zold and go to my proper bed."

Her parents exchanged a wondering look. "Er... wow," Lee said after a moment. "Okay. That would be great. And could you..." He paused, then went on experimentally, "Could you possibly wash your face, clean your teeth and change into your pyjamas?"

She nodded earnestly. "Can."

She wasn't exactly a chatterbox. Like her late attempts at walking, speech seemed to be something irrelevant, a chore for ordinary mortals. Lately, though, she'd begun small homely tasks for herself like getting dressed and making sentences, and before Gideon could begin to wonder about this latest development, she'd slipped neatly off the bed and headed for the door, Isolde at her heels like a hairy shadow. "Bloody hell," he observed. "Should we let her?"

"I'll go check on her in a few minutes. Alice *Rawle*, Gid?"

Lee was pale with shock. Gideon really would have kept his big trap shut if he'd had time to think. "I'm probably wrong. But you said I should subtract four, or four and three quarters, from some words you kept saying—*she certainly gave it her all.*"

"That's a bit cryptic, isn't it?"

"I know. But I think, when it's a particularly bad one, your mind tries to make it as abstract as possible."

"So abstract I can't work it out myself? What's the use of that?"

Don't say that, don't say that. Don't ever ask what the point is, the use, if you can't see the future or unmask a beast or whatever impossible task the world's laid on you. Gideon held him tighter. His own world rocked sickeningly on its axis whenever he thought about Lee doubting himself in those terms. "You don't *have* to work it out. You have a handsome, incredibly intelligent husband to do the thinking for you."

"Oh, that's right. I forgot." Lee shifted to see him. "Go on, then."

"Okay. If you take away four and a bit words from *she certainly gave it her all*, that leaves us with *all*, and the R sound before it. And the wonderland part was obvious—I just didn't want to think about it. Or her."

"Oh, shit. You're right. Alice Rawle."

"I don't get it. She's nothing to us, isn't she?"

Nothing but a memory from Lee's childhood, and a minute on a sunny afternoon outside the school gates. Gideon kissed his brow. "Look, she might've been one of your stray signals, right? A dream."

"Right. Or Sergeant Smartarse might've read my clues wrong." A first trace of daylight was silvering the air. Lee pushed against Gideon's shoulder, turning his face to the light. "I don't think you did, though. And she's *not* nothing to us, no. Because..."

"Because I should've followed up on her. On whatever the hell General Bolton-Reeves was doing, driving her into Dark village like a bloody guided missile. Why didn't I?"

"I don't know. All I remember is that he didn't get far with his plans, because..."

"Because of *our* little missile. Maybe that was it. I couldn't cope with anything more to do with our kid at that time, so I..."

"Shelved it? We both did that. Not just you."

Gideon shivered in gratitude: what a bloody blessing it was, never to be left alone with the tough stuff! "Okay," he said, reaching a hand to Lee's spine. "It's still weird, though. I should've chased her up, made sure she was with that buttoned-up blimp of her own free will."

"I don't see how you could have. The blimp's top brass. You'd need much more than a nosebleed and suspicions before the army would let you near her, even as a copper."

"Maybe. But I didn't even try. Never went after David Rawle, either, to see why he lied to us about her."

"It is weird. Not too late, though." Tensions gathered in Lee's shoulders, an inner straightening of a spine that had carried too much of late. "If you can't get to Alice, maybe I can help you reach Uncle Dave. He lied about his missus being alive. I can help you find him, at any rate. I can..."

A hot splash hit Gideon's chest. Gideon gasped and sat up, grabbed a tissue from the box on the bedside table: shifted to kneel over and immobilise Lee, and dabbed the fresh blood from his upper lip. "No."

"No what?"

"Listen to me. Do you remember last year, when this whole household was in meltdown over Dave Rawle and his bright ideas, and you told me that I could..." Gideon paused, settled a bit more of his weight. "That I could *put my foot down* with you? That I was the only person who could?"

Lee stared up at him. "I remember."

"This is me doing it."

"Oh." One corner of Lee's mouth quivered. Colour gathered under his skin. "Really, Sergeant?"

"None of your kinky stuff. I mean it. I want you to stop."

"To... stop?"

"Yes. In a minute, I'm gonna go call Tollgate Road and get them to clue the Launceston lads in that their schools intruder might be Alice Rawle. That discharges my responsibility *and* yours, as far as we can do that in the middle of the night with nothing more to back us up than your hallucinations. Okay?" He waited until Lee had accorded him a nod and a pallid smile. "Okay. And then, just for a few weeks—the rest of this summer, say—you're going to stop. Pack in your cold-reads, your police work, everything. Let all the monsters alone. I know you can build walls to shield yourself."

"The walls cut me off from you and Tamsie, last time I tried that."

"Build 'em differently this time. I'll deal with the monsters, I swear. You do think it was Alice who came creeping around that Launceston school today, don't you?"

"Yeah. Not sure I'd ever have got it without you, but yes."

"Right. I can find grounds—solid, boring, everyday reasons— to talk to David. I'll be subtle. I can start by finding out why there were armed guards at the gate of that school of his. Take it from there."

"Gid, you're gonna have to be careful. He was freaked out all the way about Alice last time we met him. Scared and full of threats."

"I know, and I haven't forgotten that he wanted to add Tamsyn to his collection of so-called gifted kids. That's where you come in."

Lee wriggled his hips. "Oh? I do have a job, do I, in this new regime of yours?"

"You do. Excuse me turning into Victorian papa, but here it is. Stay at home and mind our kid, or take a summer job on one of the yachts where you can bring her along with you."

"What? I can't just... *retire*."

"Not retirement. A sabbatical." Fires of resistance rose in Lee's eyes, and Gideon began a slow burn of his own. What was the point of all the loving protection in the world, if Lee wouldn't consent to be protected? "Look, I don't care how you do it. Cancel your clients. Put your TV work on hold. Anything that connects you to all of that, just... stop it. Stop."

His growl of authority startled them both. Would have brought an answering roar from Lee any other day. *Who do you think you're ordering around, Mr Policeman bloody Badger?* Gideon should have been alarmed at the sudden surrender in the wide green gaze fixed on his. Instead relief swept him, and a rushing sense of power. Was he—just for once, here and now when it really mattered—about to win an argument with this man?

He had to. A fresh stain of scarlet had appeared on Lee's upper lip. "Just stop," Gideon repeated, the growl mitigated now by tenderness and a kind of fearful pride. "I don't care how you do it. Sit in a deckchair in the garden. Have naps. Give yourself a break, sweetheart, or all of this is gonna break *you*, and I can't bear that." He bent down to kiss him, words rasping in his throat. "For God's sake, Lee, please. You're still bleeding."

***

The admonition must have worked, or something was working at any rate. Morning came, as lovely a moorland daybreak as ever had cheered the heart of a copper getting ready for his daily rounds. Lee was having a pleasant dream. Gideon, much to his surprise, found himself in it with him.

He felt capable of anything today. The world lay before him like a series of problems that longed to be solved. David and Alice Rawle, Rufus Pendower, monsters in the Launceston schools... All these would tumble like ninepins if he hit them right. There was nothing that couldn't be done by a local bobby with determination and energy to spare.

Such strange energies! They ran through Gideon like soft fire. He sat down on the window seat, uniform cap in hand. Lee, stretched out on his front in the bed, was also lying blissfully on top of a vividly detailed dream image of Gideon himself.

They were on the clifftop near Drift. Dropping his cap, Gideon bit back a bark of laughter at the weird double vision: that he could be here in his bedroom, neatly buttoned and ready for the day, and at the same time flat on his back on the sunny turf, knees drawn up, in a state of such absolute abandoned sensuality. A pale moon rode in the blue sky, only a little way past first quarter. It was safe to growl a little, show his teeth. Lee pinned him down: spoke deep into his mind. *All right, love. Yes, show me that. Let me see.*

What the hell did that mean? Shivering, Gideon pulled away. He had no right to be watching, and if eavesdroppers heard no good of themselves, what would become of feckless souls who looked into their lovers' dreams? A long time ago, Lee had offered a changing-room metaphor to describe how his gifts worked: even if someone left the door open, he didn't have to peer inside. Would struggle not to, but...

Depends on who's in the changing room, Gid.

He smiled at the memory. He'd been Lee's irresistible temptation then, so it seemed only fair that now the tables were turned. Lee was behind the open door, defences down, laid deliciously bare. The soft-fire energies surged again, something to do with the growl and the gleam of pointed teeth, an urge to push and pounce. *I'll show you.*

Yes. Let me have it.

Lee groaned and grabbed at the pillow. One fist closed on the cotton, and Gideon felt it like a clench around his balls. Gasping, sitting forward, he checked that the bedroom door was shut. Although the room was drenched in sunlight, he'd just heard his watch beep six o'clock: early hours, even in the busy Tyack-Frayne household, and no chance of interruption from his kid or the dog. Morning shift at Bodmin station didn't start till eight, but there was backlogged paperwork to tackle. He had time.

Still he had no business here. Or if he did, if Lee was working up his morning glory in a sexy dream about him, Gideon should clamber into bed and make it an honest reality. Nothing Lee liked more than a tussle with his copper in full uniform while he himself lay naked as day. Gideon shivered with laughter. He'd have given a month's pay for a photo of the two of them last time they'd done it that way, Lee perched elegantly on the edge of the bed, wearing Gid's cap at a jaunty angle and nothing else, while Gideon knelt between his thighs, hoping the come stains would sponge off his best dress pants.

The memory swept him past a point of no return. He unzipped, and Lee writhed on the bed. The duvet was tangled around his thighs, exposing his backside, as powerfully erotic a sight to Gideon now as it had been in the first days of their love. Muscles bunched as he thrust down. He let go of the pillow with one hand and reached beneath himself. Too much for Gideon, who surged like a wild Atlantic wave into the dream, shuddered and grabbed at his cock and climaxed with a broken-off yell. He caught Lee up in the rush and the break of it, the wave's beautiful death.

Lee's movements quickened. He gave a grinding wail. Gideon knew it so well, dearly loved to be its cause. His gentle, quiet-spoken husband, almost beside himself with pleasure, letting loose that animal sound as he went over—Mr Tiger indeed, blazing through all of his stripes... "Gideon," he rasped afterwards, voice a raw shadow. "Oh, Gideon. Gid..."

Steadying himself against the window frame, Gideon got to his feet. The room was swaying around him. The window seat was a favourite spot for lovemaking: one of them had left a box of tissues there, and he quickly mopped up. Fastened his zip with clumsy, tingling fingers. By the time Lee raised his head, he was back in his skin. He could—just feasibly—have walked into the room five seconds ago, to give Lee a kiss before leaving. They'd omitted that ritual only once in all their time together, on the day when Gideon had run onto Alan Tremethick's knife-blade in Bodmin, and almost put himself beyond the reach of that sweet mouth forever.

It was odd: he'd scarcely thought about Tremethick in four years, not to the extent of recalling his name. He'd persisted in his refusal to press charges, so presumably the poor bastard had vanished back into the world he'd come from, that swamp of drugs and desperation. Another line he'd failed to follow up on, a darkness he'd set aside in favour of life and light with Lee... "Morning," he said, cheerfully casual. "Got a peck on the cheek for your old man, before he goes off down the tin mines?"

Lee emitted a faint snort. "Old man?" he echoed incredulously, propping himself on his elbows. "You're an untamed force of nature, you are, even in my..." He looked up at Gideon, a sudden blush painting him from collarbones to the roots of his hair. "In my dreams. Oh."

"Oh?" One more effort of evasion was probably worthwhile, and Gideon leaned innocently in for his kiss, hoping his own colour wasn't too high. "Dreaming of me, were you?"

"Yeah, only I... I really thought you were here." Lee shifted his hips and coloured more deeply still. "Oh, great. Like a bloody teenager. It's been years since I did that."

"Well, nothing wrong with it, is there?"

"No, apart from the bedlinen." He planted a thoughtful kiss on Gideon's mouth, as if tasting and testing the flavour of his words. "Are you on the dawn patrol, handsome?"

"Nope. Just going in early to catch up on some admin."

"Will it wait?"

"For you? Forever."

"Good. I'll fix you some breakfast."

***

A working breakfast, Gideon reckoned. These were regular events in Chy Lowen, one of the many reasons why it remained a house of joy. If school or behaviour issues were involved, Tamsyn would be upright and serious in her booster seat, Isolde perched beside her, like a hairy secretary ready to take notes. Sometimes Zeke and Eleanor would be there too, the twins in their high chairs. The big square kitchen with its scrubbed-pine table became a boardroom, a space for voicing concerns before they could burrow their way underground.

Just Lee and Gideon today. Silence still drifted from upstairs. Tamsyn at rest spread ripples of quiet around herself, expanding rings of peace. *Every home should have one*, Gideon reflected, reaching back into her serenity. *Dream on, sweetheart.*

The boardroom had certain rules: that food should be respected, and the time to eat it, no matter how urgent the business in hand, and so Gideon made appreciative short work of his fry-up and toast. Lee took his usual seat opposite and ate too, from time to time glancing up at him. Even after five years, Gideon could struggle to read his expression, and this morning's was an enigmatic mixture of amusement and reproof. Add in a strong dash of embarrassment and remembered pleasure... "All right," Gideon said at last, harpooning a mushroom on his fork and proffering it across the table like an olive branch. "What's bothering you?"

Lee leaned forward. He bit the mushroom off the fork, speared a remaining tomato for Gid in return and held it out. "I ought to put you over my knee."

Gideon choked on the tomato. He grabbed a napkin and pressed it to his mouth. "God almighty," he complained, coughing. "I'm due on duty in half an hour. Do you want to send me in there with my cock like a telegraph pole?"

"Tough luck if it is. What do you mean by muscling into my dreams?"

Gideon gave a second's thought to playing confused. A carnal, rosy heat had risen into his face, though, and Lee could see through him, front to back and out the other side. "Sorry," he growled. "I just walked in, and you were dreaming, moving your hips and making such nice sounds. I sat down to watch you. I suppose that was bad enough. But then something happened. I was in there with you. I was inside."

"Not the first time that's happened. We've shared dream-space, visions. This was different."

"Yeah. I felt like I was in charge of it somehow. I... pushed." Suddenly the wrongness of that stung Gideon like a whip. "God, I'm sorry! I'd never normally have done that. What was I thinking?"

Resting his chin on one hand, Lee surveyed him. "I shouldn't think you were thinking at all. Pass me the calendar, would you?"

Gideon reached behind him to unhook it from the wall, almost too distracted to wonder why Lee wanted it now. "What's up? Did I double-book something?"

"No. Just want to check..." Lee ran a finger over the page, crowded with Tamsyn's after-school activities and social obligations as well as Gideon's late shifts, his own cold-read clients and the phases of the moon. Whatever he was looking for, finding it made his expression soften and a strange, bright compassion replace the half-hearted anger in his gaze. "Never mind. Forget about it, sweetheart."

"I can't. I crossed a line. I—"

"Hush." Lee pushed out of his chair. He padded around the end of the table and to Gideon's astonishment hitched himself onto his lap. He ran a hand over Gideon's hair, searching, soothing. "It doesn't matter, big man. Everything's okay. No need to worry."

"Are you sure?"

"Absolutely. Look, it wasn't *all* bad, was it? Clearly."

"Okay." A reluctant chuckle rumbled out of Gideon's throat. "We didn't half make each other come!"

"Like wildfire. Are your uniform pants decent?"

"Yeah, just about. You're shivering, though. What's wrong?"

"Nothing. Nothing." Lee rubbed his face against Gideon's, something feverish in the contact, an unshaven rasp of skin to skin. "I'm a bit tired, that's all. I tell you what—I am gonna do as you told me last night. I will take a break."

Startled, Gideon held him. He'd been expecting much more of a fight. "Really? Am I becoming an overbearing brute of a husband?"

"No. You're just right about this. You do know why I've been pushing so hard, don't you?"

"Because that idiot Dave Rawle said you were... battery-packing for Tamsyn, boosting her signal or some such nonsense. You told me yesterday in the car."

"I just about remember that part. I'm not sure it *was* entirely nonsense, not for a while. I've had time to think since, though, and... if she ever was using me like that, she's stopped."

"Did you talk to her about it?"

"Well, we never talked about her starting, so... No, she's just worked it out, like everything else she does that might be a problem for us. The dads can't cope, so she switches whatever gift it is off. Are we repressing her?"

"I don't think so. I reckon she looks around and sees what all the other kids are doing or not doing, and she wants to fit in, so she regulates herself. Then we enforce certain things for her at home, like bedtime and vegetables and not floating the dog, so that's her framework here." Gideon shifted slightly, holding Lee harder, giving him the faintest comforting rock. "I tell you what. Your uncle Dave was full of opinions about gifted children in Cornwall, wasn't he? I will find a reason to see him. And if he knows anything that might be useful to us about what the kids can do, I'll have it out of the bastard."

Lee sat up, as far as he could in the loving cage of Gideon's embrace. His eyes were dark with trouble. "You can't go throwing your weight around with him, Gid. You know you can't."

Gideon considered this. Yes, on one level he was perfectly aware that he couldn't track Rawle down and frighten the truth out of him. On another it seemed so easy. Rawle had come here, sat in the kitchen chair Lee had vacated. A kind of shadow-shape of him was still left in the air. If he tried, Gideon could recall with eerie precision the scent of his aftershave, the underlying hormonal tang of his anger and fear. As for the frightening, all he would have to do was let go a nuance of self-control, unfasten a binding *here* and *here*, and...

"Gideon!"

Lee was bolt upright, hands braced on his shoulders. Gideon could barely read his expression—the mix of love in it, laughter and stark fear. He smiled up helplessly in return. "What's the matter?"

"You. You were just about to tell me how you planned to interview Dave Rawle. Quietly and legitimately, in the course of police business."

"Oh. Right. Well, I never did find out what banner he's running that school of his under. Even private academies have to answer to the government's inspectorate. I bet Lawrence might be interested in an unregistered educational establishment right in the middle of her turf."

"You don't know that he's unregistered."

"True enough, but finding out might be a job for Lawrence's finest sergeant. You know—the guy with the Queen's medal."

Lee's brow creased. He tilted his head a fraction. "Wow. I never thought I'd hear you mention that again."

Gideon hadn't thought he could. He'd been proud of the honour, but the process of travelling to London and standing in a gilded ceremony room had been a mortification. And the more he'd thought about it, the more it had seemed irrational to pin upon him awards and decorations for doing his barest duty. The medal, and all further reference to it, had been best tucked into his sock drawer and forgotten. "Yeah," he said, puzzled himself by the lapse. "But you mentioned my weight. Throwing it about, I mean, and I don't mean to do that, but... if I do have any weight with Lawrence, maybe that's part of it. Maybe it can help me get things done."

He liked the sound of his own voice saying that. Confidence rushed through him, a bounce like the wind off the sea. He put a tender hand around the back of Lee's neck and drew him in for a kiss. "Worth my weight in brass, I am. No, forget that—fourteen stone of solid Cornish gold. And you, my handsome, are going to lay back and let me get on with it. Sit in your deckchair in the orchard and watch the apples grow. Right?"

"Wrong," Lee informed him smartly, fixing a powerful grip on his collar. "I'm getting our kid up and ready for school, and then I'm recording an end piece for the show to make up for yesterday's disaster. After that, though, I..." He relaxed a little, a surrendering movement that brought his brow gently against Gideon's. "I'm going to cancel off my clients, and that house-cleansing job I had lined up in Liskeard."

"Really?"

"Yes. I do listen to you, you know. Jory Stark wants that boat of his fixed up over in St Wylloe. I might take that on, if it won't sink *our* boat—our financial one, I mean."

"We'll be fine. That's a great gig for you, love. You'll be out in the sun all day, and you could work your own hours."

"Yeah. I'll fit it around Tamsie's school, and she can come with me in the holidays."

That was great. A hush fell in the sunny kitchen, warm with the summertime whisper of the wind, the voice of the orchard and the moor. Gideon listened to it, and to the outside edge of his lover's thoughts, the places where the changing-room door always stood welcoming wide. They were a happily married couple starting in on their fifth year, both of them pleased to have found and solved a problem. Unable to help himself, impelled by the new, soft fire, Gid pushed deeper. "God almighty, Lee. What's wrong?"

"What? Nothing." He recoiled a little. "Nothing *you* ought to be able to... Oh, hell. I'm so fucking scared and tired, Gid, and I don't even know why."

Gideon opened himself up—arms, heart, big broad shoulder—to receive his tired fall. To make the catch with everything he had. His throat filled with hot salt, that Lee had finally confessed this, admitted to trouble in paradise. The trust was enormous, but Gideon wasn't afraid. He was proudly, hotly sure that he could make it right. "I know why," he rumbled, enfolding him in the deepest embrace he could, the one Lee had once described as *consuming*, a way of being joyously eaten alive. He kissed what he could of the damp face being pressed against his neck. "My stupid brother's right for once. You *have* done too much, for Tamsie's sake or for every hard-luck story from Land's End to Launceston. But all that's gonna stop now, isn't it? You're going to leave everything to me for a while. Going to rest."

Lee nodded shakily. He untangled, flashing Gideon a tearstained smile. Tamsyn's latest joy in life was dinosaur paper napkins: he wiped his eyes with a stegosaurus and blew his nose. "Bloody hell. What a mess. I'd better get that kid out of bed, or she's gonna be late for school."

The door creaked. Gideon restrained Lee's raw-nerved jump. He didn't want to start his day by yelling at one of his neighbours, but they had to learn to knock... "Oh," he said, on an outbreath of relief. "Tamsie! Morning, my flower of the moors. Lee was just coming to get you."

There was no need. She was dressed, from floppy straw sunhat to sneakers. The combination between them was eccentric: patchwork jeans teamed with one of Ma Frayne's ferociously frilled handmade shirts, but perfectly acceptable for a school day, buttoned and zipped. "Wow," Lee said, putting out an arm to invite her into the huddle on the chair. "Look at you. You did it all yourself."

"Was easy, Lee." She scrambled up to join them, planted a noisy kiss on each face. "Had a shower, too."

"You... Er, okay, but next time call me or Dada, all right? Do I even want to know how you reached the controls?"

"*Didn't*, Lee." Her brow creased at his failure of imagination. "Used the attackment. On the bath."

Gideon broke into laughter. "Oh, my God. The attackment? You are something else, Miss Tyack-Frayne. I thought you didn't even like that shirt."

"Don't, but Gammar's coming."

"No, she's not, sweet. We won't see Grandma until Saturday."

"Oh, don't challenge her, Gid." Lee stood up, depositing the little girl on his husband's lap, wan smile gaining conviction as he looked down at the two of them. "I'm gonna put the kettle on, just in case. How long have you been up, honey?"

She dug in the pocket of her jeans. She seldom used words when an action or gesture would get the message across, and Gideon had noticed, with a puzzled, fleeting concern, that she seldom referred to herself, habitually dropping the *I* from her communications. With an otter's unlikely wriggle, she extricated a handful of leaves. "That's not really an answer," he said, examining the latest offering. He glanced at Lee in mild alarm. "Or... is it?"

"Well, these are feverfew. Latin name, Tamsyn?"

"*Tanacetum parthenium!*"

"And this from a girl who can't say *shower attachment*. The nearest clump of these is quarter of a mile away, in the lane behind Sarah Kemp's house."

"Saw Sarah. Saw Wilf. Waved."

"And did they wave back, or were they too busy calling social services? Can you say *government care order*? That's a bad thing to do, Tamsyn Elizabeth—wandering out of the house on your own like that. Dangerous."

"Wasn't alone. Had Zold."

Yes, there she was, grizzled nose poked cautiously around the door, not prepared to commit herself until she saw how this confession went down. "Nevertheless," Lee said. "I know you understand me. You mustn't do it again."

She listened carefully. Lee had been right, Gideon thought. Maybe she'd been doing this for months, and today was just the first time she'd been busted. She hadn't known it was wrong because the moor was her oyster, her garden, her world, and nothing could touch her there. Now she'd found out that her journeys bothered her parents, though, she would stop—without resentment, simply accepting the limitations of *their* world, like a well-mannered alien tucking away its tentacles so as not to frighten the earthlings.

That was nonsense, of course. She was just a little girl. And the idea that nothing could touch her was purest fantasy, a father's wish-fulfilment dream. "Hoi," he said, trying to sound halfway like a responsible adult. "Did you hear your dad, you monkey? What do you say?"

"Won't do again, Lee. Promise."

"That's a good girl." Gideon rumpled her curls. "What's this latest offering for, then? What does feverfew do?"

She seemed disinclined to answer. She was watching Lee with unsettling silver-eyed attention. "Feverfew's good for all kinds of ailments," Lee said uneasily, after a few seconds. "Toothache, infertility, labour pains. I don't have any of those things, sweetheart, not as far as I know."

She stretched up her arms to him. He bent to meet her embrace, but she planted one little hand gently on either side of his skull, drew his head down and rested one ear against his brow as if listening. "What's this about?" Gideon asked, a scrape of laughter in his voice. "Are you trying to hear the cogs whirring?"

"Feverfew's good for headaches too. In fact that's its main application. I don't have a headache either, though, chick." He looked up at Gideon, face a picture of amused mystification. "It's almost as if she thinks I *should*. Oh, Tamsie—what's up?"

He hoisted her into his arms. "Crying," he whispered over her shoulder, in response to Gideon's alarmed glance. The poor kid didn't like to be caught short, preferring to deal with her problems than weep about them, knowing she had staunch allies to help her get the job done. "Oh, dear. Is this about yesterday, when you knew I'd had a bad day at work and you were worried? All that's over with, my honey. Lee's gonna take the summer off, spend all day with Tamsie, go work on uncle Jory's crackpot old boat at St Wylloe. No headaches, no nosebleeds. No ghosts."

That was an odd old lapse, too. Gideon surveyed his husband and kid. Gone were the days of Tamsie, Dada and Lee: all three of them had conscientiously worked past the baby-talk third-person in order to meet school and the adult world halfway. *We say 'I', we say "you". We take responsibility for ourselves and each other.*

Ah, he loved them so much. Love for them rushed through his blood like Sennen surf. He got to his feet in the joy and anguish of it, hauled them both into his arms. "Lee's right," he growled. "Nobody is to worry about anything, okay? Dada will take care of it all."

The doorbell rang. Isolde sprang out of her guilty half-crouch in the doorway and began the huffing bark which meant friend, not foe, even though she still felt obliged to make a point. Gideon let go of Lee and Tamsyn and took a big step in front of them.

But even the dog had more sense than that: was dancing and waving her tail in the hallway. He drew a steadying breath and went to answer.

He pulled back the door, and Ma Frayne tumbled over the threshold in a welter of fragrance and lace. Making up for lost time, was Ma, and she now possessed an eye-popping wardrobe and an array of the perfume samples bestowed upon her by her many friends in Boots. "Don't worry, boys," she cried, patting Isolde, waving to Tamsyn and dropping a large paper bag on the floor. "I know it's early, and I'm not here to disturb you. Mrs Harle took us out to Torquay Dinosaur World yesterday—I wouldn't have gone, seeing plenty of dinosaurs as I do in the living room at Roselands every day, but I was thinking of Tamsyn Elizabeth. And they had such a gift shop!"

Gideon retrieved the bag. "What have you got in here, Ma? A baby T-rex?"

"A stuffed one, yes! As cute as could be. You pull a string in his back and he roars and bellows like anything, and then he sings a song."

"Oh, *great.*"

"And some napkins—I know she likes those—and a backpack, and a lunch box, and... Oh, she's wearing that sweet blouse I frilled for her! She looks lovely. Did you put it on her specially? But you couldn't have done. You didn't know I was coming."

"Her choice, Ma. She dressed herself this morning."

"*Did* she? But she's rather young to do that, dear. You couldn't manage *your* buttons until you were—"

"Ma, please."

"Oh, I'm sorry." She beamed unrepentantly. "I mustn't embarrass you, must I, not when you're in your nice uniform. My, when I see you together with Ezekiel in his Sunday best, I could just about pop, I'm so proud of you both."

"Church and State. That's us."

"And Lee just looks lovely whatever he wears. Good morning, Lee, dear."

Lee blew her a gallant kiss across the top of Tamsyn's head. "Morning, Ma."

"Anyway, I must be off. I'm helping out with a counselling session at the Pink UK community centre in Liskeard this morning, so I just had my taxi bring me up here on the way." She paused for breath, lifted one hand to shield her eyes from the sunlight blazing through the kitchen's southeast window. "But she's *crying*, Gideon! What on earth have you been doing to her?"

Chapter Five
A Day in the Lives

Lee saw Ma Frayne off in her taxi. Gid followed rapidly in the police truck, revving and bemoaning his lost paperwork hour. Ma, for all her good intentions, had lingered helplessly over her grandchild, causing the cabbie to beep and tap his watch until Gid had gone to glare at him through the kitchen window. Thereafter he'd sat frozen like a rabbit in headlights, huddled behind the wheel.

Tamsyn waved gaily from her perch in Lee's arms. She'd recovered her equanimity with a thoroughness that was typical of her. Dinosaurs and a change of subject usually did the trick, but there was more to it than that: as if, although tossed about in life's teacup storms like anyone else, she could see beyond them into a broad blue ocean where everything would be all right. Lee set her down, and she took his hand and towed him indoors to resume their morning routine.

He set out twenty minutes earlier than he needed to, allowing her to botanise to her heart's content along the verges of the lane, Isolde snuffling at her heels. The morning had risen to a perfect moorland stillness—barely a breath of wind, the gold of the gorse giving back the sunlight until the whole landscape seemed ready to melt and dissolve, a single lark holding position directly overhead to pour out her song. Lee's body wanted to sing back to her. Right or wrong, Gideon's push into his dream had made him come like a spring tide with an onshore gale behind it. He felt like... Striving for a comparison, a way to describe to himself what his husband had done to him, he shivered with laughter. He felt like Truro cathedral, that was it. In the moments just after a thundering organ recital had stopped. Empty but sanctified. Vibrant. Last note still shaking the air.

He walked Tamsyn into the village and up to the school gates, where headmistress Prynne intercepted her, then he watched in pleasure as she was borne off among a chattering crowd of her teachers and friends. Now his working day should begin. Hard to find shadows on a day like this, but he could set up his camera gear in Chy Lowen's attic space, stand against the wall with the most cobwebs and crumbling plaster, and record an atmospheric outtro for Anna. After that he'd drive across to St Wylloe to see Jory's boat, check out the scale of the work and give him an estimate. He had a load of laundry to do, some hoovering, beds to make. Gideon was good about splitting the housework, but if Lee took him at his word about a total break from all labour, the place would be a wreck within a week.

The lane back up to the house was empty. Without his kid to distract him, he set off briskly, determined to steal a march on his tasks and enjoy a vigorous swim in the stream of life prepared for him. He was almost at the top of the hill, Chy Lowen's orchard treetops broaching the horizon, when the campions and long grasses stirred in the verge by his feet, and an unmistakeable cat shot out and across his path: Bill Prowse's, of all unlikely visitants, a beast once black but marked with a landscape of bald patches after an outbreak of mange, missing since Bill's decease and presumed dead too. Half a tail, one eye. Nothing much had thrived in the Prowse home, though Gideon had occasionally trapped this occupant and dragged it off to the vet with much the same weariness as he'd collared the children and steered them in the direction of doctors, social care and school.

Bill's house was inhabited again. Nature, abhorring a vacuum even more than she did a Prowse, had just provided a replacement—Bill's cousin, who rejoiced in the improbable name of Marple, eerily like him except twenty years younger and with that much more time to plague the life out of his neighbours. Lee supposed that the cat, like the unknown Prowse ancestor's obsession with names from Agatha Christie, was a curse coming home to roost. What had Bill's middle name turned out to be? Poirot?

He considered texting Gideon to tell him the Prowse moggy was back. Their days often contained weirdly parallel experiences: if Lee had encountered a cat, maybe Gid would too. A good subject for their one-a-day exchange, that would be; would make him groan and laugh among the parking tickets and petty crime of his beat. Lee knew it wasn't all car chases and heroism, although Gid had never looked back since discounting CID from his career path, as if he'd seen into the dreamworld of plainclothes, alternate history, a terrible outcome of grief and disaster in the streets of...

Kerdrolla. Lee stumbled to a halt, breath catching in his throat. He pushed his fingers into the moss on the top of the drystone wall. He had to hang on to this world, not that hellish dream. Gideon *didn't* remember, and that for Lee was the whole point. If he ever did, if he recalled John Tregear, firelight and fever and a burning church, Lee would lose him. Simple as that. Because Gid could bear all the world's badness, would put on his uniform every day and go out to set it right, but his whole faith depended on his belief that he himself was a good man. Beleaguered sometimes, hot-tempered and horny around the full moon, but deeply, essentially human and good.

Ah, Lee had stuck his head in the sand just as much as Gideon had last May! He'd pushed Kerdrolla onto a back shelf in his mind along with Dave Rawle, and Rufus Pendower's crush, which had turned from a joke to a dangerous obsession, and Lee had been glad to set the poor stricken sergeant aside because Rufus remembered Kerdrolla too.

He didn't want to take any of it down from the damn shelf now. He was suddenly, overwhelmingly tired. Aftereffects of the mickey his kid had slipped him? If so, he was almost grateful. The deathly streets of Story-town faded out into sunlight. The children had lived, and Gideon had run with the bomb the length of the harbour at Falmouth and pitched it out into the sea. Lee's shining saviour cop, who up until this morning had grumpily discouraged all mention of his heroism!

He let himself in through the garden gate. Poppies with heads the size of Gid's fist had opened since yesterday alongside the path into the orchard. *Somniferum*, those were, as Tamsyn probably knew. Dorothy would've struggled to get herself stoned amongst the pretty little red ones in the *Wizard of Oz*. These were what you needed, pink and purple silk with ripe pods that wept white sap like semen. Maybe Lee was irresponsible to let them grow in his garden, but Tamsie was far too advanced in her wortcunning to come to any harm.

Wortcunning? Smiling, Lee made his way through the sunlit shade of the apple trees. He and Gid had run the risk of leaving out a pair of old deckchairs overnight, inviting Bodmin fogs and creeping damp, but the weather had stayed fine. Where had he picked up an outrageous old witch-word like that? From Mrs Coulter, probably, that nice old lady Elowen had discovered in the village and who brought his little girl books on botany and comparative religion. Tamsie was off with her after school today, for a reading session or whatever they got up to, so he didn't even have to worry about getting done with his chores in time for the half-past-three run.

Maybe everything could go on hold for an hour or so. What had Gideon told him to do? *Sit in a deckchair and watch the apples ripen.* "Sorry," he whispered, yawning, pulling the message close to himself so it wouldn't reach through their link and disturb Gid at his desk. "Can't even manage that much, love. The deckchair part, yes, but..." He sank down into the gaudily striped canvas cradle, tipped his head back and stared at the leaf-dappled blue until a veil seemed to cover it, a darkness. *The apples will have to look after themselves.*

***

Gideon spent his morning amongst the good, the bad and the bewildered of Dark and Bodmin town. He was rostered for a morning shift in the village every Tuesday and Friday, usually long enough to mop up any small villainies there, especially now that Bill Prowse was gone and Ross doing time in Exeter jail. Darren, too—off to a shady new job in London, Lee had said, an unlikely escapee from the far-west poverty trap.

Gideon missed his lanky, conniving presence with an unexpected pang. In his absence, all he had to do to discharge his duty of guardianship was help Mrs Waite fit her new security alarm, and retrieve Kate Salthouse's prized ragdoll cat from the culvert drain under Cros-an-Wra lane. The creature hissed and spat at him tremendously as he squeezed his bulk through the tunnel. He took her as gently as he could by the scruff and squeezed back out. Once in his arms, her pedigree kicked in and she flopped like a swooning debutante, leaving a silken imprint of herself in long white hairs all over his uniform shirt.

His utility vest—they were encouraged not to talk or think of it as a stab vest these days—covered the worst of that damage. Not, alas, the lipstick kiss-mark planted on his face by the grateful Kate, which he failed to notice before Jenny Spargo pointed it out with a whoop in Bodmin car park. He fended off the flak from her and the half-dozen other officers sent to form a thin blue line against three hopped-up boy racers tearing up the tarmac amongst the grannies and kids. A flying fender missed his kneecap by half an inch. He chucked a stinger to Jenny, who was better placed to deploy, and she tossed out the strip with a matador's grace just in time to spike the Subaru's next charge.

After that—reabsorb the adrenaline, wipe off the grit from your face, such being the life of a uniformed town bobby. Suddenly Gid had a flash of Tamsie's book from yesterday. He saw himself marching about in the guise of a tubby, black-and-white Mr Policeman Badger, and was shaking with laughter when he went to pick up the next call from the Rover's dashboard radio.

A summons to the high-street butcher's, where to his grief he recognised one of the smaller Prowses, now eking out a breadline existence with his mother in one of Bodmin town's council estates, caught literally red-handed with a half pound of liver down the front of his coat. Gideon retrieved the bloody package. Disgusting, but he was suddenly faint with hunger. He slipped the kid a fiver, gave him a look he wouldn't soon forget, and released him to scamper away. Mr Kyger the butcher showed signs of outrage, so Gideon gave him the look too, slapped the meat down on his counter-top and added another fiver to pay for it, reflecting that he'd come off this shift in the red if this went on.

Blood, dirt, fur. At lunchtime, back at HQ, he cleaned himself up as best he could and went to look for his boss.

He didn't have to wait. She was prowling the corridor, evidently in search of him. "Sergeant," she rapped out. "Where on earth have you been? My office, please—now."

Gideon followed her, trying to control a junior constable's sinking of the heart. But there was no need: once the door was closed behind them, Lawrence rounded on him with a beaming grin. "Alice Rawle!" she declared, venturing to slap him on the arm. "Arrested in the grounds of Godolphin Road Primary in Launceston early this morning, loitering with intent, although intent to do what, God only knows. She's not our usual profile for kiddy-school stalkers, that's for sure. Distraught, extremely violent, confessing to yesterday's incident faster than Sergeant Lennox could take notes. Sit down, Gideon, sit down."

He obeyed, head spinning a bit at the onslaught. "They caught her?"

"Are you awake, Sergeant? Yes, they caught her, thanks to a late-night tip-off from a Bodmin-station team member of mine."

Remembering his manners, Gideon took off his cap. Ragdoll Suki's fur had got onto there somehow too, and he absently tried to brush it off. "Hardly that, ma'am. The tip-off was no more than a name."

"Ah, but the *right* name, Sergeant! Karen Lennox thinks we're bloody psychic over here." Lawrence sat down with a contented bounce on the far side of the desk. "Speaking of which, she is *exceptionally* sorry for her treatment of your other half. She's been doing her homework and watching some *Spirits of Cornwall* back episodes. I think she's sending flowers. Station politics aside, that was bloody good work—nobody wants a predator near any of our kids. How is our local prophet today?"

"Off-duty," Gideon told her, with an unintended rasp that made her eyebrows rise. "Sorry. He's okay, but yesterday was rough on him. He's taking a few weeks off."

"Well, much deserved, although I'm starting to wonder how this department would function without him. And you. You're a formidable team. Who came up with the name?"

"Lee did." In fact Gid was proud of his own work on Lee's puzzle, but that was irrelevant. Lee did the seeing and the suffering. Only Lee bled. "We've had a run-in with that family before."

"What family? Alice Rawle's?"

Are you awake, ma'am? "Yes. The father is a long-time friend of the Tyack family, although that hit the rocks last year when he came to visit us. He runs a school for what he calls gifted children, and I gather the gifts are more than a penchant for algebra or the violin."

"Oh. Gifted in the same way that... Lee is gifted, for example?"

She'd been going to say *Tamsyn*. She had been in charge of the Montol crowd-control op in Penzance three years before. Or maybe Pendower had talked to her, his once-staunch character springing all kinds of leaks these days. Whatever she'd seen in Gideon's eyes, it had made her veer off from his child. "That's right," he said, allowing her a grateful nod for the discretion. If she didn't ask, he could speak. "Dave Rawle thought Tamsyn might be better off in some kind of... academy or institution for children with that kind of ability."

Lawrence's eyes widened. "I bet that went down well."

Better than you think. "We asked him to leave. I haven't seen him since, but I did a little digging around while Lee was helping us out with the Clem Atherton case. The Rawle school is off on the other side of Bodmin moor, conveniently isolated, and the last time anyone looked, there were armed guards at the gate."

"Nice of you to clue me in on your investigation. Who did the looking?"

"I did, ma'am." No need to drop gallant Jenny Spargo in the soup. Had he been unfair in raising the ghost of poor Clem? Lawrence had blushed at the name. He hadn't needed to remind her of the body in the Pascoe cornfields, and the shocks and revelations in the lanes around the farm, the cherry of which for Gid had been the discovery that his buttoned-up inspector was a lesbian.

Well, leverage was leverage. Proudly front and centre on the wall behind Lawrence's chair was her framed certificate for support services for gay and transgender officers in the southwest. She'd even risked a photo of herself and Morwenna on the desk, not in a clinch or anything but undeniably together. She touched the photo frame now, like a talisman in difficult times. "What do you want, Sergeant?"

"To go and look again, officially this time."

"And how do you plan to justify that?"

"I'm not sure the place is licensed."

Lawrence shrugged. "I can check that with a phone call to Ofsted."

"Listen. Dave Rawle started that school because he had a gifted kid of his own."

"Oh. Alice?"

"Yeah. And whatever she is now, twenty years or so ago she was there as a kind of teenage assistant and guide to the younger children. She could do what they could, but she'd learned to control it."

"Does she, though?"

Gideon drew a deep breath. "I last saw Alice just over a year ago in Dark. She was in a bloody spook car with a top-brass general from the military base on Dartmoor. I think she was there voluntarily, but I don't know. She tried... Whatever it is she can do, whatever influence she exerts, she tried to exert it, but... something stopped her."

"She must weigh eight stone wet through. Is that why you said she was dangerous when you called in last night?"

"Yeah. The Launceston lads had trouble with her, didn't they?"

"Only the conventional kind. She didn't levitate their squad car. She's sick and debilitated, even though she did put up such a fight—Lennox is having her assessed at Derriford hospital before they press charges. Do you recommend a secure wing?"

"I do, ma'am."

"I'll pass that on right away." She steepled her fingers, rested her chin on the tops of them thoughtfully. "It's probably best if you just tell me what you need."

One direct approach deserved another. Gideon met her eyes. "I want to know why a school—any school, even one for kids who can float cars—has gun-toting rentacops at the gate. If Alice is anything to go by, I want to know what happens to those kids, because I don't think it's always anything good."

"A link between David Rawle and the military?"

He nodded in relief. "Yes, ma'am. It's refreshing to find that you're almost as paranoid as I am."

Lawrence sighed, visibly surrendering. "Very well. I'm allowing you this as a personal favour, mind, because Lee is involved, and we owe him a lot more than a bunch of bloody dahlias from Launceston. Take Spargo. She can keep her mouth shut, as I'm sure you already know." She pushed up and came back round her desk to stand in front of him, brow creasing in disapproval. "I can see that you've discharged your morning's duties—most of 'em are still on your uniform. Get a fresh shirt and vest, Sergeant. Brush down that cap."

"Er... yes, ma'am."

"You know that this kind of task is more appropriately CID work, don't you?"

Gideon surveyed her. She had folded her arms and was staring down at him with a new and troubled intensity. "Possibly," he said cautiously, not wanting to lose this fight on a technicality. "I can go plainclothes, if you like."

"No. Because you're *not* CID. Are you?"

"I... believe I remember you sitting by my hospital bed in Trelowarren and telling me I'd never be fit enough for that kind of work. Which was fine by me, because I didn't want it anyway. I belong in uniform, on the street."

"I tend to agree. And God knows you're needed there, but... the thing is that you *are* fit enough. I don't know how, you damned prize bull, but you've climbed back from your injuries as if they'd never happened."

Unease crawled through Gideon's veins. "Ma'am, respectfully—if I'm to get over the moor and back in time to finish off my other work today, I'd better start now. Will this discussion wait?"

"In one way, yes. In others it feels as though nothing will." Lawrence's intensity increased, new lines of weariness tightening her face. "I'm fighting a battle out there. Hate crime against every minority we've got is on the increase. Violence and street brawls and mad right-wing allegiances across the board. And everything's gonna get worse as we crawl towards this feckless devil's deal to take us out of Europe. I don't want to be here just reacting to it all in the aftermath. I want to get ahead and stop it, Gideon. I want to get upstream."

Gideon recoiled. Something to do with that damned word: *upstream*, as if he were a migrating salmon, expected to leap against every flow of his nature or die trying. But *his* death wouldn't be the issue, would it? Blood would fall like rain. Children would drop beneath the unseen blade of a scythe, rainbow banners turning scarlet on the cobbled streets of...

"Sergeant?"

He started upright in his seat. Had he fallen asleep for a moment? Cold sweat was standing on his brow. "Sorry. I... It's nothing. Just a bit of a headache." With a grinding effort, he smiled. "You've got good CID officers tumbling out of the woodwork around here, haven't you? Jim Cardew and his partner are keen as mustard, and if you're looking for... er, fresh meat, there's Jenny Spargo. She'd bite your hand off for a chance."

"Fresh *meat?*" Lawrence echoed wonderingly. She rubbed nervously at one wrist. "Have you had your lunch, Sergeant?"

"I'm sorry?"

"You can go to this academy of yours. Keep a low profile, and there's to be no biting of any kind, thanks very much. Get something to eat first, for heaven's sake. You look hungry."

Maybe that was all that ailed him. He thought with queasy desire of the juicy steak sandwiches Mike's roadside van would be serving up in the Bolventor layby right now. He and Jenny could stop off en route. "I'll see to it," he promised, getting up and settling his cap back into place. "Thanks for stretching a point for me about Rawle. And, er—don't think I don't appreciate it, about CID. That you think I'd be good enough, I mean."

"I'd back your application tomorrow. You're the kind of officer we need out there. You're smart, you're disgustingly fit, and you know this blasted sock-toe of a county like the back of your hand."

He paused, one hand on the peak of the cap. He wanted to salute her, laugh at her, and back off crossing himself all at once. "I couldn't," he said hopelessly, wondering why his mind added, *never again. I never could do it again.* "I'm sorry, Christine. It's not for me. I'll be the best uniform copper I can, but not that." *Not that, please God. Never again.*

***

Sergeant Spargo finished her coffee, glanced across from the driver's seat and gave a disgusted chuckle. "Lor', Gid."

"What?"

"Well, it's not like you're a messy eater or anything. I was partnered up with Alfie Trengwainton last month, and we were both practically *wearing* his lunches by the time he got done." She patted the powerful Rover's wheel in satisfaction. "*And* he never let me drive."

"Your point being?"

"Well, one minute your food's there, and the next..." She picked up the wrapper Gideon's extra-large steak sandwich had come in. "The next it's gone. It's like you evaporate it."

"What can I say? I was hungry."

"Oh, I'm not complaining. You're very tidy. Alfie used to put me off my salad." She reached over and gave him a friendly poke on the hip. "Then you just metabolise it, you bloody monster. Not a spare inch on you."

Gideon wondered if he ought to apologise. He could've put away another of Mike's sarnies and not have felt it touch the sides. He looked wistfully at the wrapper, then folded it away with Spargo's napkin into the car's recycling box. "Want to give me your carton?"

"No, it needs a rinse. I'll take it home." She grinned. "Gone are my days of coffee and doughnuts for lunch, and chuck the packaging over my shoulder into the back! Wouldn't dare do that in this rolling cathedral."

"I know. I gave someone a right old blast on the windscreen wipers yesterday in Launceston. Still, a Saturday-night shift or two around the Redruth clubs ought to take the shine off her."

She chuckled. "Yeah, that'd do it. My cousin Prue at Moor Lane told me you'd had to go over to fetch Lee. Is he all right today?"

"He's better. You and Steven should come for lunch sometime soon. He'd love to see you." He watched sympathetically while she pursued a last leaf around her carton. "Not sure that's gonna sustain a hardworking copper through a tough day, Jen."

"What, my mega-berry super-salad? Highly nutritious, that was. Palaeolithic or something." She leaned an elbow on the open window frame and inhaled the savoury scents still drifting from Mike's van. "Mind, so was yours. It's no good, though. I'd double in size if I so much as looked at what you just tucked away. What's your secret, Sergeant?"

Gideon wished he had one. He'd have used it in the wake of his injuries at Falmouth, when enforced rest and comfortable married life had threatened his waistline. Men of his build had to work for it, he knew. But he'd healed with ferocious rapidity after that, as if his body had learned how, regaining function in hard-packed muscle and speed. "Just pushing Tamsie's buggy around, I reckon."

"Oh, great. If I have to wait for Steve to get around to helping provide one of those..." She shook her head. "Come on. Let's go and have a snoop around Bowithick, if you're refuelled."

She switched the Rover on, gave the engine an appreciative rev. Gideon resisted an urge to ask for the driver's seat. Immediate appetites satisfied, he was hotly impatient to be on the road and in action. Jenny was one of the Devon & Cornwall's best duty motorists, though, and would enjoy a bounce across the moor. She'd get him there just as fast as he needed to go.

Suddenly her very willingness touched him behind the heart. Her readiness to help, her cheerful, laid-back competence... He patted her wrist, and she shivered oddly. "Look, Jen," he said. "You've been my partner-in-crime over Dave Rawle before, getting your dad's mate in Camelford to check this Bowithick place. There's something hinky about the whole deal. We've got a green light from Lawrence this time, but I heard around the Tollgate canteen that you're looking to make CID."

"What, and you think buggering about on the backroads of Bodmin with you might tarnish my shiny record?"

"Yeah. So if you want to stay in the truck, working on some nice plausible deniability..."

"Gideon Tyack-Frayne!"

He blinked. She was the calmest and best-natured of his colleagues, imperturbable even in riots and fights. She was staring at him now in frank outrage. "Sorry, Jen," he said awkwardly. "Sorry."

"I should bloody well think so too."

***

He needn't have worried. Only the wind lived at Bowithick now. Behind the high walls and hedgerows, the site was vacant, blank-windowed buildings giving back his own bewildered stare.

Spargo strode straight off to quarter the grounds. No-one had stopped them at the gates, and Gideon wondered if the armed guards there had been a figment of the Camelford copper's imagination. Bowithick—the countryside around it, dreaming in postcard-perfect serenity, a landscape of tiny lanes and dairy farms and soft-eyed Jersey cows—met every bucolic expectation a weary town-dweller might bring to it. Jenny had nimbly dodged dozens of them en route, the mid-life brigade out on their holiday jaunts, hiking the roads with actual paper maps in hand and expressions of dazed delight.

Everything ended here. Whatever Lee and his sister had found when they'd come to this place as children, now it was vacant. Gideon didn't need to break locks and enter the low, box-like classrooms and halls to know that Dave Rawle's academy had been turned to purposes of the rawest, most ruthless utilitarianism. *A factory*, he thought dully, coming to a halt in the middle of a strangely marked concrete playground. His head ached and his vision blurred. *A factory for little lives like my Tamsyn's. Dear Christ, what did they make?*

Footsteps scraped on the far side of the yard. Spargo appeared from behind one grey block, smiling, raising a hand. Her shadow, sturdy and neat as the brave soul who cast it, marked out her shape on the ground.

Gideon's ears popped. Something twanged in the air, a short-lived, high-pitched shriek. Spargo jerked up on her toes as if seized by the collar. Then she fell.

There were three sacks of quickset sand on the ground. When Gideon ran to her, he found these instead of her bleeding corpse. All were oddly marked, as if someone had used them for target practice from within. The impact craters blossomed on their surfaces, sickeningly inside-out. He couldn't remember his run across the yard. Fit or not, he'd never make a CID cop, and Lawrence was stupid for insisting. Gideon had seen the training videos, taken part in a couple of live-shooter roleplays. Had seen how Jim Cardew and the other hard young lads ducked and repositioned, strategised and kept their heads low, even in scenarios with an officer down.

Maybe they'd act differently when it was real. Maybe like Gideon they'd just blaze across open ground, getting picked off like idiots in their turn. He was stupid too. But this had been Spargo. Jenny was the officer down.

Not real, not real. By the time the footsteps scraped again—and the first time they had been nothing, only the rasp of tarmac and dust heating up in the sun—Gideon was hunched on a step a couple of yards away from the bags. He tried to stop drawing breath in rattling, freaked-out backward moans, but he'd left it too late, and Spargo paused once in her easy stride, glanced around for trouble—already a better CID guy than Gideon—and belted over to his side. "Gid? What's up?"

"Nothing." He coughed, wiped a sleeve across his mouth, lurched upright. "Nothing. I thought I saw something, that's all."

"You look terrible. Not a case of roadside-caff revenge, I hope."

"No, no." His sarnie, which had briefly threatened a return, settled back, and the red sparks faded from across his visual field. In their absence Jenny Spargo looked so good to him, such a perfect piece of living, breathing existence. A fucking miracle. "I'm fine."

"We should get some pictures around here, you know. I think the place is empty, but it's bloody weird, not like any kind of school I've ever seen. There's not much equipment left, but these bags are everywhere—sand, I thought, but it looks like some kind of mix that would set once the outer skin's pierced. They're all full of these weird looking holes."

"Yeah. Get pictures. Take some video footage, too, of the..." He fell silent, pressing his fists to his hips. What did he want her to capture—the desolate vibe of the place? A replay of her own fall? No reason for him to be giving her orders, either; it had been years since he'd outranked her. Spargo didn't care about things like that, though, provided she was dealt with courteously. "Just film around," he went on, voice still rough. "Get the layout and anything that looks disordered, as if there might have been a struggle. Please."

She was already loading up her phone cam. "No problem. I don't think anyone stormed the joint, though, Gid. Just looks like they closed it down."

"Right. Er, Jenny?"

She spared him a glance. "What?"

He couldn't tell her, not in words. Instead he took her, camera and vest and peaked cap and all, into his arms. She emitted a squawk. Briefly she stiffened, and then some hormonal, deep-brain message reached her, beyond gender or rank or the daily restrictions of their lives, the awkward shells of their protective gear. She rested her head on his shoulder, put her arms around him in return and patted him. "There," she said unsteadily, as if to a lost kid she'd plucked out of a fairground crowd. "What's all this about? There, now. You old softie, Gid!"

***

Lawrence had left for the day by the time Gideon got back to HQ. His normal shift hours were almost over too, but his mountain of paperwork was threatening a landslide, so he took off his cap and utility kit and sat down behind his desk with a half pint of coffee.

His mug had Tamsyn's baby footprint immortalised in paint on the side. The big modern office space was quiet, the night crew not yet mustered. Paperwork was a misnomer: Gid's backlog lay in wait for him on his desktop PC. That was good, environmentally sound and all that, but the screen's pallid gleam wasn't the light he wanted. Made him feel hot and scratchy inside, for all the open-plan and glass walls.

He'd brought it on himself. So Spargo had said when he'd stopped to drop her off to meet her boyfriend. Sergeants who stayed on top of their admin could go romping around the glamorous streets and restaurants of Bodmin town, she'd reminded him, slapping him on the arm as she got out of the truck. She hadn't questioned his distracted clamber behind the wheel on their way back from Bowithick. Neither of them had talked much, and the cabin had filled with their subtly freaked-out hush. In Bodmin he'd watched her in his rearview, pretending to wait for a gap in the traffic, enjoying the prosaic living sight of her striding away down the kerb with Steve.

He'd offered to write up a report about Rawle's school. That could be the tip of his iceberg tonight, he decided, and he set about it briskly. There wasn't much to say. Police reports were not creative essays, and over the years he'd developed a terse copper's style that got the job done with clarity. No speculations, no questions. *Just the facts, thank you, Sergeant.* That was fine with him. *The site appears to have been abandoned. All buildings are secure. Some unusual equipment is extant; see photos and video footage separately logged.* He added an eyes-only email for Lawrence. *Recommend you make that call to Ofsted, ma'am. If Bowithick was ever registered, there'll be records of the children who attended. I'd like to think they went quietly back to their local schools and colleges, but it would be good to know that for sure.*

The email brought Gideon to the borderline of his remit as a beat copper. Further investigation would be work for Lawrence's CID team and admin liaisons. If something about the place, or the heat, or the state of Gideon's rippling, hypersensitised, air-sniffing innards had served him up a bloody hallucination, that was his own problem.

Oh, great. He was having another. His mate Peter Briggs had just walked in, and he was wearing a silver balloon for a crown.

Halloween pranking was a long way off yet. Briefly it skimmed Gideon's awareness that midsummer was rising, Granny Ragwen's blasted gate presumably swinging wide, but he and Lee had spent their last two solstices in calm domestic bliss, barely noticing the dates as they came round. Bill raised a hand in cheerful greeting. "Still here, big man? Your lad'll be waiting behind the door with a rolling pin for you."

His voice faded off into the wind-rush of Gideon's blood. He wasn't wearing a crown, of course. Gideon had lost a nameless, irrecoverable tranche of time in the nauseous computer light. It was half past nine, and a bright full moon had risen behind Pete's head. Getting up, Gideon snagged the car keys off the desk. He retrieved his jacket and shrugged into it, even took a moment to put on and straighten his cap.

Pete, like Jenny, spent long hours at the gym without making much headway against the pasties and sausage rolls. He was one of Gideon's best friends. Just now he was only fifteen stone of obstacle between Gid and the moon.

He gaped as Gideon took him beneath the arms. If he cried out—yelled, swore, broke into laughter—Gideon didn't know. He'd gone deaf to all but the moon-beat in his ears. That was the light he wanted. Effortlessly he lifted Briggs off his feet and set him aside.

He ran down the stairs, taking five at a time, dropping round the turns with barely a touch to the rail. His hearing prickled back into hyperfunctionality and he became aware of his own silence. Of the armour-plated rustle of a woodlouse on the stairwell wall. The squeaking, silvery pop of a daisy bud in the turf between the HQ building and the car park. He opened up the Rover and climbed in, his breathing deep and easy, lungs and mind filling up and flooding with sacred light. He turned right on Priory Road and began his journey home.

Chapter Six
Into the Heart of the Night

The golden apples of the sun. Lee had been dreaming of sunlight. He liked his Yeats, and for the first minute of waking lay still, recalling what he knew of the words. *Though I am old with wandering // Through hollow lands and hilly lands...* Yes, he could imagine such a time. The fogous and barrow graves and tors, or just the hollow or high places of the heart—yes, he would come to an end of them one day.

Peace still lay along his bones. He never had feared journey's end, and since he'd met Gid, he'd known he'd never have to get there alone. *I will find out where she has gone // And kiss her lips and take her hands // And walk among long dappled grass // And pluck till time and times are done...* Lee's orchard spirit was a sturdy *he*, and never had anything less ethereal charged through the trees than Gid in pursuit of his child or the dog. Apple blossom in his hair for sure, but only because he was so tall that he knocked it down. Lee shifted in the deckchair, smiling.

God, it was damp, though! He came to surface with a choked-off gasp. His whole body clenched in a shiver. *The golden apples of the sun...* No, no. Silver apples of the moon, clustered over his head in mystical profusion, like clustering orbs in a graveyard, invisible to everyone but him. It was dark. Night had come down in the garden. He'd fallen asleep, abandoned his work and his plans and his duty, his household tasks and...

His child. Lee catapulted out of the deckchair and stood swaying in the moonlight, grabbed a low branch to keep from falling. His limbs were sluggish, one arm—he'd had it tucked behind his head, for God knew how many hours—numb and useless, first pins and needles trickling into his hand. "Shit," he got out, voice like sandpaper. "*Tamsyn.*"

He ran for the house. Scenarios flashed at him. The best was social services, a verdict of neglect, utter disgrace. The worst was that headmistress Prynne had waited with his girl after school, turned her back to deal with some other crisis and lost sight of her. The worst was Tamsyn alone on the moors.

He skidded across the dew-damp lawn and onto the drive. Cornering, he saw that lights were on in the kitchen. Christ, perhaps all he had to deal with was Gideon, and somehow that was worst of all—his husband, his first and most sacred trust, coming home to find an empty house, his daughter lost and betrayed. A sob scoured Lee's throat. *Oh, not that. No.*

No. Tamsyn was comfortably seated at the kitchen table. Way past her bedtime, but someone had washed her, brushed her hair and put her into her pyjamas. Lee scrambled to a halt, hands on the window ledge. Home-alone scenarios flashed through his head, where the poor kid had done it all for herself, but then another figure appeared in the lamplight, a reassuring shape in floral skirt and pink pullover. *Last year's M&S,* he thought irrelevantly, but the idea skimmed off the surface of his waking mind. The old lady placed a glass of milk in front of Tamsyn, then settled on a chair beside her. Both turned their attention back to a huge book lying open on the table. "Oh," Lee said. "Mrs Coulter. Thank God."

He let himself in through the back door and scullery, hands clumsy on the latches. Before he could open his mouth, the old lady raised tranquil eyes to him. "Ah, there you are," she said. "Don't be afraid. You can see all's well here."

"I... Yes." He stopped short against the cabinets. He wanted to run to his child, but he felt as if he'd forfeited the right. "I can see that. I'm so..." His voice faded off in a croak, and he tried again. "I'm so sorry."

"Why, now? You needed the sleep. Tamsyn and I came to see you when I brought her back here after school. Didn't we, girl?"

Tamsyn nodded enthusiastically. She slithered down off the pile of cushions on her kitchen chair and met him with her usual joyous tackle-hug. "Did, Lee. Had my supper, had my bath. Reading with Ganny."

He swept her up. "That's Mrs Coulter, love, but you're a very good girl. And she's extremely kind to look after you. I'm sorry I left you alone."

"Not alone."

"Why didn't you wake me up, when you found me asleep in my chair?"

"Did try. Ganny said Lee was Sleeping Beauty."

"Well, she was half right."

"Buy a hose!"

"I beg your pardon?"

Mrs C began to chuckle. "*Briar Rose*, child. What a card you are! You really mustn't worry, Lee - we've been fine."

"Next time just tip me out of the chair."

"No, no. We thought your Prince Charming might get back in time to do the job. Speaking of which, you'll need to keep your strength up. I made a little chicken broth for Tamsyn, and there's plenty left. Come and sit down."

Lee did as he was bidden. He was deeply shaken, at being invited to sit and eat in his own house, at the necessity, his own incomprehensible neglect. "What on earth time is it? Where's Gid?"

"On his way. Here, eat this up, dear, and drink this glass of milk."

This was ridiculous. What next—cookies, and pyjamas of his own? Before he could protest, Tamsyn snuggled contentedly deeper onto his lap. She planted one forefinger on the open page of the book, which was richly illustrated and adorned with what looked like original handwritten notes. "Pentacle!"

"Pentacle?" Lee reached around her and drew the book closer to him. He turned a few pages, careful with their ink-laden fragility. Amusement reached him despite his guilt. "Mrs Coulter? Comparative religion is one thing, but this... this is a grimoire."

She reappeared at his shoulder. "Oh! Here, let me just set these things down." She deposited a glass of milk and a bowl of savoury soup in front of Lee, then dealt the book a sharp thump with her fist. "Grimoire? Glamour! There, now. Look again, dear—just a lovely book of herbs."

Lee gave it up. He had enough on his plate, or at least in his bowl. Mrs C had whipped up a delicious brew in his cauldron—or a broth in his kitchen; he couldn't remember and it didn't seem to matter. He dug in gratefully. "Did you have to go shopping for any of this? Do I owe you anything?"

"Heavens, no. Everything I needed was here. Let that warm the damp out of your bones, and..." She took up a seat opposite him, laid her hands palm-up on the table. "Let me take the child home with me tonight."

"What? No. Why?"

"Because he *is* on his way, your fine man. And he's been good as gold lately, hasn't he? But a full moon this close to solstice will test his reserves to the limit."

Lee met a lot of nutcases in the course of his work. He was tolerant on the whole, but he had limits of his own. He forgot the absurdity of the whole conversation—forgot the grimoire now gleaming with innocent berries and leaves—and answered Mrs C on her own terms. "If you're saying he'd harm Tamsyn, I'd rather you just left now."

"*Harm* her?" She gave a caw of incredulous laughter. "Of course not. But she needs her sleep as much as you did today, and she won't get it here tonight. Will she?"

Cupping his hands around the bowl, Lee conjured a vision of the night to come—of Gideon with used-up reserves of goodness and self-control. "We never disturb her," he said, barely meaning to speak the words aloud. "Her room's off down the corridor, and... I don't know why I'm telling you this."

"Because your husband's coming home, and you have to serve him and save him, and the sounds of that will waken her, even in a great wolf's lair such as this. You meant to send her off to Sarah Kemp's for... What is it you call that weekend?"

Lee chuckled richly, pointed at the child in his lap, who pointed merrily back at him. "Not something I can say in front of *her*."

"Well, never mind. It's always the one nearest full moon, you make sure of that. I'll have her home before your husband wakes up in the morning. He'll never know she was gone."

"As if I wouldn't tell him! I... I tell him everything. No, Mrs Coulter. We don't even know where you live."

"Ah, you do. Think about it."

"I don't." Lee gave the last spoonful of broth a swirl around the bowl, and then in an abandonment of his table manners lifted it and drank the dregs off. "Wait, yes. Of course I do. Pellar Street, in Granny Ragwen's old house... No, that's ridiculous. Madge lives there now."

"Madgie has her flat above the betting shop in Liskeard. Prefers the bustle and bright lights, she does. Let the child come with me now, dear. It's almost time, and, you know, she's..." Mrs C paused, rapped her knuckles off the table-top, coughed hollowly. "Glamour! She's done it many times before."

Of course she had. Suddenly Lee couldn't work out why he was making such a fuss. "Sorry," he said, and looked down at the smiling little girl in his lap. "You love your nights with Mrs C, don't you?"

"Yes, Lee." Her expression became tender, reminding him oddly of Gideon's. "Do love."

"I'll make you up a backpack, then."

She pointed at the floor. Her overnight bag was standing open, her favourite plush toy—the one Ezekiel had given her years ago, half-bald with cherishing but still recognisably a little planet Earth—ready on top, together with the basic two-button phone loaded up with her home number, Zeke's, and the family mobiles. "But she's in her pyjamas," Lee said, in a last attempt at objection. "It's way past time she was in bed."

"And so she will be, the moment I get her home. My car's just outside—did you think I was going to march her down the lane in her slippers? I have a child seat. Many children come to me for shelter."

"She doesn't need... This is her shelter, right here."

"I know. And I know you're tired and scared, and you don't want to hear about the damn solstice door. But *you're* part of the Frayne brood now, Locryn. Mind it's not you who falls through."

"I don't understand."

"You will. You can understand without thinking. You can hear without listening. Hear now."

Lee sat still. The moon had risen, sudden and vast, squarely framed in the southeastern window. If he let go of the ordinary noises of the night, placed his senses beyond them, he could detect...

Yes, an engine. He hadn't known that he could pick out the note of the police truck from every other car in the village, and certainly not at this distance. He knew, surely as if he'd been a hawk on a thermal above the moor, that Gideon had just passed the St Cleer turn-off and was five minutes from home.

He grabbed Tamsyn in one arm, her backpack with his free hand. He hustled and herded Mrs Coulter to the door, suddenly assisted by Isolde, who'd trotted in from business of her own in the garden and was wide-eyed, hackles raised, looking anxiously over her shoulder through the open door. "Will you take the dog too?"

"Yes, of course. I'd best, hadn't I? She'll only howl."

***

The bedroom was painted in moonlight. The twin chests of drawers from Drift farmhouse, lovely in their carvings and their battered coat of white paint, the huge funereal wardrobe which had been Gid's doubtful contribution from the parish house, reconsecrated by Tamsyn, who used it as a play-house, a castle or cave, depending on the needs of the game—all these had been silvered along their southeastern corners and panels. Through Lee's eyelashes the solid old pieces became spectral, only their shining parts real. The transmuting light altered everything. Mrs C's VW Beetle, the modern kind that resembled a vegetable anyway, had looked like a pumpkin rolling away down the lane.

He leaned his back against the wardrobe. The Rover's growl became a reality, a normal disturbance of the air: headlamps strafed the ceiling, and everything began for him, the ordinary, holy routine of his husband's return from work. Lee had to maintain that normality, as far as possible within his moon-racked home. Christ, he was scared! And so turned on that he could barely breathe, his cock heavy and stiff in his jeans.

The inner door clicked. Lee hadn't bothered to close the outer one. What was the point, on this fairytale night of grimoires, pumpkin coaches and a wolf who could blow the house down, a wolf whose bigness and badness were surely only a matter of perspective, surely still in Lee's hands to control? He listened to the soft-footed approach up the stairs, so different to Gid's normal homecomings, the cheerful yell from the door. Oh God, this potency in the air, this weight and heat...

Gideon stepped into the room. His back was to the moon, his detail drenched in darkness. Lee couldn't see his face. All he could hear were the sounds he was making—the faintest whispering purr on each outbreath, the shadow of a growl. Over a year ago, Lee had taken him into a dream, and there in the place beyond the Men-an-Tol portal Gideon had understood, fearlessly at last, what he was. He'd almost known the real name of their home.

But he couldn't bear the knowledge back into waking life. Lee couldn't help him, not yet. On some level Lee knew that his failure to do so was building up a price for both of them, a terrible forfeit. "Gideon," he whispered. "Can you listen to me? Can you still do that?"

The great head tilted slightly. Now Lee could see his eyes, amber fire like solar flares around the iris, moonlight through rich Cornish brown. Lee saw his small nod of assent. "All right. My fine... my fine man. Do you remember, you wanted us to dance at Zeke's wedding—properly, not just shimmying around? So you bought that DVD, and we... we were hopeless, weren't we, taking turns to have our back to the TV and falling over the furniture. But then you just *got* it. God, you took me in your arms, and you moved, and suddenly I could do it too, because you were holding me so close." Lee swallowed a fiery dryness in his throat. "You were so passionate, but so... perfectly, perfectly controlled. Can you still do that?"

Another nod, faint this time, just the slightest movement of the sleek dark head. Lee felt the weight of his attention, the honour of it. That Gid would hang on for him. "All right," Lee whispered. "Come and dance with me, then. Dance."

He held out one hand. Gideon strode forward and took it. He'd left his jacket and vest behind somewhere and was vibrantly warm in his T-shirt. When he laced his fingers between Lee's, his touch was only human. His arm around Lee's waist was only loving and strong. He'd been the natural lead, when their dance DVD had detailed the waltz steps, the lead and the follow, and Lee had rolled his eyes but stepped back to accommodate that powerful first movement. Gid's left foot to his right, the guiding push of his thigh, the place where their hips met, their first successful practice melting into a frantic roll-around on the couch. How stately they'd been at the wedding, not even daring to look at each other for fear of re-igniting the fires! A safe two inches between them, from nose-tip to corsage to cock.

Not tonight. Tonight Gid moved like the ocean, like a wave on the beach below Drift, the waters of Earth pulled high by the sun and the moon. He held Lee close and swept him once around the limited space between the bed and cabinets. He didn't look to left or right, avoiding the furniture with a blind precision that made Lee close his eyes in a shallow-lunged ecstasy of trust that did not end when the dance did, when the bedroom wall impacted softly against his spine. Shuddering, he looked up into the shadowed, still-human face. "Yes," he said. "You controlled it. Now show me who you are, my beauty. Take your clothes off, all of them. Let go."

And after all, Tamsyn could have stayed in her bed at the end of the hall. The bats flitting back and forth beyond the inched-open window were not disturbed in their patterns, and the second brood of fledgling swallows continued their peaceful occupation of the nests in the eaves. Not a leaf, not a star, not a breath of air was altered because Guardian Frayne had come home. He was Lee's own man, and the deep-laid tracks of his nature—his lifetime's habits of gentleness—had channelled his transformation, wolf to Lee's lamb.

Nonetheless, Lee let his eyes close again, and this time kept them shut. He pushed down his jeans and briefs, stepped blindly out of them and kicked them aside. *Up against the wall* had always been a favourite fuck for them both, with roots right down into their sacred beginnings, the parish house and the beast outside the door. Always this way round, because Lee, tough as he was, could never hoist Gideon high enough and pin him there. Familiar ground, a sense of homecoming, everything sweet and the same, except that now the beast was in Lee's arms.

He gasped when Gid lifted him. He was an armful, he knew, and Gideon would grunt and chuckle at the effort. Now there was only that whispering silence, and the knowledge that he weighed nothing to his lover. "You don't have to hold off," he said, surprised at the everyday sound of his own voice. "I saw to myself earlier—with the lube, I mean. I didn't think you'd want to stop."

I wasn't sure you could. Lee was ashamed of that now, and scared at himself: whatever the hell had he been thinking, ready to plunge into those black waters, even with this man? On some level he must have known, a fathomless, untapped resource of trust: *no* would mean *no* between them always, *wait* and *stop* and *don't*. With that much settled in his mind, Lee could let it all go. He burned up into *yes*, from his scalp to his clenching toes. *Now* and *yes* and *do it*. He would have closed his eyes anyway now, wanting nothing but the sense of Gid's penetration. He tipped his head back. The slow push inside him, riding easy on the lube, went on and on, until his breath shattered with a threat of fearful laughter. *Why should I be surprised that you're fucking huge? Did I really think it would just mean broader shoulders, bigger hands cradling my butt, the tips of what feel like— oh Christ—knife blades, delicately catching and scratching my skin?* Lee hitched his thighs up in a passion of acceptance. His eyes were closed, and so if the face next to his should be set in new lines, that meant nothing. His arms were locked so tight around Gid's neck that he was clutching at his own shirt sleeves, and so if those great shoulders should be coated with silken fur, that meant nothing. He was riding and rising to the point where he wanted to cross his ankles behind Gid's back, to hold him close and maximise the strain and squeeze inside, the divine bloody friction, and so if hot fur was rubbing at the insides of his thighs and the backs of his calves, that meant...

Lee had no idea how to get himself out of that one. The heat and the rasp were real. They meant everything. He stopped his frantic efforts at denial and inner escape. He was starting to come, in a flare like sweet death, and although Gid was ramming so hard and fast into him, a mouse building its nest in the wall behind them need not have felt alarmed. Those hands on him, their perfect, absolute restraint... *Guardian, Guardian, what big hands you have, what a huge human jewel of a heart—all the better to love me with, to keep us both safe and sane.* Gideon jolted and snarled, rhythm breaking, and Lee, eyes still closed, held him fast. "It's all right, my love," Lee choked out. "Everything will be all right."

***

And everything was. The moon sailed serenely over Bodmin Moor. She visited the houses of Dark with her light, an incomprehensible mother making last rounds of the grown-up children of earth. She smiled through Mrs Waite's chintz curtains, pleased to see that lady sprawled in passionate relief and solitude after the death of her husband, right in the middle of the marital bed, where she'd never been made to suffer but equally had never known a moment's true pleasure or love. The moon looked into the Prowse house, where Marple's few sticks of furniture stood on the bare boards left by the council's cleaning brigade, and she filled up with her light the vacancy left by Bill's chair and the little bunk beds where his children had taken such shelter as they might.

An impartial mother, she lit up the activities of one Pol Teague of Pendethy, who had finally managed to steal his ex-girlfriend's spare set of car keys and was letting himself into her back seat, where he intended to lie beneath a blanket and wait, rope and a knife at the ready.

She followed the stifled giggles of Sarah Kemp and Wilfred and shone her blessing on the patchwork quilt, beneath which new life—despite all sensible daytime vows to the contrary—was being conjured. In Pellar Street she peered through the fancy lace-pattern nets Granny Ragwen had used to favour, and into a bedroom where Tamsyn Elizabeth Tyack-Frayne, cross-legged on a rug, expression rapt, was turning and turning a vast crystal sphere in mid-air, beneath the watchful gaze of the old woman in her wickerwork chair in the corner.

As if saving the best for last, the moon paused by Chy Lowen. There, the window which had been inched open to admit the summer air was now thrown wide. The doors remained closed, the sacred sealed gates of the kingdom, but there in the wide double bed—unlike Flora Waite keeping to his own side, the space beside him sacred too—Lee slept alone.

***

At exactly half eight in the morning, the pumpkin car crunched back up the lane.

Lee jerked bolt upright. Between swinging his feet to the floor and pausing by the window, he registered messages from his body. No pain—of course not; he'd been in the hands of a loving moorland god—but extraordinary sensations from head to toe of having been torn apart and reassembled...

He looked outside. There were Mrs C and Tamsyn already on the drive, the dog dancing around them. He ran for the bedroom door. Stopped short: whipped round and grabbed the nearest covering to hand, a crumpled blanket from the floor. He didn't have time to look, but the room was full of sunlight, and he pelted downstairs with the image burned onto his retina of Gideon sprawled on his front and smiling.

He flung the blanket around him, hoping the effect was more Highlander than escaped lunatic, and opened the door. "There you are, dear," said Mrs C, smiling. "It's all right. I wasn't about to knock. Run along now, Tamsyn—you know what to do."

Dazed, Lee bent down to receive his little girl's hug. He kissed her brow, noting distractedly that she was glowing with her usual weekend-morning contentment, then watched her run silently off across the hall and up the stairs. "I'm sorry, Mrs Coulter. She should have stayed to thank you for having her."

"No, no. We had everything arranged. If she pops upstairs now, she'll be there before he wakes up. That's why I kept her in her pyjamas."

Lee shivered in the cool morning air, and tugged the blanket across his chest. He had no idea why he felt compelled to justify himself to this old lady. Still, she'd been a social worker: perhaps it was one of her gifts, and he hoped she'd seen families more chaotic than his own without declaring them broken. "I never set out to deceive him."

"Of course not. It was all my idea, if you recall." She took a step closer to him, put her head a little on one side as if listening. Her cheerful face softened into a new compassion. "But you have to be careful. There's something terribly wrong."

"You don't understand. I don't know how you come to know the things you do, but there was no need for either of us to worry. He's incredible. He's in control."

He shut himself up with an effort. What on earth was he doing, unfolding the secrets of the night in this sunny morning hour? But Mrs C was nodding, as if his words were nothing more than she'd expected. "We believe as we must, I suppose," she said gently. "You're in the hands of time, child—most of the time, anyway—and time will always unfold. As it happens I don't mean him, though. Gideon's becoming what he should be. I mean wrong with you."

"Me? No. I've been working a bit too hard, but I'm going to take some time off now. The whole summer."

"That's good. But when you come to think about it—as I did, in the cold light of dawn—would you *ever* have let your girl go off with a stranger, no matter how spellbound you were?"

"Spellbound?"

"Under a glamour, then. Hypnotised, if you want to take a modern view."

"But you're not a stranger. You're..."

"A random old bird who flew into your village a few years ago."

"But Gid had you background-checked."

"So he believes and would swear in a court of law, with that big paw of his upraised, and blind Justice herself laying her head on his shoulder for comfort. But it's not like you to miss a point, or evade one, either. Is it?"

Lee rubbed his eyes. No, it wasn't. "No," he said, a chasm opening up beneath him. "No, I never would have let her go. Oh Christ, what did I do?"

"Let's make the best of it. No harm done, so now let's complete the charade. You'll forget this conversation. Glamour!"

"Bless you," Lee said politely, convinced that she'd sneezed. "I'm sorry. Forget what?"

"All of it other than this—take care, little prophet. Have your summer. You can call it your... What did we call them, those few mad months in the sixties when we all thought that peace had a chance? Oh, that's right. *The summer of love.* Go on with you now. Glamour. Glamour!"

Lee turned around. He couldn't just forget things on command. That was ridiculous. But when he looked into the hallway, he could see only the dancing light of Bodmin summer, leaping from window to mirror to the crystals in the dusty old chandelier. From upstairs came the joyous racket of his daughter and his husband beginning their day, a weekend morning when Gideon had time to chase and tussle and toss the little girl about to her squealing, delighted heart's content. Already Isolde was joining in the chorus. Shaking his head, as often inwardly thanking God they didn't have neighbours, Lee let the door shut behind him and set off to join in the fun. Why should he look back?

Chapter Seven
Lee Tyack-Frayne's
Summer of Love

What a time he'd chosen for it, with the rest of the world melting down in hate! Families and friendships blew apart over Brexit, an anguished civil war of the heart. In the States, the hellish political carnival raged on. Lee wondered if he wasn't supposed to notice when Gideon stepped in front of the TV, or claimed a sudden interest in Jazz FM during a radio news broadcast in the kitchen. Probably he thought he was being subtle. And Lee couldn't bring himself to call him on his manoeuvres. Being shielded was too pleasant.

The moon got small again, and Lee collaborated, closing down his social-media accounts, which he'd only used for work anyway. They'd tortured him sometimes, the rush of the world's badness on top of everything he already felt. He rose to whatever bait of distraction Gideon chose to dangle: sunset walks across the moor, days out with Tamsyn and Ma Frayne on the riverboats around Kelyndar. Night after night of the kind of loving most men only dreamed about, because once the moon had waned, Gideon was only Gideon once more—his normal self, if that self had been set some kind of exam on the art of pleasing his other half in bed, and was anxious to get in all the practice he could. Lee went about his days with his bones half-melted with delight, his skin tingling.

He could barely stay awake, and blamed his disrupted nights for the honeyed languor that would steal over him around noon. Once Tamsyn's holidays began and he was on full-time dad duty, these episodes became easier to conceal. Gideon was usually out, and Lee could time his naps to coincide with Tamsyn's, Isolde keeping her own drowsy watch in the orchard, living room or bedroom or wherever they'd crashed out together.

A hot July opened up, and he began his boat-repair job for Jory Stark in St Wylloe. After a few days, passersby got used to the fact that Lee Tyack-Frayne, famous TV psychic, was sanding planks in Jory's garden behind the church, and stopped asking him for lottery numbers and tips for the Saturday races. He became just another working man amongst them, with his dog and his wide-eyed little girl. Tamsyn, having learned her lesson about lifejackets on the Kelyndar excursions, insisted on wearing one on deck: a boat was a boat, after all. She wanted Lee to wear one too, and when he laughingly declined, went solemnly to sit in the prow as if on watch. Lee could scan most of the sunny, overgrown churchyard from the deck. He kept an eye on her while she and Isolde scrambled about amongst the gravestones and the flowers. From time to time she brought him crowns of feverfew and willow, to cure the headaches he kept reassuring her he didn't have, but otherwise she seemed happy, her little air of watching and waiting no more than an ordinary child's expectant view of life.

Rings of contentment spread out from her. That was how it struck Lee, as he chaperoned her about her business in Dark and beyond. Everyone within her sphere of influence flourished.

Elowen and Michel had moved to England for the time being, renting a house in Bodmin town. This news would once have made Gid's hackles rise, but Elowen was becoming famous for her archaeological discoveries around the Hurlers. Success suited her, seeming at last to settle her old sense of injustice at being—helplessly, beyond poor Cadan's control—her father's second-favourite child. She had dug her way through Sarah Kemp's garden and into her kitchen, recompensing her handsomely afterwards with a landscaping job and a state-of-the-art refit. Now she was eyeing up Chy Lowen, which also lay on the alignment of circles, but it would take her a while to get there, a stay of execution, though Gid had declared he'd gladly let her plough on through if he too got a brand-new aga and all the trimmings.

Baby Cadan continued to contribute to Elowen's peace of mind by taking steadfastly after Michel instead of her complicated, painful Tyack relations, right down to the sophisticated Gallic manners: Lee would come upon him munching his rusk with the air of a Montmartre demimondaine, admiring passing ladies, who returned his attentions delightedly, stopping to make a fuss of him at every pass. Tamsie was a hoyden by comparison, but they loved each other. She helped out in the trenches when she could, more for the joy of the mud than the antiquities, as far as Lee could see. She called Elowen *Lowen*, and Lee contrived to forget Rufus Pendower's theories about the sound of those two syllables in Breton dialect. With a little mental rearrangement, he managed to forget Pendower himself. Forgot Launceston and Alice Rawle, who was safely locked up in a high-security unit somewhere in Devon, and might as well have been on the moon. Even Gideon had set her aside. David Rawle was missing, and the investigation of his abandoned school had stalled out amid a rush of more urgent work, as the concept of Brexit shone a more and more lurid green light for every racist, xenophobe and—inexplicably;

perhaps just part of the general tide of hatred for all that was different—gaybasher on the peninsula.

A summer of love for Lee despite all this, a Woodstock, a night hand-in-hand with the women of Greenham Common, forging a human chain around the cruise missiles. Tamsyn created the space and Lee occupied it, too tired for once in his life to question the process. And like that long-ago Woodstock summer—like all frail hopes in a bad old world where the hawks ate the doves for breakfast, dinner and tea—it couldn't last.

***

"Ugh," Gideon said, turning over the pages of Monday morning's *Herald*. "Poor Jenny Spargo. That's right on her home turf."

The day was so fine that they'd taken their early breakfast outside into the orchard. Neither had bothered much so far with clothes, and the place was a rare kind of Eden, all serpents welcome under contract to bring only the knowledge of good. This sounded to Lee like a breach of the rules. He came round to Gideon's side of the trestle table, clambered onto the bench beside him. "Nothing up with our Jen, is there?"

"No, but a body's been found up near Pendethy. Been identified as..." Gideon paused, then actually began to chuckle. "Pol Teague! I don't bloody believe it. My God, talk about good riddance."

"I know that name, don't I?"

"Yeah, you do. Brother of the less famous Jim, who happily killed himself in a single-vehicle RTA a few weeks ago. Pol's been in and out of the papers for years. He's a stalker, and a right slippery bastard too—drove one girl to suicide, and a couple of others had to change their names and leave Cornwall to get away from him. Everyone knew what he was doing, but there was never enough concrete evidence to pin the little fucker down."

Out of habit Lee glanced over his shoulder, but Tamsyn was safely out of reach in Uncle Zeke's house, ready for a trip with her cousins and her Gran to see the fossils at Chesil Beach. "Fuck the little fucker, then," Lee agreed, hooking his arm through Gid's. Odd that after all their intimacies, such an ordinary gesture could feel so hot, the satiny rub of skin fresh from the shower. "What happened to him?"

"Pissed off the wrong boyfriend, maybe. Or knowing those Pendethy ladies, maybe the wrong girl. They found him in his latest victim's car, only the car was at the bottom of a ravine just outside of the village, which is why it hasn't come to light till now. The roof of the car had been... Let me see, how did our intrepid *Herald* reporter put it? Oh, yes. *The roof had been peeled back like the lid of a sardine tin.*"

"Crikey," Lee said comfortably. Gideon's bare shoulder felt like a flank of the moor this morning, a place to stretch out and rest all day in the sun. "Is the girl all right?"

"Fine, thank God, singing the praises of whoever knocked Teague off, although I dunno about that—sounds to me like a case of a big nutcase versus a little 'un, and that's not good. Still, they found rope and a knife in the guy's pockets. They reckon he was waiting in the back seat of her car for her to come out of her new boyfriend's house."

"Jesus. Why is it Jenny's problem, though? She's working with you out of Bodmin, isn't she?"

"Ah, she's in the same boat I am here in Dark. Pendethy born and bred, and she still lives in the village, so everyone there thinks it's her job to look after them. She won't mind too much, I reckon. She's gunning for CID, and cracking a case like this would sort her out handsome."

Something cold touched the back of Lee's throat, as if he'd woken up alone on his moorland hill and found that the world had dropped into winter around him. "When did this happen?"

"Oh, about three weeks back. Girlfriend didn't think too much to it when she came out of the house that night. Just thought someone had nicked her car. What's up, morning glory? Not getting any kind of flash about this, are you?"

"Nope. Sticking strictly to my holiday rules. Jen will have to do her sleuthing on her own."

"Good. And you know what? I hope she doesn't find a thing, CID or no CID. Who cares about any of these guys—Pol Teague, or John Tregear, or that creep over in Bodinnar last year who turned out to have a cage and shackles in his garage, and not the fun kind? If some vigilante's taken to cleaning them up, more power to him. Who cares?"

Lee wriggled round on the bench. Then he hitched himself up onto the table to sit in front of Gideon, taking care to move his paper, tea mug and the remains of his toast out of the way. The cool press of the planks on his bare backside was a distraction, but he pushed it aside. He had to keep his mind out of his genitals for five minutes at a stretch, even with Gid staring up at him in open-mouthed, sleep-dishevelled wonder. "The weird thing is," he said, reaching to stroke the dark head, "that *you* used to. Care, that is, about all these creeps and villains. You'd bust them, but then you'd come home and tell me how this one never stood a chance with the family he'd had, or this other one was an addict or never got sent to school, or this one was abused himself and was passing it on."

Gideon sighed, blowing out his cheeks thoughtfully. "Yeah, I suppose I did. Not much point to it, though, was there?"

"Well, you wouldn't sneak into Bodmin jail at night and let any of 'em go. But you did make recommendations for their custody, for rehab and psychiatry if you thought that would help."

"I still do most of those things. You're right, though—I *don't* care, not the way I used to." He laid one hand to each of Lee's knees, carefully, as if weighing up pros and cons. Then he ran both palms warmly up his thighs. "There's just so much to *do*, love. I'm getting cases wrapped up faster than I ever did before. I've got so much energy, and I feel clearer somehow, less distracted. Let me be that kind of man for you."

Lee was losing track. The breeze was rustling in the apple leaves overhead. He was in his life's brief summer, and the air was sweet. "What kind?"

"The kind who doesn't worry too much. Who takes care of everything while you rest."

What a dream. Who ever got to hear that, in a world that demanded everything twice over from most families, then asked for the cherry on top? Gid was watching him, the picture of health and contentment, all brightness and bounce and readiness to pounce. Lee gave it up. "All

right, Sergeant. What's on the menu today?"

Gideon grinned in unashamed anticipation. "Don't you mean *who*? Some nice juicy morsels for starters. Members of *Kernow Glan Nowydh*, will you believe, setting up shop in Bodmin. So far they're all about sticking flyers on lampposts and telling anyone with a tan that they have to fuck off home now, but if they're modelling themselves on the original movement, we have to keep an eye on 'em. *New Cornish Purity*, my arse."

Lee sketched him a salute. "Go get 'em, copper."

"Then I'm on my beat for the rest of the afternoon unless I get called up to Pendethy. I tell you what I will do at lunchtime—

I'll swing by Liskeard and see Rufus Pendower. I've been meaning to."

"Yes. Do. Wait, though—he's not one of the morsels, is he?"

"No, not at all. I know we kid around, but I'm worried about him. One of my mates in the Devon squad says he's been missing work. I'll be nice."

"Course you will." Lee sat back a little. He was in no place to lecture Gid about caring. He should've gone to see Rufus himself, straight away after their encounter at Beaumont Hall. He should offer to join Gid in Liskeard. Sleepy arousal swept through him instead. "Did we ever do it this way before?"

Gid's eyebrows flew up. "I, er... don't think so. Over the table and under it, but not with you sitting there." He gave it thought. "I could suck you off something beautiful. You'd have to scoot back a bit, though. Mind out for splinters."

Lee obeyed. His cock was stirring. In the space between beginning and completion, erection and orgasm, he would be safe, his mind full of windblown apple blossom and stars. He'd been hiding there for weeks, he suddenly understood: since the solstice full moon, in deep trenches of sleep, between the waves of pleasure Gideon could pull from his flesh. "No," he whispered, and Gid, who'd been leaning in, glanced up enquiringly. "No. I'm sorry, love. I know I started it, but..."

Gideon surged off the bench. He scrambled onto the table top with Lee, almost knocking him off the end of it with the force of his tackle-hug. "What does it matter who started it?" he demanded. "You can say no at the top of the craziest fuck we ever had. Mid-flight. Anytime. Christ, Lee—you do *know* that, don't you?"

What a question! For six years, Lee had known that his slightest word and smallest twitch of discomfort would halt Gid in his tracks. He could have said no in the light of the full solstice moon and stopped the avalanche, he was almost completely sure. "Course I know. I'm sorry to stop you, that's all. But you've shagged me out, big man. Gonna have to let the wells fill before we go for another round."

He huddled into Gideon's arms. He was suddenly cold despite the sun. He didn't want his lover to know, but Gid gathered him up with the irresistible warm strength that seemed to be summoned by such changes, the answer to unexpressed need. Lee rubbed his cheek against the broad, fine-skinned shoulder. Baulked of arousal, all his body wanted now was to shut down into sleep, and he fought the reaction unwillingly, swimming against the tide. Gideon's morning scent, soap and clean moorland air and the tiny, subtle, thrilling undercurrent that marked him out as himself, pure Gid, wrapped Lee round like a cloak. "You'd better go," he whispered, half-hoping he wouldn't be heard. "You'll be late."

"In a minute." A chuckle shook the big frame. "Oh, wait. Are we getting there?"

"Where?"

"You know."

Lee did. He was charmed that Gid found it charming, a goal to be aimed for in their marriage: the time when sex dropped down their list of priorities, when one or the other or both of them would be too worn out to get it up, or do anything with it if they did. Lee loved the idea too, for his own reasons. If he and Gid ever got to that stage, they must have had time together—acres of time, buckets and rivers and truckloads, time enough to wallow in and run like precious gold dust between their hands. "I think we have to be indoors for that," he said, making sure to keep his tone light as Gid's mood. "Outside on a picnic bench is a bit too sexy."

"Oh, right. That's it. We have to be falling asleep on the couch in front of the TV."

"That's it. Right pair of old farts. Oh, I want that, Gid."

"We'll have it." Gideon held him fiercely. "We'll have every minute of it, I swear."

"Go on, then. You'd better keep earning your fat police pension. *My* ghosts and monsters aren't gonna keep us in our ripe old age." Lee swiped a slap at Gid's backside, let go of him and reluctantly released himself. "Fresh uniform's on the back of the bedroom door. Get lost."

He watched him stride off across the lawn. He left something in the air behind him—a trace of that scent, perhaps, or just a warm vibration, but Lee seldom felt wholly alone when he was anywhere on the premises, as if he could turn the whole house, the very air, into an extension of his embrace.

Lee closed his eyes, considering this. Before he could formulate any coherent thoughts on the subject, the man himself was back anyway, smartly kitted out from cap to boots and on the run. He took the steps from the French doors to the garden in one leap. "It's all off," he yelled, waving a hand at Lee as if trying to flag him down and heading towards him at a jog. "All off. Forget it. I looked at the calendar. We've got bigger fish to fry."

"We do?"

"We do. I forgot. It's your appointment day."

Lee blinked at him. Dentist? The car's MOT? It took him long seconds to grasp at the answer, and when he did he broke into laughter. "Oh, what—my brain scan? That doesn't matter."

Gideon crunched to a halt by the bench. He put his hands on his hips and rocked back on his heels, the very picture of an outraged village bobby. "It bloody does, you know. We missed your last two."

"Yeah, I know. But everything was all right, wasn't it? This one will be fine as well. I'll go along on my own."

"No way. Part of my conjugal duty, this kind of thing is."

"Oh, you're more than paid up on your conjugals, handsome. Look, it's completely routine. I'd way rather think of you knocking Kernow Glan's crew-cut little wooden-top heads together than waiting round in corridors with me. A much better use of your time. Besides, you couldn't get the time off at this short notice."

"Bugger that. Let 'em fire me." These words out, Gid appeared to reflect on them, and perhaps upon the pension, too, and the practicalities behind the dream of growing old with the man he loved. He pushed his cap a little way back off his brow. "Having said that, I *might* have a bit of a struggle to swing it past Lawrence. Are you sure?"

"Absolutely. I'll call you if I need you."

"Do you promise?"

"On my heart." He traced two short lines on his own chest, and then two upon Gideon's, just over the blue police badge on his utility vest. "There. A St Piran's cross to seal it for both of us. I swear."

***

The Kernow Glan interviews turned out to be the easiest part of Gideon's day. The worst of the bad old lot had gone down with John Tregear, part and parcel of the fantastically damning mobile phone that had been posted to Bodmin HQ in the wake of the Falmouth bombing. *Attempted* bombing, Gideon corrected himself with a surge of satisfaction, revving the police truck and peeling away off the Twelvewoods roundabout towards Liskeard. If he'd remained becomingly modest around Lee, his boss, the press and even Her Majesty, when that lady had stepped forward to present him with his medal, that didn't mean he wasn't blisteringly proud. Or not even proud, exactly—just *happy*, in a hot, enduring way he'd never experienced before. A detonation in the Pride parade would have killed dozens, maimed dozens more. People were alive and whole today because of him. His heart rose in his chest. He'd growled and glared at this new bunch, the ones calling themselves *Nowydh*, across the interview tables, and they'd crumbled and given one another up with frantic enthusiasm.

Villains weren't what they'd used to be. At least the likes of Bill Prowse and Tregear would've put up a fight. They'd been sure of their hatreds, bitter and unashamed. The new ones swung like compass needles in a magnet factory, confusing their racism with homophobia, refusing to understand that the Brexit they'd voted for wouldn't prevent the appearance in their streets and pubs of the brown and black faces they despised. *How far do you think Europe goes*, Gid had demanded wearily on the fourth or fifth futile go-around, attempting to reason. *The Middle East? Africa?* Their goals were stupid and small, a grab at imaginary spoils: jobs they couldn't do, money they hadn't earned. John Tregear's rage would've set the whole planet on fire. Christ only knew how Dev Bowe had managed to kill him.

Gideon's world jolted on its axis. He missed the junction with Lanchard Lane, and only just braked down in time for the twenty zone in the town centre. His enjoyment of the day and himself flew out of the Rover's windows like birds from a cage. He swallowed hard, grabbed at the wheel with suddenly sweat-damped hands. Something somewhere was terribly wrong. In Gideon's world his fears always began in the same place—well, two places now, two beloved epicentres, and he took the next right, doubled back and pulled over in the nearest available space.

He got a loving earful from Lee, who'd almost managed to parallel-park in a tight spot outside the hospital until distracted by the buzzing of his phone. He was fine. Tamsyn was fine too, as Zeke's texted photo confirmed, grinning with her cousins over their haul of ammonites and shells. Gideon hung up smiling, shivering slightly with relief. His fit of the horrors ebbed, probably nothing more than a touch of indigestion anyway. Inwardly vowing to quit his new habit of roadside-caff lunches, he looked around him.

By luck, he'd stopped more or less outside Pendower's house. He and Lee had been here several times before, for awkward, well-intended dinners with Rufus and Daisy. The neatly paved drive was the same, the little brick wall and the gate.

Everything else looked wrong. The lawn was overgrown and starred with dandelions. Orange geraniums—ugly customers at the best of times, but a favourite of Daisy's—had collapsed and were lolling over the sides of their pot by the front door. Someone had pulled the curtains at random across the windows, a kind of half-measure that would do for night or day.

Not Daisy's style at all. She liked boundaries, set breakfast and dinner times, especially since the birth of her little boy. Curtain ties, potted plants, manicured lawns. Gideon pushed open the Rover's door and cautiously got out, examining the building's facade. A chunk of render was missing from under the eaves, and someone or something had cracked a small pane of glass in the bedroom window. On instinct he avoided the front door, raising the latch on the side gate instead to let himself into the yard.

He found Rufus sitting in one of the two striped deckchairs set out in the afternoon shade. At first glance he appeared perfectly content. One of his huge folklore texts was open on his lap, and he was leaning on one elbow, as if to share the book's contents with an invisible companion in the other chair. He looked up at Gideon tranquilly. He was thin and unshaven, but for long moments he seemed much younger than his years, as if revisiting happier times. "Hello, Gideon," he said, a bright smile dawning. "You should've knocked."

"You wouldn't have answered. Would you?"

The effort of telling the truth chased the fantasy away. Gideon could almost see it go: the empty chair, the sense of vanished affection. "No," Rufus said, face clouding. "I'm taking some leave. I'm not well."

More than Gideon's life was worth to settle in the deckchair beside him. He perched uncomfortably on the low wall surrounding the wheelie bins. "Not what I hear from my mate in Plymouth. He says you've been AWOL. It's not too late if you pull it together now, sort yourself out and turn up for duty tomorrow with your hair brushed and your boots nice and shiny. I came to see if you'd like some help with that."

"Would you polish them yourself? Brush my hair?"

Gideon considered the tone of this question. There was yearning in it as well as a bite of sarcasm. "If you like," he said levelly. "Everyone needs to be taken care of sometimes."

"Do you do those things for Locryn?"

"No. Lee's pretty much on top of his personal hygiene." Anger flared in Gideon, a heat he'd been suppressing for too long. "I meant to approach this nicely, but since you've dumped us both into the middle of it, Lee doesn't need you hanging about his sets and locations like a stalker. You need to back off."

Well, there it was. Rufus gaped. Gideon rubbed his eyes: he really had come here intending to be gentle, not to slap down the still-beating heart of his problems with Pendower on the cracked cement paving of the yard. "Shit," he said remorsefully. "I didn't mean to say that, believe it or not—not yet, anyway. I do want to help you. Where the hell's Daisy?"

"She took the baby and left."

"Oh, Christ. When?"

"It was after that day in Launceston. I came home, and I couldn't stop myself from talking about him—what he said, how ill he'd been, how insane it was that he'd been arrested for doing nothing but try to help and tell the truth. I couldn't shut up, even though Stevie was cutting a tooth and wailing, and Daisy needed me to take him off her hands. She was exhausted, and she asked me if I loved her, and..."

"Please tell me you didn't say no."

"I did. And I told her we were quits, because she didn't love me either. I had proof, because I'd seen how she looked when she was in love by then, so I could tell the difference."

"Don't be absurd. That girl never so much as glanced at anyone but you."

"Oh, not like that. I mean in the maternity ward, when they put the baby into her arms."

Gideon sighed explosively. "Women have all kinds of love. She's not gonna look at you like her precious firstborn son, no, but—"

"Are you *seriously* about to lecture me on the subject of women?"

"Oh, right. I'm gay, so I wouldn't have a clue? I work with women, Pendower. I've got a mother, a sister-in-law and a little girl, not to mention the dozens of victim-support groups I've worked with over the years, the battered wives and the rape victims. If you think my sexuality excludes me from any of that, you're as bad as the knuckleheaded Kernow Glan brutes I've been grilling all morning."

Rufus doubled over in his chair. He fastened his hands together at the back of his skull. Running out of breath and scorching words, Gideon didn't blame him. What the hell was he doing? Why did this poor bastard, deserted and clearly half out of his mind, bring all his own sore spots to the surface? "Sorry. Sorry. Look, for God's sake don't sit like that. Look at me, and I'll start over, if you'll let me."

Not a flicker from the hunched-up figure in the chair. Surrendering, Gideon got to his feet. He strode past Rufus, briefly dropping one hand to his shoulder, and let himself into the house through the back door.

The kitchen was a sordid mess. There but for the grace of God went Gideon himself, if he'd never met Lee—the bachelor habits and self-neglect, discarded food packets, half-eaten ready meals for one. Oh, he'd have tried, but loneliness would've dragged him down in the end. Nature hadn't built him to be solitary and unloved. He took a long, assessing glance around him, and then he went to work.

Quarter of an hour later, the surfaces were clean, the sink disinfected, dishwasher chuntering over a full load, cardboard and tins set aside for recycling, a few unspeakable horrors exorcised from the fridge. Normally he found such tasks tiring, far more of a pull on his energies than a chase around the streets after villains. Horses for courses, he'd always thought, but maybe he'd just been making heavy weather of his half of the domestic routine. He had bundles of energy now. A glance into the living room revealed extensive wreckage there too. He could bet that the bed was unmade, and the bathroom didn't bear thinking about.

Action was better than thought in such cases. He blazed in. He felt like cleansing fire, the kind that certain trees and heathers needed to make them sprout afresh. He didn't stop to consider the intimacy of turfing another man's underwear out of the wash basket and into the machine, of rinsing traces of his toothpaste and whiskers off the sink. Like any other messy job, it was best done fast and well. Once finished, he bounded downstairs, half convinced he could take the same arm's-length, merciless approach to his colleague's state of mind. He snapped the kettle on, rattled tea mugs out of the cupboard. "Get your arse in here, mate," he called cheerfully through the door, not looking out.

"Tea's up, and your kitchen's no longer a biohazard. The land of the living awaits."

No response. At last he went to lean in the doorway. Rufus was sitting exactly as he'd left him, hands still clenched at the back of his skull.

His unchanged stillness made Gideon's sense of reality skitter and slide. Perhaps there were two worlds: one full of action and benefit inside the house, and another out here, where time had slowed to treacle, and no-one gave a damn anymore. As often when uncomfortable with his own decisions, he compared his last forty minutes with how Lee might have spent them if he'd been there. What that quiet, gold-hearted soul might have done.

Probably he'd have pulled over that crate from the corner of the yard, put it in front of Rufus and sat down. He'd have allowed his one-off brand of receptive silence to expand around him, filling the dreary little space until curiosity or the need to speak overcame Rufus and he unfolded, rejoining the human race because he wanted to, not because some overbearing lump of a copper had ordered him to be cured.

Well, maybe it wasn't too late for a little Tyack magic. Gideon grabbed the crate, dragged it over and sat down. He put his head on one side, tried for the receptive silence.

Somehow it turned the air around him to crackling static, and Rufus looked up with anything but mollified curiosity in his eyes. "Why are you still here?"

"I... don't know, really. I tidied up for you a bit inside, chucked some stuff out of your fridge."

"Did I ask you to do any of that?"

"No. But I remember, when Tamsyn's mother changed her mind about letting us adopt her and took her away, Lee cleaned our flat. I came back from work and found it all done. It didn't make anything less dreadful. It was just easier to feel rotten somewhere clean."

The grim face softened slightly. "That was when I first met him. Elowen had taken Tamsyn the day before, and he was being so brave, out in Farmer Bowe's fields trying to do his work. Of course I didn't know what he was going through, not until you explained. I'd got such a shock when you'd said you were married to him, too. When I look back on the way I reacted, I'm ashamed. I must have seemed so ignorant."

"No, never that. A bit naive, maybe."

"I'd worked with gay officers before. Just not married ones who called each other *husband* the way you two did."

"Well, for me and Lee at that point it was go big or go home, you know? Other coppers might need to be more discreet. I was lucky—I had family to support me, an understanding boss. But we're talking about me here, or Lee at any rate, and..." Gideon spread his hands. "And I think it needs to be about you. Have you been seeing Amber again?"

Rufus nodded, not visibly fazed by the subject change. "Yes, almost all the time. She was here when you arrived. We were reading my book together, though I never was interested in any of that stuff until after she died. If she could come back, you see—if she could talk to me and seem so real, maybe all the things I'd dismissed as paranormal garbage could be true as well. So I began to study it all, to try and understand, which is why I ended up in John Bowe's barley field with you."

Sergeant Weird-Shit. Gideon had coined the name to make Lee smile on a dark day, but now it seemed trite, for a man who'd acquired his expertise in such a way. For such a reason. "I'm so sorry that you lost her."

"Well, these days I don't feel as if I have. You distracted me from her for a while, which is why I was angry. But she came back." He cast a smiling glance at the deckchair beside him. "I must sound insane, talking like this."

No, you don't. I saw her too, on the clifftops at Drift, and I still can't explain how, except that I was within Lee's nimbus of vision, and he was holding open the gates between the worlds. She was wearing a dress you bought her with tulips on, her favourite. "Living with Lee," he said awkwardly, "I've learned not to have too many boundaries, about what's real and sane and what's not."

"You're so lucky. To live with him, I mean. You could never deserve him."

When Zeke said something like that—made the caustic observation that Lee was worth a hundred of him—Gideon could accept it. There was even a weird pride in it for him, knowing that Lee loved him despite his unworthiness, knowing that he meant to spend his life redressing the balance. From Rufus, it was a red flag. "Pendower," he rumbled. "You've got feelings for Lee, and I don't blame you. He's not about to return them, though, and it seems to me you've chucked away the love you *did* have for the sake of some dream that can never come true. You do get that, don't you? Never."

That last word had been a verbal punch. Gideon was sorry as soon as it was out: there'd been no need. He saw retaliation gathering in Pendower's eyes. Well, he had it coming, and better to let the poor bastard get a good one in. "All right," he said resignedly, when the hush that had gathered in the little yard was threatening to drown them both. "You've got something to say to me, go ahead."

"He'd break his heart and die for you."

Pain passed through Gideon's chest, a dull pang, as if the breakage had already begun. "We'd die for each other. But his heart's in my keeping. I'd never abuse that trust."

"You damn well abused it in Kerdrolla." Rufus knotted his hands together. His eyes fixed on a point behind Gideon's shoulder, as if some spirit had emerged from the brickwork to reproach him—not Daisy this time, Gideon was sure. "I'm not breaking my promise. I'm not! I only promised about Dev Bowe."

Gideon couldn't keep up with this. "What has Dev got to do with anything?"

"He couldn't have killed John Tregear. You know he couldn't."

"I think about that often. I believe you're probably right. But if you know anything, and you've been holding back—"

"Oh, God, Gideon. Don't lean on me to find out the last thing in the world you want to know."

"You've lost me. As for Kerdrolla..." The word fell heavily into the stifling air. "I dreamed about a place with that name when I had flu a couple of years back. Lee said it meant... Story Town, or something like that. Did he talk to you about it?"

"No. I was... That is, I remember..."

Again that frightened glance beyond Gideon's shoulder. Was some angel with a fiery sword standing there? Whatever Pendower was seeing, it stopped his tongue, or altered whatever had been about to come burning off it. "He must have spoken to me about it, yes. He knows how much I like place names and their origins— maybe he thought I'd be interested to hear what your brain had come up with when you had a fever. I'm sorry, all right? I wasn't going to tell."

"Rufus, who are you talking to?"

Pendower made a massive grab for normality. "You, of course. Who else?"

"Yes, mostly. That last part, though, and when you said you weren't breaking your promise—who else do you think is here?"

"Nobody. Nobody. But listen to me, Gideon, and I'll try to tell you as much of the truth as I can, not because I'm jealous or angry but because I'm afraid for you both. I'm not stupid. I know you're joined at the hip for life, and it's not your fault if I've got a stupid schoolboy crush. The only things that can hurt you are the secrets you keep from one another."

"What are you talking about? I don't keep anything from him."

Frowning, Rufus focussed on him, his gaze suddenly forensic. "You really don't, do you? You really don't know."

Abruptly Gideon had had enough. He couldn't believe he'd engaged with Rufus to this extent. Like arguing with a drunk or a crackhead, except that his colleague's incapacity was mental illness and he therefore deserved all the sympathy and help Gideon could provide. He felt like a storm in Rufus's teacup, the yard and the house tiny, painfully restrictive. "Okay," he said, pushing to his feet with a force that sent the crate clattering over behind him. "That leaves Lee keeping secrets from me. You know, for someone who claims to love him, you don't know anything about him at all."

"You're right. I'm sorry."

Jesus, was Rufus trying to *pacify* him? A bit bloody late for that, but Gideon summoned all his patience and professionalism, ignoring the need to jump over the wall of the yard and run and run until he found wide moorlands and clean air. "No, *I'm* sorry. I've been chewing your arse off here, and you're not well. I tell you what I'm going to do. I picked up a bit of shopping on the way over here, and I doubled up on milk and bread and some other basic stuff just in case you were running low. So I'm gonna go and fetch that, and then I'll phone the welfare office. Look, it happens to us all from time to time, and they helped me a lot when I was out of action." Remembering Beth Squires and his own complete refusal of that worthy officer's services, Gideon made a face. "Well, they would've if I'd let them, and you will. Don't worry, it's not Squires anymore. They've got a psychologist called Treece now—I hear she's really good."

He didn't wait for Rufus's reaction to any of this. Whatever Rufus thought was irrelevant now. He'd proved himself unfit for duty, and the rotting food in his kitchen had told a wider story: maybe the poor sod needed to be in care. He strode off to the truck, letting the gate bang behind him. Thirty seconds sufficed for him to pick out the duplicate groceries and sling them into a bag. Rufus watched him serenely enough as he swept back through the yard and into the kitchen, much as he might have watched a wave break over Sennen sands, or any other unstoppable force of nature.

Briskly Gideon unpacked. A crumpled scrap of paper on the counter top caught his eye, and he flattened it out: an invoice from a local firewood company, three bags of kiln-dried, stove-ready birch, payment overdue. Household finances had been Daisy's remit, Gideon recalled from one of the interminable dinner parties, Lee good-naturedly manufacturing conversation by comparing his domestic arrangements with hers. The bill was only for thirty quid. Gideon had that much left over from his grocery run. He fished his wallet out of his pocket, peeled off a twenty and a ten and secured these, along with the invoice, to the front of the fridge with a magnet. Briefly it occurred to him that he and Lee had enough bills of their own to pay, but he felt lordly. Bountiful, brimming over with beneficent power.

He made a quick call to the Tollgate Road welfare office. Finding Squires' replacement at her desk, he explained that although Sergeant Pendower was on secondment in Devon, he was better known at the Cornwall HQ, where his courageous actions were a matter of local legend. Smiling to himself, Gideon recalled them: his dash around the barleyfields on the night of

Guldize, collecting stray children until a lightning bolt had struck him, forever destroying the smooth, neat lie of his hair. His extraordinary tackle-run to knock Gideon out of the way of a gas-leak blast in Dark. His fearless arrival at the burning church, bringing Tamsyn in his arms...

Wait. Where the fuck had that last one come from? Keeping the mobile clamped to his ear, Gideon leaned his elbows on the counter. That had been part of his dream, hadn't it—the Kerdrolla dream, where Story Town had exploded and Zeke's chapel had burned to ashes in the glowing heart of a midsummer night. He rubbed his brow with his free hand, and gradually became aware of the welfare officer repeating his name down the line.

He pulled himself together. Pendower had been under pressure, he continued, and was showing signs of depression. He was a good officer and a friend. Treece made empathetic noises at him, promised a personal visit later that afternoon. Could Gideon stay with Pendower until she arrived?

He wanted urgently not to. He was grateful for the text he'd seen before placing the call, summoning him up to Pendethy after all. Treece was understanding, and he hung up with the sense of a job well done.

He turned to leave, and found Pendower blocking the doorway. "Okay," Gideon said cautiously, hoping to God this mission of mercy wasn't about to devolve into a ruck. "Treece is coming out to see you later today. You'll let her in, won't you? You definitely need help."

Pendower didn't respond. He was surveying his clean kitchen: the well-scrubbed surfaces, the tea towels folded over their rail. At last his gaze fastened on the cash attached to the fridge door. A miserable, humiliated flush suffused his features. "I hate you for this," he said softly. "I know I shouldn't, but I really fucking do."

"Godsakes. The place was stinking."

"My stink. Mine to make, mine to clean up."

"Agreed, but you weren't cleaning. You don't want to add enteritis to your heap of problems."

"My fucking heap."

"Pendower, pack it *in*. And stand aside out of that doorway, unless you really want to piss me off."

"It'll come back on you threefold."

The words were familiar. Gideon racked his brains for the reference. "Wait. Our local witches in Dark say that—not old Granny Ragwen and the likes of her. The young ones in the coven on Watchover Hill." He had to repress a chuckle. "The Threefold Law, eh? What's gonna come back on me—all the detergent I used to scrub out your kitchen? I'll be sure to keep some aside for you in case this happens again."

"No. Your little girl did something after that day in Kerdrolla. She did something to make everything all right. I don't know what—I can't remember that part properly at all. But it was huge. And nobody can *do* that, don't you see? Not without making the universe lash back."

Two choices now faced Gideon. The first and most tempting was to drop Rufus cold with a roundhouse punch for daring to drag his child's name into this. The second—because he'd done enough damage here today, despite his best intentions—was to make one final attempt to talk to this struggling, lonely man. Rufus's own frame of reference might be the best way in. Gritting his teeth, Gideon aimed for the high road. "Best we don't talk about Tamsyn, all right? But Lee says something along those lines too. At least, he'd say that you can't do an action without causing a *re*action, that you can't move something around without something else moving in to take its place. I get that, kind of. I can even see how it works with the laws of physics, in a way. Why threefold, though? That doesn't make any sense at all."

"Why don't you ask your coven witches? Or better still, ask Tamsyn."

"Pendower, I warned you."

"Yes. Sorry. Ask Granny Ragwen, I should've said." Now it was Rufus's turn to laugh, a sick, frightened sound. "You think she was killed in Penzance, don't you? In the warehouse, when she got up into the rafters."

"Nobody knows what happened to her. She's... missing, that's all."

"How can you not remember? Locryn does. I do, and it *haunts* us, Gideon. It's going to haunt us till the day we die."

Chapter Eight
All Too Short a Stay

Meredith Parker was a nice woman, her sarcasm only superficial. She had been in charge of Trelowarren's radiography unit for many years, and she and Lee knew each other well. "Good of you to grace us with your presence," she said, scrolling her way down his records on her computer screen. "You wouldn't have thought that half an hour twice a year was *such* a brutal schedule."

He made a wry little play of wincing. "Sorry, Doc Meredith. How many have I missed?"

"Just the last two. Oh, and one the year before, and we didn't see you at all in 2015." She laid off, pushing away from her desk to face him. "That was the year after your baby was born, wasn't it? How is she?"

Lee got out his latest photos, and he and Meredith exchanged notes on Tamsyn's and her grandchildren's various misdeeds and accomplishments. "Well," said Meredith at length, with an air of resuming business. "I suppose I should be grateful you've made time to see us now. How did your scan go?"

"Fine. Usually freaks me out a bit having to lie still for so long, but I didn't mind it today. Think I might've gone to sleep for a few minutes."

"Nice that you feel so relaxed around us. Don't you usually have your other half to help keep you awake? Where is he today?"

"He couldn't get the time off." He saw Meredith's eyebrows on the rise. In another world, he'd have been faint with astonishment himself. Gingerly he let the two planes of being touch and overlap. If he let himself think about it, Gid might forget an appointment completely, but never in a thousand years let Lee attend on his own, no matter how... *No matter how spellbound*, an old woman's voice breathed past his inner ear, and he snapped the connections decisively. Just as well that in *this* world, Lee's beautiful summer, everything always turned out all right, and appointments like this were routine. "It's just routine," he reassured Meredith and himself. "No point dragging him along. He's got loads of stuff on at the moment."

"Off saving the nation single-handed, is he? I heard about that business at the Pride parade in Falmouth, and his Queen's medal. Cornwall owes him a lot."

She still couldn't bloody well believe he wasn't here, Lee could tell. "My heroic husband," he said brightly, trying to believe it himself, dismissing hungry shadows of desolation from the air around him. "Still quite human, though. Likes his nights in front of the telly and his pasties and chips, just like always."

"Is he exercising? I heard he was quite badly hurt in Falmouth that day, on top of his other injury. Men of his build need to watch themselves, after their mid-thirties."

"Oh, you should see him. He's more than back on form. Cutting a swathe through the hearts of the southwest."

Meredith began to laugh. "Jammy sod. But never mind him—how have you been, Mr Tyack-Frayne? Still hearing voices? Seeing things?"

Lee nodded. "Outrageously."

"I should think everything's fine, then. We always ask what's normal for *you*, you know? Has anything been different?"

"One thing, I suppose." Lee felt mildly guilty for complaining about what had overall been so pleasant. "I seem to be sleepy a lot of the time. Gid's making me take the summer off work, so it's probably just the relief of that. I'm kind of... *stupidly* chilled out, though, like I'm not worrying about a whole bunch of things I should be."

Meredith considered this. "Are you taking any new meds? Growing some nice Cornish weed in that orchard of yours?"

"You're kidding. Poor Gid would have to arrest me."

"Well, whatever ails you doesn't sound *too* awful." She eyed the heaps of files on her desk. "Feel free to infect me if you like. If there's nothing else you'd like to talk about, I'll let you get on with your day, and we'll mail your results to you as usual."

"Great. Thanks, Doc."

He was putting on his jacket when one of Meredith's technical assistants cracked open the office door. Lee recognised the young man from his many previous visits, and was startled by his pallor. Well, times were tough for everyone, apart from his own spoiled and sheltered self. He tried for a smile and a wave, but the assistant only cast him a scared glance. "Don't you knock, Joe?" Meredith enquired pleasantly. "I've still got a patient in here."

"Yes. I'm sorry, Doctor. Could I see you for a minute, though? It's, er... It's a bit urgent."

Meredith shrugged an apology. "Well, you know your way out, Lee. Take care of yourself, all right? Give my regards to Gideon."

He followed her into the corridor. Joe drew her off to one side and began to speak to her in a fraught whisper. Lee pushed his hands into his pockets and continued towards the exit, noting the scuffed lino tiles beneath his feet. How many would he be allowed to cover, he wondered, before Meredith's voice rang out again? She was a kindly soul, but fiercely professional. She wouldn't mess around. He counted ten tiles, then five more, and then because he was calm as a water-lily floating on a pond, but still quite sure of what was about to unfold, he came to a halt and waited.

"Lee? Could I just call you back to my office for a minute or two? I need to speak to Joe, but then I'll be right with you."

Lee turned and smiled. No need to make this any harder for her. "Okay," he said. "Don't worry, all right? Take your time."

In the office, he settled on the window sill and leafed through a copy of *National Geographic*. He'd have thought this would be one of the situations where he'd stare unseeing at the pages, but his brain worked differently these days, and in fact he became absorbed in an article on deep-sea life forms in the Marianas Trench. When Meredith came back into the room, he looked up with gigantic single-celled amoebae and bioluminescent jellyfish fading from his field of vision. "Sit down, Doc," he said gently, putting the magazine down and stepping over to pull out her chair. "Just breathe for a minute. Everything will be all right."

She thudded into the chair as if her knees had given way. She was a consummate professional, but she'd had a great shock. He turned his back on her to let her recuperate; busied himself with the office kettle and tea-making things. By the time he turned round with two steaming mugs in his hands, she was back in her skin. "It *will* be all right," she said, with just the faintest tremor remaining in her voice. "But I need to know something, Lee."

"I'll tell you if I can."

"In all the time I've known you, I've never encountered the... the things you can do. I was always rather scared by the idea of them, and I imagine you probably knew that and kept them out of my way. I just treated you as any other patient with auditory and visual hallucinations. But they're not, are they? Not hallucinations at all."

"That's subjective, I suppose. They're real to me."

"Yes. So if you tell me things will be all right, is that... Are you using your powers? Do you *know*?"

He set the mugs down on her desk, being careful to avoid the keyboard and mouse. Then he sat back down in the chair he'd occupied before this little earthquake had struck. "I seldom know anything for absolutely sure. My signals get scrambled. Did you ever tell your children or your grandchildren everything would be all right, even when you really had no idea?"

"I... Well, yes. I suppose I have done that. Is it wrong?"

"No. I think sometimes you have to. Maybe I mean it in that way. It's basically a benevolent universe, so things will eventually unfold for the good, for somebody somewhere."

"Is it? Benevolent, I mean?"

"I have a biased view. I have Gideon, so the world looks good to me, *is* good to me. Whether or not that's going to continue is something you'll have to tell me, and I'm so sorry to put it on you, Meredith."

"Why? Why are you consoling me because I have to grow a backbone and do my job? I've broken far worse news in this room."

"I've been coming to see you for almost twenty-five years. For the first half-dozen or so of those years, I came and went clutching my dad's hand. You were a good friend to both of us." He hesitated, sorry to have called tears into her eyes, but prey to unforeseen hope. He swallowed a mouthful of tea so that his next words would come out clearly. "It's not the... *very* worst news, then?"

She jerked her head up, suddenly her brisk, sharp self once more. "Christ, no. There's every chance that we can save you." She grabbed the blue cardboard folder she'd brought in with her and withdrew a sheaf of CT transparencies. "I'm going to put these up on my lightbox so you can see. You have to be very brave, Lee. Do you want to call Gideon here before we go on? Because I should talk to him too, and you mustn't drive yourself home."

A lie rose in Lee's throat, so complete that he must have been brewing it up along with the tea. "I've called him. He's on his way, but I'm gonna need time to absorb whatever this is before I see him, so I can tell him in my own way. I'd rather meet him outside."

"All right. Let me show you what we're up against here. Remember I can get you an emergency counselling session, right away if you'd like it, or..." Her voice scraped dryly. "Or there's the chaplain, if..."

"Didn't you just say I *wasn't* about to die?"

"Yes, but—"

"Let's cross that bridge when we come to it, then, eh?" Lee thought he'd rather make that kind of crossing hand-in-hand with Ezekiel, and he had to swallow laughter at the comedy and comfort of the idea. What a catch Zeke would think he had made—the conversion of a lifetime! "Show me these head shots, Doc. Please."

She got up and clipped the first of them to the box. The hum of the backlight filled the room. Lee tried not to recoil from the weirdness of this sudden view down through the top of his skull, a shift of perspective disconcerting enough without the eerie pale mass afloat on the left side of his brain. He locked his hands together in his lap. "Not my best angle. What the fuck is that?"

"You have a Bechstein's meningioma the size of a tangerine growing over your parietal lobe. If I say it's low-grade, that just means it's probably not cancerous, but it's putting all kinds of pressure on parts of you that can't safely be squashed. I've never seen one this big in someone who was still walking around. And you say you've had no pain?"

"No, though my kid's been bringing me headache cures for weeks."

"You said you feel sleepy all the time. Perhaps your brain's been protecting itself in some way, trying to keep you shut down." Meredith folded her arms and looked at Lee grimly. "I wish you *had* had some. It might have sent you in here sooner."

"Wow. How is that monster not gonna kill me?"

"Because we can probably get it out. But you have to listen to me carefully, and I'm going to write all this up for you in a letter you can show Gideon."

"You don't have to do that. I'll just tell him."

Meredith switched off the box, dropping the room into silence. To Lee the sun seemed wan without the neon's edge. He watched without much interest while the doctor resumed her seat opposite him. "You're in shock," she said, "even if you don't feel as if you are. You won't take everything in. Let me write."

"Okay. Um... what else will you say?"

"You're on the very, very far edge of surgical viability. I want you in here, assessed and in theatre by the end of this week at the latest. If we do this, follow this schedule exactly, your chances are good."

Lee would have preferred something better to take back to Gid. A plain *good* would do little to take the loving terror out of his husband's eyes. In the moment of imagining their conversation,

Lee knew he would never have it. How could he even begin? Perhaps if he had more time... "Isn't there a waiting list?"

"This kind of thing bumps you up it."

"And I don't suppose—in the letter you're going to write for me, you couldn't say my chances were *very* good, or... or excellent?" He managed a smile. "I know you've got a crack team."

"I do, and I'll place you with full confidence into their hands. But I owe it to you, to your family and your friends, to make a realistic statement of the odds. Bechstein's are very operable. Seven out of ten surgeries are a success."

If Lee had got seven out of ten in a maths test at school, Cadan would have called it *very good*. Rumpling Lee's hair, steering him off to do his homework: *very good, Locryn. Now go and look at the ones you got wrong and try for an eight next time. I'll come and help you later if you're stuck.* He said, flatly and without emotion, "I miss my dad."

Meredith twitched with empathy. "Oh, shit, of course you do. Times like these make us realise all over again how much we needed the people we've lost. Please let me get you that counselling session, Lee."

A refusal would drag things out. Lee was beginning to long for sunlight not turned sallow, for air not recycled through ventilation ducts. "All right. Yes, please, when I come in for my assessment."

"Good. I'm going to try and get that sorted out for you now—tomorrow, if we can." She misread Lee's silence and held up a hand. "Don't tell me about your commitments. Nothing's more vital than this. This is the one thing you have to do. Is that understood?"

"Yes. Of course, yes."

"I have to make a couple of calls. Just sit quietly and finish your tea."

"Do you mind if I wait by the window?" *I was quite enjoying that article on the Marianas, and I might not suffocate or go nuts there.* "I can look out for Gid coming into the car park."

The strange thing was that Lee could almost see him. He eased down onto the sill, nursing his mug of tea. The worlds overlapped again—this one, and the place where Gideon would have moved heaven and earth, postponed his whole bloody life, to come with him to the hospital today. He closed his eyes, expecting to hallucinate him jumping out of the police truck, threading his way impatiently between cars at a run. Instead he saw him in a little brick box, face to face with Rufus Pendower.

Not a box, no. The yard of Pendower's arid, somehow ghastly little house. Of course Lee had bad associations with the place. He'd fugued out in Kerdrolla, expecting Rufus to drive him home, and found himself in Liskeard instead, almost too sick with grief to draw his next breath. Rufus could be difficult. Whatever he was doing now to make Gideon angry and sad, Lee was having none of it. He glared at him over Gid's shoulder. *Mind how you tread, sunbeam. I'm sorry for you, and I know I owe you, but just bloody watch it, okay?*

Rufus met his eyes and blanched. Satisfied, Lee retreated. Blinking his vision back to normal, he saw that his breath had made a patch of condensation on the glass of Doc Meredith's window. Signs of life... He drew a tiny St Piran's cross, and suddenly wondered what had possessed him to choose that of all symbols for his promise to Gideon that morning. *I'll call you if I need you, I swear.*

The cross, the smudge on the glass, wouldn't last long in this heat. Across the room, Meredith was finishing up, the printer beginning to whirr. With that one lie accomplished—a lie to his husband as they'd sat face to face in their Eden orchard—the rest of the truth could go hang as far as Lee was concerned. "He's here," he announced, with just the right mix of fear and relief to suit the occasion. "I've got to go."

"Wait. Here's your letter. I've booked you in for two o'clock tomorrow afternoon—just as an outpatient, you can go home afterwards and sort out anything you need to. But I'm requesting your surgery on Friday. I'll phone you as soon as I know."

"Right. Thanks." Suddenly that seemed a poor return to this old friend for her years of kindness, and he stopped by her chair on his way to the door: took the letter, then leaned over her and pressed a kiss to her cheek. "I mean it. Thank you, Meredith. All of this must have been so hard for you to do." He crumpled the letter into his jacket pocket, and he ran.

***

Monday night was chef's night at Chy Lowen. Gid and Lee had used to cook for one another daily, but Tamsyn's arrival had stealth-bombed that civilised arrangement, and weekends could devolve into takeaways and ready meals from Tesco. Now that their girl was old enough to sit with them at the table and enjoy proper food, they'd both made the effort to start their week off right with a home-cooked speciality meal, taking turns to rustle up old favourites and invent new. These endeavours usually ended up with the whole family in the kitchen, Tamsyn suggesting hideous flavours for ice cream for dessert, the dog taking advantage of each moment of chaos to snitch scraps from tabletop and counters.

Gideon, resplendent in a 1950s flowered pinafore, strode about the kitchen. Szechuan chicken in chilli garlic sauce was his goal this evening. His own turn at chef's night had used to make him nervous, but like most other things it came easily to him now. All it took was good prep, a scientific approach, confidence and a big dash of flair. Nice free-range birds from the farm down the hill. The recipe book Lee had bought him as encouragement when he showed signs of culinary talent. The pinafore he'd found in the back of a drawer when they'd first moved in, worn first to make Lee laugh and then in the hope that the spirit of its previous owner would guide and domesticate him, keep him no less and no more than the good dad and husband he aspired to be. He cherished such outward symbols. Sometimes he had strange longings for garments that would contain and restrict him, a suit of armour or some kind of whole-body corset, but he dismissed these visions as an idle BDSM fantasy, and wondered at the workings of his brain.

He'd thought he might enjoy the peace of an empty house, but his skin was crawling with unease. He'd had the strangest of days. Lee would help him decompress, take thorns out of his paws. When he'd started his sabbatical, he'd offered to take over Gideon's chef's-night duties, but there'd been no need. What with renovating Jory's boat, looking after his kid and listening to his husband rant and moan, the poor bugger was hardly on holiday at all, and Gideon had more than enough energy to work and cook too.

He glanced at his watch. He wasn't worried. Lee had texted to say his appointment had gone fine, and he was treating himself to an afternoon of idleness in Falmouth. He and Tamsyn were both due back around six, by which time Gid's chicken ought to have reached a state of tender perfection. He put together the ingredients for the sauce: rice-wine vinegar, soy, sesame oil. The kitchen was a bit of a wreck, though by contrast to Rufus Pendower's it was a haven of hygiene and contentment. All the mess was evidence of happy family life: Tamsyn's toys, Lee's books and script notes piled on the table and chairs, his own trail of chef's-night destruction. For the second time that day, he set himself to tidy up.

He wouldn't draw any further comparisons between this world and Pendower's. He'd left Liskeard in a squeal of tyres, shaken to the bone. Stupid of him to have succumbed. Rufus was delusional, that was all. He'd picked up on *Kerdrolla* and run with it, his obsession with etymology fuelling the fantasy. Try as he might, Gideon couldn't imagine Lee—who guarded his subconscious as faithfully as he did his waking mind—sitting down with Rufus to chat about his husband's fever dreams.

As soon as he was back, Gideon would tell him all about it. Together they would explode the mystery in loving common sense. Having settled that with himself, he switched on the radio, flicked it to Kernow FM and allowed the undemanding banter and hits from the noughties to disengage his brain while he worked.

He was hanging the last copper pan on its rack when Lee's Escort bumped onto the drive with its characteristic roar. *Have to get him a better car,* he thought affectionately, and then: *don't go out to meet him. He wants to make an entrance.*

Where on earth had that come from? Gideon leaned back against the sink, wiping his hands on a towel. The signal had been so strong, there was hardly any credit due to him for picking it up, but still he was pleased with himself, and more than happy to cooperate. What had Lee been up to?

The kitchen door swung open, and he saw. He folded his arms, exhaled in a long, appreciative whistle, then broke into a grin. Lee flushed in pleasure and embarrassment. He'd stopped in the doorway to allow Gid's inspection. He'd been to the barber, for once not just for a haircut but to get his couple of days' growth of beard elegantly shaped. His neat frame was picked out in a new, closely tailored sea-green shirt. "Well," he said, spreading his hands. "I couldn't go and visit Ma, so I had to put my time in somehow. And I just thought, what with running around after Tamsie and being a house-husband, I might've... let myself go a bit."

To Gideon, Lee looked like pure domestic heaven whether he'd just rolled out of bed or was ready to fall into it at the end of a long exhausting day. Still, this was the cherry on top and no mistake. Even the silver chain he wore around his throat was gleaming brightly against his tan, so familiar a sight to Gideon that he'd ceased to take conscious notice of it years ago. Seeing the direction of his glance, Lee raised a hand and touched the links. "I even got this polished up at the jeweller's."

He would have had to take it off to do that. For some reason the idea filled Gideon with unease. "I only ever saw you without it once," he said, as lightly as he could. "You were scared I'd... thrown down the gauntlet to a hostile spirit in your Falmouth flat, and you put it around my neck to protect me." He chuckled. "Even though I started it."

"Well, as you said this morning, who the hell cares who started it? Come on, you big dork. Are you just gonna stare at the goods, or come over here and get 'em?"

Gideon pushed off the sink. He took two strides towards him, and Lee broke stillness and dashed to meet him more than halfway. Gasping, Gid caught him. The sensation was extraordinary. If Lee had been an air-drowned fish and Gideon deep still waters, or a warm safe bed for a man deadbeat with exhaustion, a hole in the earth for a fox... Lee *dived into* him; there was no other way of feeling this impact, this reunion. The honour and joy of it almost knocked Gideon down, but he didn't understand: if Lee had been away for weeks in mortal peril of his life, they might have met like this at the end of it. "Didn't I just see you this morning?" he asked breathlessly, laughing into the fragrant, freshly cropped hair.

"So? Isolde does this to you when you've been away for five minutes."

"Once upon a time. I could drop off the face of the earth now and she wouldn't bat an eyelid." Deciding that he didn't *have* to understand, Gideon put both arms around him tight. If Lee needed him to be water, he'd part like the Red Sea to let him in. He'd be the most welcoming of beds, the deepest of foxholes. "You weren't letting yourself go, for godsakes. What made you think that?"

"I dunno. Just stupid. I love you so much."

Gideon tightened his hold. He lifted until Lee's spine popped, eliciting a grunt of relief from him. Lee's feet left the ground, and Gideon swung him slowly, powerfully round in a full circle, then because he'd started to laugh, made another turn and then a third. "Christ, I love you too," he affirmed, when they were both dizzy and disoriented. The lowering sun flashed a gilded beam through the kitchen, and just for one lucid instant Gideon knew that the haircut and the new shirt were distractions, shields. He couldn't hold on to the awareness, which Lee was guarding with tigerish energy, but he set him carefully back on his feet, pushed him to arm's length and held his shoulders. "Lee, sweetheart. What on earth's wrong?"

"Wrong?" Lee's smile was tearstained and too bright. "I'm fine. I think it just hit me when I got back, how... how fine everything is here. I smelled your Szechuan chicken and saw how you'd spruced the place up, and then I saw you. The finest thing of all."

Distractions, shields, misdirections. They bounced off Gideon's consciousness like the sunlight now blazing back from every polished surface in the room. "Stop it, you flatterer. Here I am in my pinafore, and you look ready for the cover of Esquire, the Kernowek special. I love this shirt. Where did you get it?"

"The new menswear place by the harbour. Very trendy and sophisticated—I give 'em three months tops."

"Mm, they might've overreached themselves in Falmouth. Feels lovely, though. I hope it was good and expensive."

"Tamsyn can forget her college fund. It's bamboo silk."

"Wow." Gideon gathered a pinch of the fabric at Lee's waist and rubbed it appreciatively between his finger and thumb. He was delighted that his man had gone out and spent some money on relative frivolities. *Life-affirmation*, he thought, and shook his head in puzzlement: why would a gorgeous, healthy thirty-seven year old need to do that? "Well, it's a perfect fit. You should go get five more in different colours."

Lee snorted. "Sergeant Rockefeller! You do realise I paid for it out of your hard-earned copper's wages, don't you?"

That wasn't true. Their account was a joint one, and anyway Lee had ploughed so much into their household with his TV work that he could go on a spree any time he liked.

It was just that he so seldom did. Gideon couldn't remember the last time. Not for himself, anyway: he'd been known to let rip on Tamsie's behalf when cute new kids' clothes arrived in the shops, and he seldom came home without a book or a pair of comedy socks for Gid. "I'd be pleased if you had," he said, lifting Lee's chin and turning it to admire the neat manscaping along the line of his jaw. "Go get yourself oiled and pampered at my expense any time you like. Makes me feel rich."

"Like you did at Rufus's house today. Then you remembered you weren't, and you were upset."

He hadn't altered his tone or his expression. Gideon stared. "Jeez, love. Changing-room door!"

"Then Rufus was upset too. The visit didn't go well."

The green shirt had been a perfect match for Lee's eyes when he'd first arrived. Gideon wondered if the shop sold a version in silver. "All right, you," he said. "You're okay. Come and sit down with me."

He steered him to the battered sofa by the aga, where he, Lee, Isolde and Tamsyn often piled up together on chilly nights. Lee settled quietly at his side, then flinched back into the moment. "Oh, God. I'm sorry."

Gideon put an arm around him. "Don't be. I'm sure I was broadcasting on all channels."

"Still."

"Anyway, you're right. It didn't go well. I tidied up his house and left him some money for an unpaid bill."

Lee gave him a sidelong glimmer. "You *monster*."

"I know, I know. But the thing is, I didn't ask him first, and I think I should have. Especially about the money." Suddenly Gideon realised that he too could distract and shield. This topic, Rufus and his domestic problems, was painful but safe. What had made him think he could talk to Lee about Kerdrolla? The prospect felt like a chasm at his feet, ready to swallow them both. Quickly he tucked Story Town away behind lurid images of Pendower's kitchen. "The place was filthy. But I do get that not everyone wants to be helped. I didn't mean to ride all over him rough-shod."

Lee took hold of his hand and laced their fingers together. "Of course you didn't. Please tell me Daisy and the baby weren't in the midst of all this."

"No. She left him." That was a good piece of mental armour, although Gideon would have to choose his words carefully: Lee's mouth had dropped open in shock. "I think he's still in mourning for Amber, and Daisy got tired of competing with a ghost." *And with you*, he could never add, because Lee would hate to know he'd been the innocent means of breaking up a friend's marriage. "So things aren't great for him, no. Having already stuck my nose in where it wasn't wanted and patronised him, I went the whole hog and called welfare services."

"Bloody hell."

"Do you think I was wrong?"

"No, just very bold and decisive."

"Not what you'd have done, though. You reckon we should go straight over there and help him out ourselves, not leave him in the hands of strangers."

"Is that not what *you're* thinking, love?"

"No. Okay, yes. Maybe."

A ripple of laughter shook Lee's shoulders. "That about covers it. As a matter of fact you're wrong. I'm sure I *should* want us to jump in the car and go rescue him, but I don't. The trouble is that I've got everything I want in the world right here. And I've recovered from whatever was ailing me this morning, so..."

He subsided onto his back, taking hold of Gideon's pinafore straps and hauling him down too. "Everything?" Gideon echoed a hot minute later, muffled against his neck.

"Mm. Just... Oh, yeah. Push your tongue a bit harder there."

Gideon, on top, had been better placed to hear any sounds from outside. He rose onto his arms, Lee grunting in protest and reaching to recapture him. "I would, if your in-laws and your kid weren't about to walk in the front door."

"Oh, shit."

"Yep. Everything and second helpings too, right?"

"An embarrassment of riches."

"Come on, soldier—on your feet. Respectable family men on parade."

Lee always responded willingly to such calls to action. The very best of family men, even with untucked shirt and a flush of arousal fading from his face and throat, he launched himself off the sofa and ran to intercept. Gideon watched in pleasure and pride as he went tumbling into the stream of kids and dogs on the lawn. Toby and Mikey adored him and would flail to get their hands on him whenever he appeared. They were toddling now, and made unsteady beelines for him the moment Ezekiel released them from their car seats and set them down. The dogs shared their partiality. Isolde knocked Lee sideways with a charge, and Buster, a child-safe, bomb-proof butterball of a mutt, came rollicking in for the kill. Tamsyn gave a shout of laughter and threw herself into the heap.

Eleanor and Zeke watched this display indulgently from the driveway. Gideon leaned in the doorway and looked on in amusement too. This was about seven times more family than he'd ever thought could belong to him. If you'd told the lonely copper six years ago that he'd be watching his nephews and daughter rolling about with his husband on the lawn of this beautiful house... He shook his head. It seemed so unreal at times.

Eleanor broke the spell, turning towards the door and inhaling hungrily. "Oh, goodness, Gideon. Is that your speciality chicken?"

They were at the chaotic, hand-to-mouth, permanently exhausted stage of their child-rearing. Gid remembered it well, though Tamsyn had given him the easiest of rides. Lee sat up in a tangle of kids, all of them trying to tell him at the top of their voices about the fossils they'd found on the beach. He placed a careful hand across the two nearest mouths to reduce the racket. "Any chance," he said, still laughing, "your Szechuan for two could stretch a bit?"

"Oh, no," Eleanor protested weakly. "We couldn't possibly. Could we, Zeke?"

Zeke too cast a longing glance towards the kitchen. "Oh, no. We should get the children home. I'm sure we'll find a... tin of soup and a few scraps of bread for their supper."

She elbowed him fiercely in the ribs. "Ezekiel!"

Gideon held the door wide, grinning. "I chopped extra veg, and there's loads of rice. I had a feeling a visitation like this might occur."

"Like locusts upon Egypt," Zeke surprisingly observed, and marched past his brother into the house. The kids and Eleanor followed on, then Isolde and Buster, clearly the best of friends even after a long car ride, huffing and bustling at each other playfully.

Lee brought up the rear. He stopped in the doorway beside Gideon. He picked up one of Gid's hands and kissed the knuckles, wild lights of sanctity and joy in his eyes. "Who could want more than this?" he whispered, smiling up at him. "How could there even *be* more?"

"I don't know," Gideon told him honestly, although for him, on some deep level, every part of it but Lee could have vanished forever. "It's pretty bloody good, isn't it?"

"The best. Everything, every part of it. Just this, right now. And everything is gonna be all right."

He began to move past Gideon, who stopped him with a gentle hand against his chest. "That's what you tell Tamsyn, when she's seen a horror movie with the Kemp kids or some dreadful news on TV. Whether you believe it or not."

Lee flashed him a quick, brilliant smile. He was warm from his tussle with the kids, or some other inner fire: his beautiful new shirt was damp with sweat beneath Gideon's palm. "Well," he said fervently. "What decent parent doesn't do that?"

***

"I'm a bad husband," Lee suddenly declared, clambering back up the bed to collapse against Gideon's shoulder.

Gideon couldn't agree less. He was still getting breath back into his lungs from the majestic blow-job Lee had just delivered. His flesh was vibrating like a cello at the end of a symphony. "Dear God. What the... bloody hell makes you say that?"

"Didn't get round to asking you how things ended up with Rufus. Or the rest of your day."

"You were busy helping me feed the five thousand." Gideon shook his head. "Can't believe Zeke made that crack about the locusts."

"Or about the loaves and fishes."

"I know, right? He's getting more human every day."

"Oh, he's entirely human." Lee slung a weary arm across Gideon's stomach and held on. "I love Zeke. You would tell him that, wouldn't you, if ever I couldn't..."

He fell silent. Gideon listened to the night around them: his own post-orgasmic breathing, which had abruptly caught in his throat, and beneath and above and on every side, the huge living silence of the summer moors. "Tell him yourself," he said uncomfortably, aware once again of the brink, the chasm. "Why wouldn't you be able to?"

"Apart from the fact that I can't imagine the scene... I just mean accidents, you know. Fate. Tripping on Tamsie's cauldron at the top of the stairs."

"She has a *cauldron*?"

"Well, it's the copper bowl we found here along with your apron when we moved in. She calls it her cauldron."

"I can't pick out the most disturbing aspect of this conversation. Tell her not to leave it anywhere dangerous. And as for you, be careful. Accidents and fate don't get to touch my family."

"Oh, Gid. They get to touch everyone."

"You know what I mean. By the way, if you were hoping for any return of favours here, I think you've quenched my ardour."

Lee gave a snorting chuckle. "Never mind. I think I just want to lie here and hold you, and let you talk me to sleep."

"Oh, ta." Gideon fastened a large embrace on him, the kind that could catch tired spirits as they plunged into their dreams. "I'll start with Rufus, shall I?"

"Mm, please."

"There's not much more to tell. He's had some kind of breakdown, and I think he knows on some level it's not okay to pursue you around your film sets and locations. He wasn't pleased with me for tidying up, but he said he'd be at home for the welfare officer's visit. Try not to worry about him, okay? They really will take care of him."

"Okay. And he didn't... He wasn't banging on about anything else, was he? He's got a few weird ideas in his poor spiky bonce, about the meanings of place names, that kind of thing."

Tell me about it. But relief had seized Gideon: if Lee already knew that much, maybe no more needed to be said. And weird ideas might be all there was to it. "I'm not sure. I was too busy pissing him off. But I think he forgave me before I left, and we'll go and see him over the weekend. You still awake?"

"Just about. What about Pendethy? Did you go up to help Jenny Spargo?"

"Oh, yeah. That was a bit strange too, actually. I did get called up, but when I arrived, she had the whole thing in hand. She more or less shooed me away."

"Really?"

"Mm. You know me and Jen—we've always been good mates. The best. But I guess she might well be seeing her fast-track to CID through this case, so I backed off and went to make myself useful elsewhere."

"Nice of you. Doesn't sound like Jenny, though."

"Ah, well." Gideon settled Lee more comfortably. "Let the mysteries of the day be sufficient thereto. Oh, there was one more thing. Have you seen my silver chain bracelet? I can't find it anywhere."

But Lee was sound asleep. He'd gone out with the sudden totality that was new with him, his body unstrung and abandoned against Gid's, his breathing deep. "Glad my thrilling stories aren't keeping you up, sunbeam," Gideon said, for his own benefit only. He hoped the bracelet wasn't lost. He'd always loved Lee's neck-chain, and they'd talked about getting him one to match, then decided the chances were too high of his getting grabbed by it and strangled on the streets. Lee had presented him with a close-fitting cuff bracelet instead, made in the same tough, silky-textured links.

It would turn up, he was sure. Anyway it was only a small concern, in the wash of contentment sweeping over him now. *Lee's right*, he thought, with the surreal distinctness of oncoming sleep. *If this was our last night on earth, what more could either of us want? This bed, this warm heather-laden air. Our witch-daughter dreaming her spells in the room down the corridor. Tamsyn, Tamsyn, weave the web. Draw thy circle fast around the House of Joy.* He floated effortlessly out of his body and looked down, at the house and the glimmering circle. Beyond its sacred boundary, a girl was standing, staring yearningly up at Tamsyn's window.

No, not a girl—a woman, but so frail and slight that she looked young. Frail or not, she had no business so close to his home, and he drew closer to get a better look.

She shifted. The transmuting ripple didn't scare Gideon: that was normal for a dream. The end of her transformation froze him, trapped him between sky and earth. She was still on two legs, but they bent backwards at the knee, and her face was the face of a wolf, and only then did he know her: *Alice Rawle*!

Others emerged from the heather, where they'd been hiding all along. All were transformed, but somehow Gideon could recognise them still. First came Rufus Pendower. He was in a state of halfway change, and looked miserable about it, as if trying desperately to cling to his human form. The others rejoiced to have left theirs behind. After Pendower came old man Tregear, and then Morris Hawke, then the Fisherman of Island village, his wheelchair left far behind. Last of all, Joe Kemp, as if this pack had formed along with the deepest roots of Gideon's love for Lee. No, there was one other—the runt, just as he'd been the fragile afterthought of a family of fine sons, limping and whining and running from shadow to shadow: Dev Bowe.

The pack began to run. They turned to a grey blur and whipped around the circle. Only Pendower held back. He clutched the Chy Lowen gatepost like a spar in a roaring sea, and he looked up at Gideon in love and hate and desperation. *The House of the Wolves*, he cried, in a broken snarl that still somehow sounded like himself, Sergeant Weird-Shit, neat little officer with his little book of notes. *For God's sake, Gideon! It means the House of the Wolves!*

Chapter Nine
Somewhere In Between

Lee was due on deck next morning at ten. He saw Gideon off to work, got himself and Tamsyn ready, dropped Isolde for a day of romps with the Kemp kids, and headed for the labyrinth of summer-green lanes that led to St Wylloe.

He had until one o'clock that afternoon, he reckoned. Until then, he could justify the normal unfolding of his day. Nothing would happen differently in the world around him or inside his head because he went to strip planks on Jory's boat. After that, the ways diverged. Trelowarren was about an hour's drive from the village. He could set out, arrive in time for his assessment. He'd made so many friends in the hospital during Gideon's stays there that he'd no doubt find someone to keep an eye on Tamsyn while he was poked and prodded, and he'd be home in time to get dinner ready—not delicious chef's-night Szechuan, probably just lasagne and a salad—and think up a way to end the terrifying charade of normality he'd begun the day before. A way to tell Gid he had a fucking brain tumour.

Christ, it was impossible. The second route opened up like a tree-lined avenue planted on both sides with good Cornish dope, opium poppies and Murphy's ears. The first looked like a desert beside it, a long thin bed of nails. Already running down the avenue, Lee imagined at the end of it the priceless reward of one more normal night at home. He'd pull the plug on the land line. Hell, he could yank out a fuse or two and knock out the booster box so neither of their mobiles worked, and Gid, always unsuspicious, would go into power-cut mode, light candles and the open fire in the living room, call it a romantic evening and enjoy the whole thing. Lee knew there'd been more to the visit with Rufus than his benign schemer of a husband was telling. A few firelit hours and Lee would have it out of him, and life would go on.

It would, surely! He'd lived this long, painlessly, with the Bechstein's Grand or whatever Meredith had said was growing in his brain. It was too much of a bloody coincidence that he'd happened to turn up in radiography on one of the last few days when he could be saved. CT scans could be wrong. Psychic gifts were poorly understood: how many seers and prophets of old might just have been walking around with passengers in their skulls, exerting subtle pressures, not all of them painful or deadly? Maybe some of them helped open up the way.

"Lee?"

He turned to look at his daughter. They were safely parked in the sunny village square outside St Wylloe's church, and Lee had no idea how they'd got there. He'd negotiated the lanes on absolute autopilot. "Yes, sweetheart," he said, swallowing down his fright at the lapse. "What is it?"

She was watching him solemnly from her booster. She put out her hands, and he twisted round and leaned towards her through the gap between the front seats, thinking she wanted to get or bestow a kiss. Her days were punctuated by dozens of such small gestures of love. Instead she flattened one palm on his brow:

moved him a little way to the left and the right, like an old TV set in want of tuning. The gesture reminded him of Gid's examination of his razor-cut, already blurring out this morning in new growth. Everything about him was still vigorous, from his beard to his cock. The second path beckoned, petals and leaves waving. "Nothing," Tamsyn said thoughtfully, and not as an answer to his question. "Boat now?"

Maybe he should get her to talk more. She was mostly silent in his company, and he in hers. Still, their rapport had been endlessly varied, a constant exchange of images and ideas. He thought of her growing up without that. *First path*, he vowed. Meredith hadn't written him off. At one o'clock he would set out for his appointment. "That's right," he said encouragingly. "We'll go and work on the boat now, shall we?"

She nodded earnestly. "Yes. We'll go and work on the boat."

St Wylloe was perfect today, a dream of a coastal village in the far southwest. The sun beat down on the market cross and the narrow roads around it where a few parking spaces had been marked out, the quartz in the granite dazzling. Gorefen Day was coming up, festival of summer, local arts and flora. Every inch of soil had been planted out with fuchsia; jasmine clambered up trellises on walls. The date palms clattered softly in the breeze. Lee put on his sunglasses to help cut down the Mediterranean glare, and watched in amusement while Tamsyn withdrew her own small blue pair from her satchel and did the same. They set off hand-in-hand towards the church.

Jory's back garden was more easily accessed from the graveyard than the lane, through a mossy gap in the wall. Like many of the ancient Celtic churches—like Drift, where Lee's uncle Jago had put paid to the Cornish Panther—Wylloe's sat on a circular mound. When Lee had explained this to Tamsie, she'd listened attentively, but as often he'd ended up convinced that she already knew. *Where else would you build a church, Lee, if you wanted to harness the ancient magic of the land and the circles of stone?*

After the square, the graveyard was a sanctuary. Only wayside weeds grew here, tall grasses beneath the overarching sycamores, though Tamsyn had been finding herbs hidden amongst their cool damp roots. Red campion, tricorn leek with their savoury scent and odd triangular stems, little starry chickweeds, and off to the north side, as if in benediction of the lost souls buried there, an old weeping cherry like a huge upturned bowl, leaves trailing the ground, a few rags of its splendid springtime blossom still clinging. Perched on a canopy tombstone in her civvies, elbows resting on her knees, Gid's favourite colleague and work friend, Jenny Spargo.

Surprising Tamsyn was hard, although she did her best to act the part when opening birthday and Solstice gifts. She ran over to Jenny as if finding her in St Wylloe's churchyard on a weekday was the most natural event in the world. Jen rumpled her hair, made room for her beside her on the tomb, and raised a pale face to Lee. "Hi. I hoped I'd get to intercept you here."

"Doesn't sound too good, coming from a copper. Have Jory's neighbours complained about all the hammering?"

She took his attempt at a joke for what it was worth, smiling wanly. "Not my beat, is it?"

"A long way from it. What's up, Jenny? Are you on your day off?"

"Yeah. Got my nephew's eighteenth birthday party this afternoon, but I wanted to see you first, if I could. On your own, I mean. Without Gid."

He knew what she meant. The skin of his forearms prickled and chilled. "Okay. I don't want to pry, but I can feel that you're terribly upset and scared. Will you let me help?"

"Bless you, Lee. But it's not my thing to be scared about. It's yours, and I don't know what to do."

"Sometimes just saying it is best."

She'd been pulling at the moss on the stone. When she rubbed her cheek, she left a green smear. "All right. I found Gideon's bracelet in Pendethy. In... Inside what was left of Pol Teague's car."

Lee was tough to surprise sometimes too. When he traced back through his mind—everything Gid had told him about Pol, his misdemeanours and his sudden death—he couldn't experience the faintest ripple of shock. Only familiarity, a rightness beyond human justice, a scene that had played out in moonlight and blood. "I see," he said flatly. "Okay."

She reached into the pocket of her jeans and pulled out an object wrapped in tissue. "Here. Take it."

And now at last Lee's heart gave a bump and a squeeze that sent adrenaline spiking through him. Blindly he took the heavy little package from her. "Jesus. What are you doing, Jen? This should be—"

"Bagged up ready for forensics at HQ. Yes. Listen to me for a second, Lee. I love Gideon. And if I could've murdered Pol and got away with it, I'd have done it five years ago. The first girl he stalked was my sister. She's okay now, but she's still getting therapy and she says she can never come home. So I want you to take this, say you found it somewhere in the house and give it back to him. And I'm gonna... forget I ever saw it, or had this conversation. Is that okay?"

Tamsyn's satchel was well equipped with tissues. Lee reached for it, but his girl had got there ahead of him and was already offering Jenny her pick of the pack, like a small tarot reader with a deck of cards. Despite herself and the situation, Jenny gave a gurgle of laughter. "You're a poppet and no mistake, aren't you?

I'm sorry, Lee. I probably shouldn't have said any of that in front of her."

"Given everything else you shouldn't have said and done, I wouldn't worry." Lee tucked the bracelet into the pocket of his jacket, where Meredith's letter rustled a reminder of the desert path. Jenny was getting to her feet: he put out a hand to help her, and she grabbed it and suddenly threw her arms around him. "This is your career," he whispered hoarsely. "Think about it, for God's sake."

"I've done nothing but think since I chased him off yesterday. Let him believe I'm being precious about the case. If no other DNA evidence turns up—and there's nothing so far, nothing human anyway—he'll be... There's nothing to connect him..." She gave up on trying to put the impossible into words, squeezed Lee hard then let him go. "Bye, Colin Fry. I am off now to get so drunk with my fam, they'll have to carry me home in a bucket."

***

Lee worked solidly until noon. Jory Stark derailed any reactions he might have wanted to indulge by bouncing out of the house on his arrival, leaning on the boat's hull and launching into a blow-by-blow account of his latest dispute with English Heritage. The battle raged on gaily, Cornwall not being—according to Jory, and in Lee's view too, when he had time to think about it—part of England at all, and more than capable of looking after its menhirs on its own. Lee made some noises about divisiveness, and the need for unity in the face of the loss of EU funding post-Brexit, and Jory got red in the face and puffed and blew with a force that entirely distracted him, allowing Lee to continue to prise up rotting planks from the deck in a strange kind of peace. Tamsie, not visibly disturbed by her encounter with Jen, wove a pattern through the gravestones, always staying within Lee's field of view. He wondered what she'd bring him this time. What did little witches use to close the stable door after the horse had gone?

Just a crown of daisies. He smiled at her in pure love as her odd little face appeared over the rail of the boat. The single bell in the church tower was pealing out its dozen midday notes, vibrant as ravens in the air. "Walk, Lee?" She paused, furrowed her brow and tried again. "Shall we go for a walk?"

As good a way of spending his lunch hour, the hour before the parting of the ways, as any he could think of. He was expected to wear the crown, and so he took it from her and proudly settled it over his new haircut. Where would Meredith's surgical team begin? A bone saw, he supposed, and he hid a freaked-out shudder. Really the op was the least of his problems. If he got that far, he must have managed to tell Gid, and all he had to do from there on out was survive and make his way back to him, to his life and everything he loved. For now, his only worry was looking like a daisy-wreathed dork on the streets of St Wylloe, but that too was minor: if your little girl made you a crown, you wore it.

He finished the plank he was working on, set his crowbar, hammer and chisel safely aside, and let Tamsyn lead him back through the churchyard. They stopped at the foot of the tower, a favourite place for their lunchtime sandwiches, but she squinted critically up at the pinnacles Gid called ears and drew him on. In the Co-op, the cashier smiled at his headgear but sold him a big bar of orange chocolate without further comment.

The streets were deeply sunk in midday somnolence. Tamsyn headed off apparently at random, running a few feet ahead of him, frequently glancing back. Lee followed, happy to let her set the direction and pace. Even the lamp posts had been painted in preparation for Gorefen, ivy and blossoms wreathing around one, a black red-eyed horse-skull grinning from the next. Fertility and death, forever intertwined in Kernowek consciousness, no lines drawn between, and who was he to compete with that? Existing as he had between the worlds until he'd met Gideon and fallen in love with life, he'd considered his own mortality without fear, and the essentially Pagan world-view of his family and community had always suited him well. He had no need to be afraid.

A grand theory. In practice it meant an unimaginable parting from his husband and his child. He took a couple of long strides after Tamsyn, as if that would somehow help. Quarter past twelve now, and he had to stay in the minute if he could, and use the next forty-five to good purpose. This was a perfect town for wandering, most of the streets pedestrianised or too narrow for traffic, every alleyway opening up into strange vistas: the vast turf bowl of the plain-an-gwarry with its earthwork amphitheatre seats and echoes of medieval mystery plays hanging in the warm air; sudden views all the way out to the cliffs and the sea beyond. Narrow lanes with roses spilling into them over thick, shoulder-height drystone walls. Tamsyn darted into one of these as if she'd known the place all her life, and Lee, who never let her get out of sight if he could help it, arrived on her heels at the foot of a single, huge standing stone. "Wow," he observed. "Good discovery, kiddo."

She turned to beam at him. "Willy Stone, Lee."

He clamped a hand to his mouth, turning his reaction to a cough. She could be like a little cat at times, and you couldn't always laugh at her. Besides, she was probably right: Willy from Wylloe was an easy linguistic step. More likely it was the other way round, and this stone with its undeniable angle and shape had passed into early Christianity as a local saint. "Is that its name? How did you know?"

She pointed pityingly to the large brown tourist-board sign aimed squarely at the stone. He had to be careful not to miss the obvious in the swirl and rush of life's mysteries. "All right, clever-boots. How did you know it was here?"

Her expression changed. He knew the look. Since her earliest babyhood, whenever words failed, all she'd had to do was meet his eyes. He'd experience a kind of ripple in the air between them, and whatever she needed him to know would simply manifest, clear and three-dimensional, in his own mind. What was she telling him now? That this giant standing stone was a node on the network, the ley-map of Kernow, birthright knowledge to the pellar kind?

God, why couldn't he hear her?

He went to scoop her up. He sat her on the sunwarmed wall which enclosed the great menhir and kept off the cows grazing on the common land beyond. "Chocolate?" he offered, breaking the bar in two, and waiting for her usual broadcast of pleasure, not so much at the treat as their shared enjoyment. But all he saw was her smile.

Still, their silence was companionable. He let it extend while she got half the chocolate into her mouth and the rest onto her face, and then he broke out another tissue from the satchel and gently cleaned her up. "You and I are different, Tamsie," he said carefully after a while, keeping his tone casual. "You know that, don't you? Different from your friends at school, and even from Dada, although he can do a little bit of it too. I don't mean moving things without touching them. I mean..."

"Looking inside people's heads."

"Yes, that's right." She was reaching for him again, as she had in the car. Again he leaned down for her, and stood in puzzled stillness while she once again turned his face a little way left, then right, then up and down. "I'm not very good at it, though. And I think you're *very* good. What are you doing, sweetheart?"

"Can't look today."

"Look where?"

"Inside you."

Oh, God. He hadn't meant to shut her out. Hadn't thought about it at all, not consciously: had been too frantically busy playing for time with Gid. If he'd raised his shields for his husband, though, how much further would he go to protect his child? "I'm sorry," he whispered. "Is that why you brought me here? Did you think you'd get a... a better signal near the stone?"

"Mm-hm. Moving head around, too." She let go of him, released a curiously adult little sigh. "Have to talk to you properly today."

"You're doing very well. Proper sentences and everything, more or less."

"Very dickifult."

Restraining laughter was a lot easier with an aching load of tears in his throat. "*Difficult*, honey. And I'm sure you also know by now that almost everybody else in the world has to do it that way all the time. That's why lots of them are sad and angry. They feel so alone."

She nodded. "Alone, all alone. Ganny said daisies used to be called day's-eyes."

Revelation hit Lee like a nova, a day's-eye sunburst. He hoisted Tamsyn off the wall and into his arms. "So you put a string of them around my head, to see if that would help you get a better look?"

A faint sob shook her at last. "Yes. Didn't *work*."

"Oh, my girl. You listen, all right?" He gave her a gentle jounce, cupped one hand around the back of her curly head and rocked her. "Soon—very, very soon—this will be over, and I promise I'll never keep you out again. I didn't mean to do it this time, and I can't make you understand why it happened, or why it's... for the best. Meanwhile we'll just have to *talk* to each other, like all those poor lonely-heads. Can we do that?"

She snuffled against his neck. "Can."

"Good girl. Proper sentences and everything, even if it is difficult. Tamsie—when you say *Ganny*, who do you mean?"

He could sense her giving the question thought. The answer wasn't an easy one. On any day but today, he'd have seen the possibilities running through her mind, the faces and the connections. Maybe Ma Frayne had told her about the day's-eyes. But she'd kept her baby habit of calling her grandmother *Ganmar*, and a sad day it would be for that old lady when she stopped. He waited, knowing that truth was a mobile, ambiguous concept for most children, let alone a telepath with phenomenal psychokinetic abilities.

She stiffened in his arms. "Alice Rawle!"

He almost dropped her in shock. "Tamsie, no. There once was an old lady called Granny Ragwen, and you called her Ganny. You were very little, though, and—"

"No, no, no, no, no, no!" She began to fight him in frustration. "No, not Ganny now. Alice!"

"Tell me. Just tell me with words."

Poor kid. He set her down, and she sucked in a huge breath, clutching him by the collar of his shirt and his silver chain. "Alice Rawle," she said, with perfect clarity, "is in the church. The stone gave me the signal. Alice *Rawle*!"

She can't be. She's locked up. It'll be years and years before you need ever worry about her again—never, maybe, if she ends up in Broadmoor where she belongs. None of these reassurances would come out of Lee's throat. If Tamsyn said she was here, so she was. "All right," he croaked. "Why?"

"Because she's like me."

"She is *nothing* like you, Tamsyn."

"She is. She is. And they hurt her and made her do things, things in a big empty place with soldiers. And you and Dada found her and they locked her up again. But she got out. She got out, and now she wants to pull everything down. She wants to turn the world back to the bad time. Lee, run! Run!"

In a way he was so proud of her. She'd never in her life strung so many cogent sentences together. She wriggled out of his grasp and fled back the way they'd come. Soon he caught up with her. He seized the flying tails of her little embroidered denim coat. Did she want to get back to the church? He hoisted her into his arms and she pointed that way mutely, eyes wild, so he settled her as best he could and ran on.

Only when they passed his parked car and she grabbed for the door handle and broke into wild shrieks of fear did he get it. He swung round so as not to hurt her. She was tearing at the locked door, and not for her own sake. She'd renewed her grip on his shirt collar. With her free hand she pointed again, first at him and then through the window of the car. *Get in, get in,* the gesture obvious even though words had failed. And when she'd said *run,* she'd meant *run away.*

Too late for Lee. The raven-voiced bell was ringing one o'clock, but he barely noticed. Gideon's police truck was parked by the kerb at the end of two short streaks of rubber, her lights still ablaze, her nose half an inch shy of the lychgate.

Whatever had brought Gid to St Wylloe's church in that kind of whirlwind, Lee wasn't about to add their kid to the mix. He let go of Tamsyn for long enough to hit the unlock button on his key fob: hauled open the door and bundled her inside.

Her fists hit the window as he locked her in. Her face had creased into a wildcat's mask. He kissed his fingertips and pressed them to the glass in a hopeless apology: waited long enough to check that the car was in the shade, that she had her satchel with her, her water and her snacks. Then he turned and ran for the gate so hard that his feet churned up the gravel and he almost fell. "Gideon! Gid!"

Chapter Ten
What Goes In Wonderland

Gideon rounded the northwest corner of St Wylloe's church and ran smack into his brother, running the other way. The impact was considerable. "Christ almighty," Gideon said, scrambling out of the red currant bush in which he'd crash-landed, distractedly noticing its rich catlike stink. Zeke, with small, eloquent gestures, indicated the church, his dog collar, the holy ground surrounding them, and Gideon rolled his eyes. "I'm sorry. But this time it's not so much a swear as an appeal to the local deity."

"What for?"

"Information, mostly, but you'll do. Did you call the police?"

"No, the vicar did. Apparently there's someone in the tower, throwing down stones from the turret. I came out to have a look."

Gideon took a few steps back and looked up at the squat, somehow dizzying tower. He blinked sun-dazzle from his eyes. "Is that what you're doing out here, running widdershins around the church?"

"I'm sorry?"

"Widdershins, like Old German *widar* and *sens* in French. Against the direction of the sun, and things in nature generally.

That's why it's meant to be bad luck." Gideon shook himself: Rufus must be haunting him today. "What are you doing in St Wylloe? Parish business?"

"Yes, I suppose so. The strange thing is, I can't in the least remember what it's meant to be."

Brushing pollen off his stab vest, Gideon turned to look at him. The sun was beating down. He stepped into the shade, drawing Zeke with him. "Do I need to get you a hat? Because that... tiny bald patch of yours is going pink."

"I do not have a bald patch, Gideon. Besides, if I do, it'll be yours in ten years' time. What are *you* doing here, on a callout any of the local police could have handled?"

That was a good question. Gid had happened to be in the squad room at Tollgate Road when someone from dispatch had mentioned an incident at St Wylloe's church. He'd jumped up, knocking over his cup of coffee. Had he offered to handle it, let alone taken time to get the call assigned to him? He played back his last thirty seconds at Tollgate. The duty sergeant hadn't been at her desk. He'd just run. "Lee's working here," he said, as if that was a good enough reason. "Tamsie's with him too."

Good enough for Zeke, who nodded. "Have you seen them?"

"No. That's Jory Stark's yard over there, and it looks like the back door's locked. Lee might have taken her into the church. She's pretty keen on churches, for a table-turning demon spawn."

Zeke let the old gibe slip by him. He was shadowed with confusion. "They're not inside."

"How do you know?"

"Because I've been in myself, and..."

"All right. What's inside that church, that you don't want me to go running in half-cocked and cause trouble?"

"Elowen."

The breath caught in Gideon's throat. Something about his inability to find his husband and his child, something about his sister-in-law's name—the combination of these things filled him with prickling dread, a need to lash out he could never indulge because he'd bring the house down, shatter Zeke's heaven and cause it to crash in blue-gold broken chunks around their ears. "What the fuck, Zeke?"

"I don't know," Zeke told him seriously, for once oblivious to his choice of words. "I'll tell you what happened, though it makes no sense to me. I did think I had business here, so I set off from Dark about an hour ago. I'd got about halfway when I saw Mrs Coulter in a layby."

"Mrs Coulter?"

"Yes, your child's exceptionally strange companion. She was holding... Well, I must have been mistaken, but it looked as if she was holding some kind of brush or broomstick and shaking it as if it was broken. When she saw me approaching, she threw it into the bushes and stuck out her thumb instead."

"She was... hitchhiking?"

"Yes. With Elowen."

The moon was almost full again. This time around, Gideon hadn't experienced the strange energetic surges and hungers that had plagued him before, but still he'd been sleeping badly. Maybe he'd nodded off in the squad room and was drooling onto his undone paperwork. "Elowen and Mrs Coulter were hitchhiking together on the road to St Wylloe?"

"That's right. So I picked them both up and brought them, and before you start jumping up and down, Gideon, Elowen is very upset. She doesn't seem to have much more idea of what she's doing here than... than I do myself, and she knows that any unscheduled meeting with you is going to make you hostile. It's time you forgave her."

"What?" Gideon pushed his cap back, distractedly aware of his own thick, close-cut hair, like a beast's pelt, so different from Zeke's fine strands that he had to be wrong about the bald patch. "I forgave her years ago."

"You know what I mean."

"No, I don't."

"Well, come inside. The vicar's in there, going spare about vandals and thugs in his church."

"I can't see anyone. And I really have to find Lee and..." Something caught Gideon's eye, high up in the turret. Surely nothing more than the sweep of a swallows wing, or perhaps one of the falcons employed by the council to keep pigeon numbers down. Following the movement changed his perspective, and he stepped back out into the sun, keeping a steadying fingertip touch on the granite wall. "Zeke. One of the ears has gone—the one to the southwest."

He didn't need to clarify. He'd called them *ears* all his life, the pinnacles which adorned the four corners of the towers of the ancient Celtic churches. They'd merged in his childhood with the idea of Batman, an alert, protective signal. Zeke, almost twelve by the time his baby brother had begun to talk, had made a couple of efforts to teach him the proper word, then, in an unusual surrender, had given up and adopted the childish term too. In one coordinated, silent motion, Gideon and Zeke rounded the southwestern corner of the tower.

The pinnacle had crashed down into the tall grass. It was much larger than it had looked in situ, set against the endless Cornish sky. Almost the height of a man, and it had broken neatly into three parts, the lichen-crusted ball from the top lying among the buttercups like a skull. Gideon realised that, ever since he'd heard the words *disruption* and *falling stones* back at Tollgate Road, he'd expected to find his husband and child connected with them somehow: at best, Tamsyn on a levitation spree, and at worst...

He shivered back into reality. What would Lee have been doing out here, in just the wrong place at the wrong time with his kid? If, out of the two remaining pieces, one looked like the body of a child and the other of a curled-up man trying to shield her, that was only his own pattern-making primate brain going about its work. Pareidolia, that was called. Gid had read about it in one of the science magazines Lee kept buying him, mostly for the pleasure, Gideon thought, of watching him fall asleep whilst manfully trying to plough his way through the articles. That kindly hand, lifting the magazine off his face... "They're probably in the village somewhere. Tamsie and Lee, I mean. She often takes him for a walk at lunchtime. Come on."

The great wooden door on the south side was propped open. Gideon heard the vicar before he saw him. Thin and small, cut from a different cloth than Zeke, he was trotting about anxiously between the archway that led to the tower and the row of chairs by the font, where two women were sitting bolt upright, watching him. "About time!" he exclaimed, setting eyes on Gideon. "I called the police nearly an hour ago. There's somebody in the tower."

"All right, sir." Gideon strode over to intercept him. "I'm here to help now. I saw that one of the ears... er, the pinnacles had come down outside. Was anybody hurt?"

"No. These women were in the churchyard at the time, but they came indoors for shelter, God be praised. There's a... a hooligan up there, some young layabout from one of the towns. He threw the pinnacle down, or... or *she* did. I thought I saw a skirt. I thought I saw... What is it they call the headgear the Muslim women wear?"

"A hijab?" Gideon struggled to keep up. He hadn't heard *hooligan* and *layabout* for years, though blaming outsiders for random troubles had recently enjoyed a revival on the peninsula. "You actually saw someone? A Muslim woman?"

"Yes. I don't know. There's nowhere to hide up there, but..."

Letting him go, Gideon leaned in through the archway and looked up. A narrow stone staircase followed the angles of the tower up to the wooden maintenance platform beneath the bell. There was almost no cover, though perhaps a skinny kid might be concealed in the shadows. "All right. I'll go and have a look."

"Hurry, please. And when you get hold of them, give them a good sharp shock. Discipline, that's what's lacking these days. Nobody knows their place anymore. Discipline!"

Pity passed through Gideon. What must it be like, clinging to this toe-hold outpost of Christianity where every change meant the uprooting of some long-held principle, every newcomer an enemy? "I'll do my best. Meanwhile, this is my brother, Ezekiel Frayne. He's minister of the Methodist chapel in Dark."

The vicar sized Zeke up, then clearly deciding that even a Low Church ally was better than none, held out his hand. "Reverend Charles Sawyer."

"And I happen to know those ladies over there, too. They're friends of mine. Nobody's going to hurt you or your church. Mrs C? Elowen? It might be a good idea for you and the vicar here to go outside and get to a safe distance."

The old woman looked at him serenely. She had an arm around Elowen, who was hunched up with her face buried in her hands. "That's just the thing, Constable. The girl and I don't feel as though we *can* go anywhere at the moment. It's very strange. I haven't felt so much power in years."

For God's sake. Gideon didn't have time for any esoteric nonsense from his daughter's self-appointed babysitter. He should check Mrs C's credentials. He'd done so before, of course, but when he tried to think of where and when, there was a blurred patch in his memory. And who else had called him *constable*, in that cracked, laughing old voice, long after his promotion...? "You can't leave? Are you saying that the Reverend Sawyer here is preventing you?"

Yes, there was the familiar cackle. "What, that whey-faced sprig? That mushroom of yesterday's growth, that..."

"Okay, okay. I'm sorry, vicar—she's a little eccentric." He cast an appealing look at Zeke. "If no-one's in immediate danger, I'll leave Ezekiel to look after you for a minute while I check this out. Elowen, please don't cry."

"I'm trying not to. But I want my life back."

I want my child back. That was what Gideon heard. He made a superhuman effort to set aside the static of old fears in his head; played her words through again. "Your *life* back? What do you mean?"

"My life. My own proper, real, true life, with Michel and my little Cadan."

She must be having a breakdown. Well, Gideon didn't have to like or trust her to be kind. He thought about the times when he'd failed, and he was ashamed. "Give me five minutes, and I'll hop you into the truck and take you back to them, okay? Siren and blue lights."

"You... You'd do that for me?"

"Of course I would. Of course."

She got her head up. She looked sick with fear, but as if some hope might be dawning. "When I took Tamsyn away from you, it wasn't really her I wanted. It was part of my childhood, the part where I realised my father loved Locryn best. I wanted it back so I could change it. I'm so, so sorry for all the pain I caused."

"Oh, Elowen." With a painful inner shift, Gideon understood the difference between true forgiveness and the grudging half-measure he'd doled out to her since she'd brought Tamsyn home. He held out his arms. She made a strange wriggling movement in her chair, as if fighting out of a too-tight sweater, and she ran to him. He let her in—all the way, not the stiff embrace of their usual meetings, deep enough that she could gasp out her fears against his shoulder. "There," he said, rocking her. "I'm sorry too, for what it's worth. About your dad, and for being such a dick to you myself, okay?"

She sobbed and choked, and gave the exact same bark of laughter Lee would emit when caught between joy and tears. "Okay."

"Good. Now, what's all this about you not being able to move?"

"I can. You freed me."

"What about you, Mrs Coulter?"

The old lady shook her head. "Oh, not me, dear. You haven't got anything I want enough to set *me* free. I'm surprised, you know."

"What about?"

"That there's any *greater* power. It's Alice, you see. And she's giving it her all."

Ice formed out of the warm summer air and dropped down Gideon's spine. Gently he pushed Elowen back. He took a shielding step in front of her. "Alice *Rawle*? Listen, Mrs Coulter—Alice Rawle is in custody, but if you know anything about her, or you think you've seen her here..."

"Who else? Who else could be..." Mrs C's gaze, normally cataract-cloudy blue, sparkled and focussed on the archway above Gideon's head. "Who else could be doing that?"

There was nothing to be seen. Nothing but plaster-dust in the air, catching colours from the sun and the stained glass... As he watched, the blocks seemed to shimmer, to slacken in their mortar like old teeth. A rumble filled Gideon's skull, a gigantic version of Tamsyn's innocent poltergeist percussions. "Shit," he whispered, backing up. "Zeke, get Elowen and the vicar out. I'll deal with Mrs C."

Sawyer had been looking frantically back and forth between Gideon and the old lady. "What?" he demanded shrilly. "No! I won't abandon my church. Do your job, Constable, and arrest that... person up there in the tower, that yob or—or immigrant, or whoever it is. They just need discipline. Discipline!"

"All right. Whatever. Just go."

"I... I can't."

The keystone at the top of the archway gave a weird jump and cracked in two. The pieces began their fall. Gideon shoved Zeke and Elowen out of range, but the impact, the crunch of granite on slate, never came. When he looked again, the fragments remained poised seven feet or so in the air, spinning gently. "Reverend Sawyer," he said, "I would truly appreciate it if you'd help my brother get these women outside."

"I can't. It's got hold of me too. I can't move."

Gideon lost patience. He strode through the trembling archway and planted himself solidly at the foot of the stairs. He raised his voice to reach the unseen presence above him. "Right. I don't know who *you* are, but I'm a police officer, and I've seen my little two-year-old girl float a rock the size of a dolphin over Bodmin moor. Show yourself, and maybe we can talk."

The shadows coalesced. Gideon tried to wipe his eyes clear of dust, but still they stung and ached with the effort of looking at the skinny figure at the top of the steps. Mrs C had been wrong, the vicar bizarrely right. A woman in a long abaya dress and hijab, her eyes black and terrible with despair.

All right. Gideon understood this. Maybe not the floating masonry and the ongoing whine in the air, or how these things were connected to the frail creature staring down at him, but he knew the context, the reasons. He'd had to arrest a woman called Katie Mills last year, as part of the Kernow Glan mop-up, for her merciless bullying of a Muslim *Big Issue* seller. Times were changing in rural Cornwall, and not for the better, never for the better anymore. Gideon barely recognised his brave new world, that had such people in it. "Okay," he said gently, extending a hand, palm-up. "Things have been rough lately, right? You've lived here all your life, I should think. Born and bred, and then suddenly there's people shouting at you in the street, yanking your scarf off on the bus. Is that it?"

The woman bobbed her head. She grabbed at the stone balustrade as if to steady herself. That was good. It meant that Gideon was getting through to her, an easier task than he'd anticipated. A small warmth of pride began in him, that he could read a situation so easily and well. "I get it," he went on. "Did you come here on a visit today? Look, this place is the backwoods even by Cornish standards. They're good people, most of 'em, but they don't see many brown faces. They might have stared at you. Did somebody give you a hard time, and you came in here to hide?"

He might be getting through, but the strange vibe was increasing, the bell emitting an unstruck moan of response. Still, the woman began a hesitant track down the steps towards him. If he could get her within arm's reach, offer her the shelter she'd come here to find...

Footsteps crunched on the gravel outside. Gideon swung towards the sound, keeping his outstretched hand in place, the move a practised copper's one. *You stay right where you are while I deal with this fresh piece of hell.*

No. Gideon's own piece of heaven. The church door flew wide, probably with more force and less ceremony than at any time in its centuries of quiet guardianship. Lee half-fell in through the doorway. Bizarrely for a man who'd arrived in such a life-and-death rush, he was wearing a daisy crown. He righted himself, focussed on Gideon. "Oh, thank Christ!"

Gideon had to bite back laughter. That was his own style of crime, wasn't it—to let rip with one blasphemy or another, usually in the presence of his godly brother? "Same to you," he said, relief putting a rasp into his voice. "I was worried. Where's Tamsie?"

"I locked her in the car. She's got the wind up about something happening here, Gid. She says it's Alice Rawle."

Gideon's scalp tightened. Could a short-back-and-sides stand on end? He hoped not, or he'd look like a fucking hedgehog under his cap. "It's not. It's just some poor woman who's been getting bashed by the Kernow Glan mob, or Ukippers, or Britain First, or..."

"It's not," a cold voice said, right by his ear. "It's *me.*"

He jerked back to face her. She was two inches off his shoulder, and her hijab was a fall of tangled pale hair, and her skin was as white as his own. "Shit," he breathed, having to clench his bladder in a spasm of pure fear. "What are you—some kind of shapeshifter?"

She cracked into raw laughter. "*You* can talk!"

***

The church was ready to fall. Gideon understood that. He understood that stone had been lifted from stone, the mortar between them transformed to vibrant soup, the whole structure dismantled but held in stasis for now by the thin girl beside him. There his understanding stopped. She wasn't wearing an abaya, just a T-shirt and jeans. Holding on to the thin blue line of his duty, which had pulled him through so many times when all else failed, he set aside fear and wonder in favour of getting the job done. Gunmen and suicides, hostage-takers and lost kids, the first rule was always the same: keep them talking. Establish a bond. "I feel like a bit of an idiot," he said, pleasantly as he could, "going on at you about UKIP and brown faces. I saw you as somebody you weren't. Did you make me see that? Because if you did, it was good. I'm impressed."

He'd talked a knife-wielding nutcase into submission outside the Bodmin Aldi by chatting to him for half an hour about what a great knife it was, what a smart consumer choice. But Alice Rawle had passed beyond vanity's reach God only knew how long ago. Her face was pinched with pain. Only the eyes were as Gid had first seen them, lightless and black. She was implacable. She knew his weaknesses, just as she knew the contact points between stone and stone in this church. "I did it for you," she said, not unkindly. "A glamour for Gideon Frayne. You all think a glamour's for beauty, but it's not—it's just to make you different."

"Okay. You were very different. Why was that just for me?"

"Because of the way you think. You hate what's happening so much—Brexit, the way every right-wing prick from Land's End to the Tamar took it to mean we want foreigners out, and everyone different too—that you've gone too far."

"Have I? That's extremely possible." No point in asking her how she knew. "What have I done?"

"You forget. You let yourself forget that a brown face can be a bad one. That sometimes there *is* a few pounds of semtex under a burka. That queers can be villains just as much as a privileged straight white male. I was Rima Malik up there, the Muslim girl

Katie Mills and her feral gang used to bait. If you hadn't risen to that, I'd have made her a lesbian too."

Gideon struggled not to laugh. She'd bull's-eyed the flaw in his nature, if it was one. The lesbian thing would have definitely worked. "You're talking about positive discrimination," he said. "I don't disagree with that, although you've got a fair point that I might have let it blind me. I can't speak for people of colour—the experience isn't mine—but I reckon we could offer favours and leg-ups and breaks for the next few hundred years, and not make a dent in the debt white cultures owe to the rest of the world. Not a dent." He let a smile flicker. "As for... queers, as you put it—there I *can* speak. All most of us want is to be treated like the rest of you. Heroes, villains, the usual mash-up of ordinary sods in between."

She was listening. Was he creating a rapport? The whine in his ears was louder if anything, his consciousness of the rafters and thick stone roof tiles overhead more intense. The red splash in the periphery of his vision was Lee, nose bleeding profusely in this high-frequency hell. "Sweetheart," he said, not looking at him, not caring who heard. "Can you get out of here? Ezekiel, can you take him out?"

They couldn't. Gideon knew this because he was rooted too now. Somewhere in the background, the poor shattered vicar was still ranting about discipline, yobs and immigrants: what did *he* see, when he looked at Alice Rawle? Zeke was doing what he could, though, everything Gid could have wished bar hauling Lee back into the sweet sunny world a few yards away and as distant as stars. He'd drawn Lee to his side and put an arm around him. He was holding Elowen's hand. And Lee said, with a faint lost scrape that cut Gid to the heart, "Katie *Mills*?"

"That's right," Alice returned conversationally. "The price of justice, you might call her—the kind your Gideon likes to mete out, Locryn Tyack. Got hold of some nylon tights and strung herself up in her cell a fortnight ago. She was a lost cause, wasn't she? Thick as a brick. Gambling debts, and a meth-head when she could afford it. No loss."

No loss, no loss. Gideon fought to believe it. He fought to hold on to his first, sane reaction: that Alice Rawle was just a clever psychopath, dipping into whatever she'd learned about him, picking out weapons. About Lee, too. "Lee," he said roughly. "Did you know Katie Mills?"

"Yeah. I gave her a cold-read two years ago. I got some kind of flash from her about Kernow Glan, and I sent you a text about it."

"I remember. That was the first we knew about them." Yes, the beginning—the opening of a tale that had ended at the Pride march in Falmouth, when Gideon had stopped a bomb and saved the day. Not in Kerdrolla, Story Town. "I pulled her in for assault on a Big Issue vendor, her and some of her mates."

"Right. So you just remember that, Gid. She *was* feral, a monster. It made me sick to be inside her head, even for five minutes."

Still.

The word hung between them in silence. *Still.* Gideon couldn't get inside the heads of the people he'd arrested, but he'd been inside HMP Eastwood Park. He imagined the four walls of Katie's cell. A pair of nylons smuggled in or, knowing her, nicked from some other woman heading out on probation. How had she done it? Fiercely he stopped himself: he didn't even know for sure that she *had*. "I've made mistakes," he told Alice harshly. "Overcompensated, maybe. Is that what you want me to say?"

She shrugged. The bony tips of her shoulders moved beneath her T-shirt like claws. "Not really. Rima was just my way in with you. The vicar kneejerks for foreigners as well, though not the way you do. And he's scared of big boys, largely because he thinks they might be the little ones he dicked around with in his last parish, grown up and coming to get him. So I did both for him—a hooligan *and* the girl. The hooligan knocked a pinnacle off his precious tower. I'm getting ready to pull down the rest."

"I know." Gideon couldn't understand why it hadn't happened already. His own nose was bleeding now, and his eyes and ears wanted to start. He made a huge effort and spoke through the shuddering air. "What do you want, Alice? I only ever saw you once—in Dark, last May. I think you wanted to hurt me then, so if that's the point of all this, go ahead and get it over with. Let these others go."

"Who stopped me?"

The question was a terrible one, so close to Gideon's heart and marrow and bone that he deflected it, pushing the answer away. "Who stopped you from what?"

"Hurting you. Who stopped me? Everyone else is here, aren't they?" She jabbed a finger in Zeke's direction, then Lee's, then finally back at Gideon. "Preacher, prophet, beast. Just like outside the preacher's burning church in Dark, in the time you keep telling yourself you don't remember. There's the old woman and Elowen, the mother and the crone. Where's the—"

Maiden. Preacher, prophet, beast—maiden, mother, crone. The maiden was Gideon's daughter, his own baby girl. He wouldn't let the word past Alice's lips. He grabbed her and spun her away from him, clamping one hand across her mouth. "You're a nutcase," he informed her savagely. "I don't know how you slipped your leash, but I'd better not find a trail of bodies between here and the Dartmoor Levels high-security wing. I do remember the fire, if that's so important to you. My brother's here, and Lee, but mind out who you're calling *beast*." He shook her, trying to remember that he was human. "As for your crone—you mean Jana Ragwen,

don't you? She was there too. But that's not her. That's just...
That's just..."

The air went still. The tortured vibe dropped out of it like bats
leaving a cave. Mortar turned from soup to substance once more,
and the ancient building's foundations received her. The old lady
sitting by the font—unimpeded now, neat and innocuous in the
Marks and Spencer fashions of five years ago—stood up and
brushed herself down, and she and the others watched in silence
as the hovering stones in the air came to rest in a heap on the
floor. "I'm sorry, dear," she said, turning a wry gaze on Gideon.
"Alice is right—about one thing, anyway. A glamour *doesn't*
necessarily make you beautiful—just different."

Gideon could breathe again. Properly, down to the depth of
his lungs. The inrush of oxygen felt like a high, and Lee was
mopping up his nosebleed with Zeke's big white pastoral
handkerchief, and there was just a chance that all was well. Setting
the weirdness aside, he was on balance glad to see old Jana
Ragwen again. "Granny," he said, with an unguarded break of
laughter in his voice. "I must have known it was you, or I'd never
have left you with Tamsyn. What are you playing at, though? Did
you stop all this?"

"Ah, no. No, not me, although you can let go of that poor
skinny child now, Constable—I think she'll do as I say. Put your
hands behind your back, Alice, dear, so the policeman can cuff
you."

Shame touched Gideon, that he'd kept his hand where it was.
Alice was passive in his grasp, a bomb disarmed, a suddenly
neutralised threat. He had no need to use excessive force, or any
force at all. Tamely she put her hands behind her, and he
unhitched the cuffs from his utility belt and fastened them, careful
not to hurt the raw, starved-looking bones. "Was it you, then,

Lee?" he said, puzzled at the undiminished fear in his husband's eyes. "Everything's all right now. Let Zeke take you outside."

"Not me," Lee returned faintly. "Not me, no."

"Ezekiel, then?" It wouldn't surprise Gideon, somehow, to learn that his brother had nixed the poltergeist activity around here. He'd never been a fan of it, had he? Lee and Gid seldom reminded him these days of his denouncement of their poor baby in their little flat in Dark, when he'd first encountered her gifts. Gideon did remember the church and the fire. He remembered a vision of Zeke in Druid's robes. "Don't be scared to tell me, Zeke. I don't understand, but I'm grateful, okay? Was it you?"

Zeke was still clutching Elowen's hand. Which of them was propping and comforting the other, Gideon wasn't sure: they were both white with shock. "No, Gideon," Zeke rasped. "This was not my work. I've been a fool, I know. I've lived in a limited world. Nothing is as I believed it to be."

Granny Ragwen shot him a look of pure sympathy. "Poor preacher," she said. "Down his walls tumble, one by one." She came to stand in front of Gideon, who realised in a prickling rush that Alice wasn't passive or neutralised at all: was fighting wildly inside herself, the cuffs only a symbol of a power beyond comprehension. "The trouble is this, Guardian Frayne. There only ever was, and only ever can be, one witch of Dark. So I traded my powers, such as they were, to return, and remember, and to find her and love her again. And so I have."

She stepped aside. Somewhere in the chaos, the church door must have opened. Standing there in gold and ruby light—and Gideon couldn't believe it, couldn't believe that out of all the madness and trouble of this day, this one bête-noire of his, this bloody thorn in his side, would come to put the cherry on it—was Rufus Pendower.

Rufus, holding Tamsyn by the hand. She stretched out a finger, and Alice Rawle dropped to her knees on the stone floor.

Chapter Eleven
The Weight of the Whole World

The little girl was calm. And here they all were, at Alice Rawle's command, as she'd predicted. Preacher Ezekiel, Lee with his unwilling, unwanted prophetic power. Gideon himself—the beast, as he'd tried to tell Lee in the grip of that old fever dream. Granny Ragwen, sacred crone, and Elowen, who staunchly as Gideon had tried to deny it was everything to Tamsyn in her way, flesh and blood, the sacred source. Mother to the maiden.

Rage came more easily than acceptance in this wild confluence: Gideon turned on Rufus, a growl burning out of his throat. "You brought my *child* into this place, Pendower?"

Rufus blanched. He'd made an effort today, was shaved and neatly turned out in his uniform. "She was in the car," he quavered, trying to hold up his chin. "She was locked in. It's hot. I heard there was an incident here, and I... I was frightened for Locryn. So I came, and she was beckoning to me. Asking me for help. I had to let her out."

To Gideon's surprise, Lee began to laugh. The worst of his nosebleed had stopped. He pushed away from Zeke with a grateful backward glance, and strode over to Tamsyn, who put up her arms to be hoisted off the floor. "I should've remembered," he said. "Who she is, I mean. If she'd wanted to be out sooner, she'd just have pulled up the locks from the inside. What did you do, Rufus—break a window?"

"Yes. I was careful, though. I told her to cover her eyes."

"I'm sure you did. She was waiting for you, I should think. She always tries to do things the normal way if she can, and she likes you. Don't you, Tamsie?"

She nodded solemnly. "Do like. Do like Ofus."

"Back to the baby-talk, sweetheart? You should've heard her earlier, Gid—we had proper, whole sentences for a while. And you have to hear her trying to say *difficult*. It's hilarious."

Rufus was staring at Lee and the little girl as if they'd been a ship with everything he'd ever wanted in the hold, about to disappear over the horizon. "She always did like me," he said wonderingly. "She gave me my own special name. And I was here the last time too, wasn't I, with you and Zeke and Gideon. Elowen too, and that old lady over there who looks like Mrs Ragwen, though of course it can't be. I haven't taken my meds today, I'll admit. But I belong here, don't I? I have a place in all this."

Jana Ragwen broke the hollow silence that ensued. "Goddess knows," she said, "the child tried to make one for you. She's used you as her... vector, I suppose, her channel for covering distance when she wants to be ordinary. You've been falling through the cracks, and she tried to save you from that. But some souls do just fall, as if they missed their footing at the beginning of their lives. Their timing's wrong. They fall for the dying and the doomed, reach out for what's not theirs to try and catch themselves on their way down. I'm sorry, Sergeant Pendower. You do have a place in this world, but it's with Daisy and your little boy, and that's not enough for you, is it? That's why Daisy didn't come, not this time around. She knows."

Gideon's radio crackled. The sound was so prosaic in the building's resanctified hush that he flinched, then fiercely composed himself. Whatever madness had just unfolded here, he'd arrived with a job to do. He unhitched the radio, pressed the pickup: listened while the Tollgate Road dispatch alerted all units in Launceston, Bodmin and points west that Alice Rawle was at large. Dangerous, in possession of some unknown weapon, on no account to be approached without backup. Gideon thumbed the transmitter. "Dispatch? Gideon. I have Rawle in custody inside St Wylloe's church, half a mile southbound off the Boskellan junction. She's... disarmed, but I'll take any backup you've got."

He heard the click as the dispatch officer switched to a single channel. "Gid? Get away from her. Clear anyone near her out of the way if you can. AFO's on standby in Penzance. They can be with you in ten, but you have to get clear."

Gideon repressed a freaked-out chuckle. In Penzance, the authorised firearms officer probably meant his old mate Jim Squires with a shotgun. "I copy that, dispatch. We'll try and hold out."

"I'm bloody serious, Gideon. Half the staff on her Dartmoor Levels ward are disabled and bleeding out of their ears. She must have gone via Launceston station, too—Sergeant Lennox is dead, and two of her constables. Treat Rawle as an unknown and deadly quantity. Cuff her to the pulpit or whatever the fuck you've got and get out of there. Dispatch out."

The radio's speaker-range was localised but good, the acoustics in St Wylloe's excellent. Gideon looked into the ring of shocked faces around him. Only Tamsyn seemed unconcerned. She'd taken off Lee's daisy crown and was examining the centre of one flower, little face abstracted and serene. "She's really doing this, isn't she?"

Gideon asked Lee dazedly, his voice hollow in his own ears, empty and lost. "Controlling her."

Lee nodded. Tenderly he jounced her, settled her more closely against him. "She's not even trying. Christ, Gid—Lennox is dead?"

"And God knows how many others." Slowly Gideon moved to stand in front of Alice Rawle. Not a sound had come from her since Tamsyn's arrival, but spit had gathered at the corners of her blue-tinged lips, and her eyes were wild. "Tamsie, sweetheart," he said, and Lee came to stand beside him, the child in his arms. "You're my good girl. You saved all your friends, just like you did at the Cheesewring at Uncle Zeke's picnic."

She looked up at him. Her gaze was fearless, full of love, but the wildest, blindest silver he had ever seen. She pointed to the daisy's golden heart. "Fibonacci sequence, Dada. The spirals grow outwards, all the little suns. One, one, two, three, five, eight, thirteen. Not dickifult."

Gideon choked on thin air. "*Dickifult?*" he mouthed at Lee. "Maybe not for you, kiddo. Other people... Other people might not understand. Do you understand about Alice?"

"Some things. I think she's like me, but Lee says no." She flicked a tiny gesture in the kneeling woman's direction. "She can tell you better. Alice, tell."

"Wait." Quickly, out of deepest instinct, Gideon made a gesture of his own. He met his daughter push for push, drawing on the loving discipline he'd established in her earliest childhood. "Tamsie, this is hard, because Alice would've hurt all of us. Once someone's under control, though, like you're..." He hesitated, struggling to believe that the force holding Alice Rawle still was coming from his daughter. "Like you're controlling her now, we have to treat her well. We can't leave her kneeling on the ground."

Silently Tamsyn absorbed this. He could see her measuring his words against her own ideas of justice. She nodded, as if finding a workable match, and a heavy oak chair shot across the stone flags from its place by the wall. The vicar gave a moan of pure, sick fear. "Discipline," he repeated, and Gideon wondered if that was the last word he had left in him. "Discipline. All she needed. A firm hand. But she was a boy when I first saw her. I never touched those boys in Blackwood parish. It was years ago, and anyway they were all little liars and thieves."

That was in another country, and besides, the wench is dead. Gideon and his daughter exchanged a look. Tamsyn made the smallest running movement with her index and middle finger, and Sawyer jerked upright. He looked frantically all around him for the source of the compulsion seizing his limbs, and then he headed for the door at an awkward, high-kneed trot. "Gently," Gideon advised the little girl. "He's old." She nodded, and Sawyer's pace dropped to a walk. These nuances of control were costing her nothing: the door eased open soundlessly to let him out into the sun.

Carefully Gideon lifted Alice Rawle into the chair. It was hard to touch her, like trying to handle an electric eel, all bones and repulsion. Hard to handle something that would kill him on the spot if unleashed. He had perhaps five minutes before the Penzance officers arrived, five minutes to resolve and neutralise this threat, because Alice would never give up. She'd torn her way across the county to get here and would tear on. He couldn't stop her. If he got at her reasons, would he stand a chance?

He didn't know where to start. The air warmed beside him, and he looked up gratefully to find Lee at his side. "Can you talk to her?"

"I don't think anyone can, not and have it mean anything to her. The inside of her head's like flashing knives. Tamsie, you can make her talk to us if you want, can't you?" Lee waited for her staunch little nod. "Okay. Don't force her, though—just *let* her. Can you do that?"

What Tamsyn couldn't understand was why any of this was a problem. Gideon knew the look well—the crease in her brow that appeared whenever she discovered a new lack or failing in the adults around her. Only her inborn kindness restrained her from an outright gawp. She laid a hand on Lee's chest like a protective five-pointed star: said, absently, as if more intrigued by her Fibonacci daisies, "Alice? Tell."

Slowly Alice raised her head. "You stopped up my *mouth*, witch?"

"She'll stop it again if you don't keep a civil tongue in it," Lee said unexpectedly. "Elowen? Come here for a minute, will you?"

Elowen darted to his side. She put her arms out for Tamsyn just as she would have for any other child. Whatever demons of loss and neglect had tormented her, they were gone. Gideon had a glimpse of the fully engaged human soul she could become, and his own sense of nightmare ebbed. There she was, shoulder to shoulder with Lee, his sister and comrade at last. "Do you remember us?" she asked, her voice and gaze searching, gentle. "We went to your dad's summer school one year. I thought you were the most wonderful person I'd ever seen. What happened to you, Alice?"

"Carriers," she croaked, as if the word had been dragged out of her. Tamsyn made a small, sleepy gesture, and she went on in a rush, "You two were carriers. I knew it straight away. My father wanted you both, but I said not to bother, I said to wait for one of you to have a child. Just carriers."

"For what? Psychic gifts, telekinesis?"

"Sometimes. Yours are just party tricks, though. He wanted 'em weapons-grade."

Gideon shivered. "Weapons? Is that what I found at the site of your father's school—a place where children like you were made into weapons?"

"A place where they tried. My father was frightened of me, Guardian Frayne. Frightened and broke, and you see I'd killed my mother in a temper fit the year before, so he didn't know what to do with me. I didn't have to touch her—just raised my hand, and..."

She tried, one arm twitching against the restraint of the cuffs. The air around her became bright. Elowen gave a faint gasp and rocked Tamsyn until the movement ceased. "Did they hurt you there, Alice? At the school?"

"What do *you* think? My father dropped me and his school and all the other kids there like a hot potato on General Bolton-Reeves when he came calling from his military lab on Dartmoor. Reeves had been searching for years. Something in the soil, he said it was, or the radon gas, or the quartz getting crushed in the granite, but Cornwall's always been full of carriers—pellar-kind, like *her*," she spat out, jerking her head in Granny Ragwen's direction. "Psychics and tarot readers, witches and little prophets. They were no good, though. Reeves broke dozens of 'em before he worked it out. He had to wait for their children."

Lee had stood quietly through this exchange. "Children like Tamsyn. And... and you. Is that what you were doing in Dark that day, with Bolton-Reeves? Looking for others?"

"Ah, yes, that day in Dark. He'd drive me round the villages. I could sense 'em, you see—smell them, almost, and your girl was like a rose, or a fresh-cooked pie. Oh, I wanted her! I thought maybe, if I handed him the greatest of them all, he might let me go." A terrible grin sliced across her face. "But your beast *growled* at me, little prophet. Do you remember? And your maiden picked me up like a paper doll and slammed me back into the car. I couldn't even open my mouth to tell him what I'd found."

"I'm sorry. Gideon wanted to help you. But you made the air sing, the way you were doing at the church here today. You made his nose bleed. Tamsyn reacted to that."

"I don't care why she did it. I'd found her. I'd felt her power—just the tiniest push of it. So I went back to the Bowithick school, where Reeves had made a kind of a teacher of me, showing them how to fly rocks and explode sacks of cement from the inside, to see if they could do it to human beings. I went back, and I gathered the children together, all those little Cornish daisies who were nothing, nothing compared to my new rose, and I wiped their minds clean with one sweep. I didn't want to hurt *them*. They helped me tidy the school up, then I called their parents to come and take them home. That night I got into the general's mind while he slept, and I exploded *that* from the inside. I wanted Tamsyn, you see."

"But you couldn't have her."

"No, no. Oh, how you and the beast shut me out! You wouldn't even talk about me. And you don't even know about her, not one bit! You don't know what she's done."

Sirens began to drift on the warm air. The sound recalled Gideon to himself, or at any rate to the part of himself he could understand and bear: the police officer, the working family man. If Alice Rawle said *beast* one more time, with that mad glimmer in her eyes, he'd have to shed his skin and eat her whole. "I've heard enough," he barked. "Alice Rawle, I'm arresting you on suspicion of murder. You have the right to remain silent, and you'd better bloody exercise it. Anything you say—"

"*Gideon.*"

He jumped. Lee had laid a hand on his wrist and was watching him with silver-jade eyes as eerie as his daughter's. "Don't let her get to you," Gideon commanded. "Whatever you're seeing, she's probably making you see it. Don't let her mess with your head."

"I'll try. In a few minutes, though—when the Penzance squad gets here, she'll either be taken away, or something... something dreadful will happen."

"She'll just be taken away. I don't know how she got the drop on the staff at the Levels and those poor bastards in Launceston. Maybe it wasn't even her."

"You know it was. You know who's stopping her now. I have to talk to her. There are some things I have to know."

Gideon exhaled explosively. Then, because Lee was right, and there was no ocean of denial deep enough, he nodded at Tamsyn, who was plainly looking to him for permission. "All right. One minute. Tamsie, switch her back on again for Lee. Then I'll take you home for ice-cream and a normal childhood, I swear."

She smiled at him with heart-wrenching sweetness. She always played along with him when she could. "Alice, tell."

Alice's head snapped round with the blind greed of shark. "What shall I tell?"

"Tell me, Alice. Please." Lee dropped to one knee in front of her. It was his sympathetic posture when talking to a child or a grieving parent sunk onto a sofa or bed, but somehow there was pleading in it, a surrender. Gideon wanted to haul him back upright. "Tell me about the Launceston schools. What were you doing there?"

"*You* were there, little prophet. I was riding your mind. Wherever you go, these children of old Kernow—not the carriers but *their* children, Tamsyn's generation—they start to shine, and I can see them. If I couldn't have Tamsyn, I'd have one of them, I'd take it and train it and aim it the way I was taught."

"But I didn't sense a child like that in those schools."

"You didn't have to. Does a horse have to know its rider's destination?"

"Oh, God. The ghosts of Beaumont Hall."

Alice emitted a faint, whistling laugh. "Oh, yes. Everyone loves you, don't they? Even the spirits you've come to exploit for your shitty little show, even them, Peg the housemaid and sailor Johnny. Old Colonel Henry, trying to warn you! I took his wolf's-head staff, the one with the flute inside, and I blew it for you, little prophet, and someone who loves you will die. Someone who loves you will die."

"That's the Beaumont curse, Alice. Not yours."

"Oh, I know. I was just playing, though that one will come true. My curse is better by miles."

Better by miles. She sounded like a boastful kid in a playground, and Gideon would've laughed if she hadn't been stopped an inch short of demolishing a building around him. "Mind what you're saying," he rumbled. "Curses have a knack for flying home."

"Who told you that? Have you been listening to the witches, to old Granny Ragwen? Not your preacher father, and not..." The knife-blade smile gleamed again. "Not your mother. Your mother loves Lee, doesn't she? Not *Ma*."

Gideon took a step towards her. Lee shot out an arm and held him back. "No, Gid. I need to hear. Is that what you're doing, Alice—cursing us? How can you do that?"

"Because I'm like *her*, you little fool! Do you think it's just *things* she can move? She's done it twice for you now, and Ma's where it started, that old girl who should've died four years ago at winter solstice."

"No." Gideon dropped wholesale into the world of her madness, because Alice couldn't know this, couldn't know how he, Zeke and Lee had sat by Ma's bedside and watched her fade.

"I made a journey. I found where the paths of Ma's life divided, and Tamsie..."

"Tamsyn was just a baby, asleep in a cot next door. She was only two and a half when you destroyed everything you cared about in Story Town, and Jana Ragwen stood in front of the burning church and asked her to lift the weight of the whole world. But it wasn't the world she turned back on itself, Guardian Frayne. It was *time*. She can't keep doing that, can she? Can't keep fixing what you break, giving you back the things you lose. Curses do come home, and miracles, too. Where's your bracelet, beast? Where are your wedding rings—yours and the prophet's? I've been *working* on the pair of you. Haven't you felt things falling apart?"

The effort not to recoil wrenched muscles in Gideon's spine. If he fell back from her—if he showed fear, he was lost. His life was beautiful, a seamless whole. As for his bracelet and his ring, the first was missing, but that was okay. Lee would find it in the house somewhere, just as he always found and gave him exactly what he needed every day. And he never took his plain gold band off. The tendons in his hands had thickened a little over the past five years, just as every part of him had solidified and grown stronger: the ring was set firmly in place. The patch of skin there felt cold, strange, but that didn't matter. If he didn't look, he didn't have to know. "We're fine," he choked out, reaching for his husband, who stumbled close to him and took a bruising hold on him in return. "Lee and I are fine."

"Well, isn't that the lie that'll send you both to hell! What if I took down the shields Locryn's raised around his mind? Tamsyn, little flower of the field—how would you like it if I did that? What would you see?"

Only love. Only love, Gideon knew that. Lee hid nothing, especially not from his girl. He turned, skin crawling, bones aching, to find his conviction reflected in Tamsyn's eyes. But she was blank-faced, clambering down out of Elowen's arms. "No, Elowen. Hold on to her. Keep her away."

"I can't. Christ, Gid, you *know* I can't, not if she wants to go."

That was true. And if Alice's power was limitless, surely the only cure for it was Tamsyn's—limitless and benign. Surely Tamsyn would take the tearstained horror from Lee's face. Lee was fighting to be away. Gideon wouldn't let him go. He had to protect his daughter, but old Jana Ragwen was limping to intercept her, arms outstretched. "Tamsie," he called, through the staticky roar in his ears. "*Can* you stop Alice—properly, forever?" *Can you take the weight of the whole world?*

She would do it. She'd do it for him, because he'd asked, and he was her father. Suddenly Gideon understood the wrongness of that. Alice was shrieking, cringing as far back as the confines of the chair would allow. In the background, Zeke was yelling at him to stop. He tried. He put out a hand, and Tamsyn, who'd begun a track towards Alice, swung towards him instead. "Sorry," he said. "Sorry, my poor little maiden. Come here."

Alice's cries morphed into thin, inhuman laughter. "Oh, you... *pussy*, Guardian Frayne. Let her try! Do your worst, brat. We'll see who's the true witch of Dark."

Her challenge—the absurdity of being called *pussy*, after all this drama—pulled the teeth and claws from her for Gid, left him fighting laughter of his own. He'd have scooped up his daughter, but Granny Ragwen had got to her and was kneeling stiffly at her side. Gideon smiled: shook his head at Alice. "Where are we— kindergarten? You do *your* worst, Alice Rawle."

Granny had got hold of Tamsyn's chin. She was stroking her face like a chalice, whispering. "Do you see," Gideon heard, and the words brushed his mind, swift as dove's wings, fluttering. "Do you see? All the flowers we've learned, all our spellbooks and grimoires, little girl. They're so we can recognise this, the true flower of evil. We weave our circle round her thrice, and cage her and keep her from harm, and so at the end of her life she goes back to the deep dust and sparkle of things, and the Mother remakes her so she may return. And we return too, to find her and love her again."

Tamsyn nodded. She turned to the old lady, smiling. "To find her and love her again."

Alice Rawle stood up. She made a snakelike movement with her upper body, and Gideon's handcuffs clattered to the ground. She rubbed her wrists and looked around her as if she'd just arrived. "*My* worst," she echoed. "*My* own curse? I can do that in three words." Tamsyn wrenched round in Jana Ragwen's arms, but Alice ignored her. She jabbed her finger in the air twice—the first time at Lee, who cried out as if the movement had gone through his heart, and then at Gideon. "*You never met.*"

Tamsyn whipped around. In her movement Gideon saw a vibrant adult power. Alice went up on her toes, as if electrified— no, worse than that. As if something had grabbed her by the hair from above, and something else by her ankles from below. These two opposing entities—God and the devil, Zeke might once have said, or in symbols from Gid's own profane mind, the horses from the Levi's ad—gave one jerk. Alice snapped. The uses to which she'd been put had made a sparrow of her, a handful of feathers barely worth the bullet. She hit the stone flags in a flurry of soft thuds and lay still.

Instantly Tamsyn reverted to the child she was. She let loose one terrified yell, and Granny Ragwen scooped her up. "Ah, no, my true flower," the old woman cried, falling a few steps back with her and turning her away from the broken heap on the floor. "That's not how it works, not like that. Ah, you see it already—

213

but what a hard lesson, my Tamsie! What a hard, dreadful scourging for us all, and more than anyone for Guardian Frayne."

Gideon shook his head. He wasn't a guardian and he wasn't a beast. He was a policeman. A husband and father too, and he had to be those three things right now. A woman had just dropped dead at his feet. His daughter was shrieking, and Lee was folding down onto his knees as if some terrible side-blow had caught him too.

He couldn't move.

A big hand closed on his shoulder. "Gideon."

His brother. Zeke was already holding Rufus Pendower by the wrist. Gideon tried to form a sentence, but his mouth and throat were numb. "What?"

"Get hold of Lee and come out of here."

"Tamsyn."

"The old lady has her. Come on." When Gideon didn't respond, Zeke's eyes flashed, a rare but recognisable storm warning. "Gideon! This is what happens when mortal men seek to toy with forces beyond their control. This is a house of God, and be assured that if evil has been unleashed here, a greater power of good will redress it. You have to come with me now. Take hold of your husband and come."

Mortal men, evil, the power of good. The start of his usual harangue. On some level Gideon had missed the rants since Zeke had acquired twin boys, some perspective and a sense of humour. There was something reassuring about his hectoring voice now, a rope of reality thrown to him across a roaring gap. Even if Gideon couldn't move, perhaps he could obey.

His colleagues were arriving. They passed him in black-clad blurs. The AFOs wore natty peaked caps, not just Jim Squires with a shotgun but a whole team of them, the Penzance and Truro and Bodmin squads combined. Jim was signalling to them with a tight-wound calm Gideon knew well: *keep it together, lads, but get the bastard. Make a perimeter.* Lennox might not have been popular, but she'd been one of their own.

The bastard was already down. Gideon tried to lift Lee away from her body. "Come away, love," he said, because that was what Zeke had said, more or less. In the background he could hear the confused shouts of the arriving teams: *where is she? Is that her on the ground? She's just a girl.*

Yes. Stripped of savage power, Alice was just what the world called a girl. Thin, under forty, unlikely to snap back with a feminist's insistence on *woman*. Her hair was in pale rat's tails on the flags. As Gideon watched, Lee put a hand to the back of her skull and gently raised her head. "Alice? Alice, can you hear me?"

"I can hear you, Locryn."

Her voice was like sand across paper. Gideon, who'd thought his child had killed her, hauled in a breath of relief and disappointment mixed and crouched beside Lee. Girl or not, safety catches were clicking off in the circle of men around them. Some crimes caused coppers to care less about intervening bodies than others. "We've got to go," he whispered, but Lee was set like rock. "Lee, please. She's not our problem now."

"She's mine. Alice," he whispered, and the desperation in his voice sent a pang of fear through Gideon, the nearest approach to panic he'd experienced since the Beast had chased him home across the moor. "Alice, do you know the story of Sleeping Beauty? The fairytale?"

She smiled, a tiny flicker. "I know everything now."

"All right. The baby princess, Briar Rose, is getting christened, remember? And the parents invite seven good fairies to give her their gifts—beauty, grace, goodness, all the rest of it. But there's this one poor old fairy who's been forgotten, and she's furious, so she says that one day Briar Rose will prick her finger on the spindle of a spinning wheel and die."

"I get it. You're the seventh fairy."

"That's right. The one who hasn't given her gift yet." Lee eased Alice up into his arms, and Gideon helplessly held out a hand to the surrounding gunmen. "She tries to take off the curse, Alice, but she can't. The old fairy was too badly treated, too hurt. So her gift's that Briar Rose will only fall into a sleep, not die."

"But you... you don't have any gifts. Nothing that I want, anyway. Not now."

"No, but suppose I changed the curse. I know you can't take it off. But you could lay it all on me."

Jim Squires had had enough. "If that woman's talking," he barked, "I want her. I don't know what's happened here, Gideon, but I need you and Lee to step away."

Gideon needed that too. He took Lee by the armpits and lifted. This time Lee didn't resist: laid Alice down, turned to Gid with a look of pure love and reached up for him. And Gideon heard Alice Rawle whisper, with perfect last-breath clarity, "All right, little prophet. Done."

Chapter Twelve
The Widening Gyre

Tamsyn wouldn't stop crying. Nor would she let go of Lee. He jounced and rocked her. The delicately chubby arms and legs of her infancy were longer now, and carting her around like a sack of animated compost wouldn't always be a possibility, Gideon knew.

Still, Lee could manage her for now. She'd attached herself to him with a baby bat's determination. Wildly abnormal for her, but such a daily-bread scene in most families that Gideon let it settle like a poultice on his heart. Everything *was* normal. Lee had carried his squalling burden into the shade of the cherry tree, where Granny Ragwen was sitting on a tombstone beside Elowen, companionably holding her hand. Ezekiel, stone face unreadable, was watching over them all. Rufus Pendower had recovered to the extent of hovering around Lee and the baby, offering suggestions to quiet her.

Lee wasn't paying attention. Seeing Gideon emerge from the church, he strode over to meet him, finding a daily-bread smile. "Everything all right in there?"

"I think I have new standards for *all right*, but yes. The paramedics are looking after Alice."

"She's not..."

"Dead? No. She's completely unresponsive, but she's breathing. It's like somebody just... switched her off."

Tamsyn's distraught cries stopped. She laid her flushed little face on Lee's shoulder, her own breath catching and hiccupping. "There," Lee told her calmly, stroking her hair. "Not the world's cutest little homicide after all."

"Stop. It's not funny," Gideon said, beginning a grin anyway. "I don't understand any of this."

"Maybe we shouldn't try for the moment. Maybe we should just get our kid home. Can we leave?"

"Yeah, the AFO chief said we could go, though Lawrence wants all of us to go through interview to try and work out what happened here. That can happen tomorrow though, or... Oh, Tamsie. Are *you* gonna tell us what the bloody hell we ought to say?"

"Swear box," Lee reminded him absently. "All right. If we can go, I think we should. I want to be at home. Did she just save up all her tantrums for today, I wonder?"

"Out here? Or..."

"In there? I don't know what happened in there, Gid, but I'm pretty sure she saved all of us. I can't think about it anymore for now. Here's your bracelet, love—I found it under the bathroom sink at home."

He was lying. Gideon knew the sound of it—rare, bright, utterly benign. Nevertheless he put out his hand when Lee spared one from their daughter for long enough to pull the silver chain out of the pocket of his jeans. "Thank you. Oh, Christ, Lee. Where are our rings?"

"Well, it's obvious, isn't it? We both left them at home. If we think about some kind of alternative to that, we'll both go nuts. So let's get back and find them, right now."

Gideon swallowed hard. His world was on its axis, even if Alice Rawle had dragged a raw-meat trail across it on her journey here today. The Reverend Charles Sawyer was raving and weeping at a bewildered community officer, and the church was full of gunmen, surrounded by sirens and blue lights, but this was a knowable chaos, a bust of the right kind, assailant disarmed and under arrest. Alive, too, which made for a better outcome than Gideon had dared hope. Still, he shared Lee's impulse to run home, to the world he and his husband had created together. "Are you okay to drive?"

"Yeah. Not sure I'm gonna be able to pick this barnacle off me, but... Tamsie, if you want to come home with me, you'll have to let go so I can put you in your car seat. Or do you want to go in the truck with Dada?"

Sometimes she loved that. Gideon waited hopefully. He could strap her booster seat into the Rover, find a quiet stretch of the backroads and switch the siren on for her entertainment. It made her sing the chorus from Eminem's *Business*. Her sobs had faded out, but when Gideon moved to lift her from Lee's arms she clenched her grip tight on him and hid her face. "Oh, dear," Gideon said, trying not to let anyone see that he was genuinely upset. "Looks like it's all about you today, Mr Tiger."

"Ah, don't worry. You know how fickle she is. She'll probably change her mind halfway down the A30."

"Well, I'll be right behind you. And Zeke will be bringing up the rear in the family hearse." Glancing over his shoulder, Gid saw his brother still in place, still watchful. "He brought Elowen and Mrs Coulter here, so he'll probably give them a ride back too. If I tell you he picked them up in a layby because the old girl's broomstick had broken down, would your day feel any weirder?"

"Weirder than when I found out she wasn't Mrs Coulter at all?"

"We should've known that, shouldn't we?"

"I'm starting to think there's a whole lot of stuff we should've known. But I'm sure… I'm just so sure that once we get home and find our wedding rings, all this weirdness will stop."

"Okay. Look, you're not worried about Alice and her so-called curse, are you? We *did* meet. And all the other things she said, about the burning church and Kerdrolla… All that was just a dream."

Lee looked up through the green shadows of the cherry tree, and memory pierced Gideon sharply of why only an agate set in platinum could possibly have graced the hand of the man he loved. "I don't think I ever heard you say that," Lee said faintly. "Kerdrolla, I mean. Jesus Christ, Gid—*do* you remember?"

"Yes. No. I… I only remember a dream."

"All right. Please let's just go." Lee shivered, holding Tamsyn close, and glanced into the car park beyond the churchyard wall. "What about Rufus? I don't see his patrol car."

"Me neither. He must've parked somewhere else. We'd better check what kind of mess he made of your window before you set off."

A shadow fell between them. Taller than Alice Rawle's, unthreatening, even a touch of anguished comedy about it, but a shadow still. "I wish you wouldn't talk about me," Rufus Pendower said, tugging off his uniform cap and clutching it in both hands, "as if I wasn't there."

"Oh. Oh, sorry, Pendower. I didn't see you. I was just saying to Lee—"

"I know what you were saying. You thought I did something wrong by bringing Tamsyn into the church, but I didn't, did I?"

No point in reminding Pendower that the kid could've picked him up and floated him and the car in wholesale if she'd wanted to. "You didn't do anything wrong," Gideon said patiently. "She stopped Alice Rawle, though I'm far from understanding how. I'm glad you brought her. Are you okay to drive back?"

"No need for that. I came by taxi. I can book another to take me home."

Gideon looked him over. His uniform was immaculate, every piece of his kit in place. "Taxi? Where's your squad car?"

"Oh, I can't drive one of those anymore. I've been put on indefinite sick leave. I think they'll probably fire me once they work out how, but an hour after the counsellor left yesterday I got the call."

"Bloody hell, Rufus. I'm so sorry. But what are you doing here, if you're not on duty?"

"I am on duty. I have a place here. I don't care what that old woman says—she's had it in for me from the beginning, and it's worse still now she's come back from the dead. I have a place."

Gideon and Lee exchanged a look. They had ordinary married couples' telepathy as well as the gifts Bolton-Reeves would call weapons-grade. *They wanted 'em weapons-grade,* Alice said again inside Gideon's skull, and he hid a miserable flinch. The General was dead or disabled, the Bowithick school, as he'd seen for himself, nothing but an abandoned shell. All that was over. *They learned how to explode sacks of cement from the inside, to see if they could do it to human beings.*

Now it was Lee's turn to flinch, a reflex of sickened recoil, and Gideon hauled them both back into the moment, their immediate problems. *What the hell are we going to do with this poor guy?* "I tell you what," Lee said equably. "You come back with me and Tamsie, Rufus. She's a bit upset, as you can see, but she loves you, and I bet you could calm her down. Play I-spy with her or something. Then you can have some dinner with us, if you like, and one of us will give you a lift home." He paused, gasping. "Tamsyn

Elizabeth, I love the bones of you, but you are gonna strangle me if you carry on like that. Won't you go to Ofus for a carry now?"

Tamsyn surrendered. The change was sudden and horribly familiar to Gideon. Usually it came in the interview room, when a suspect heard that his cronies had sold him out and were singing his name from the rooftops. When the game was up and there was just no point in holding on or out anymore. Her arms dropped from around Lee's neck, and she held out a hand towards Rufus like a small, tired socialite hailing a taxi home after a bizarre and exhausting party. Tears sprang into Rufus's eyes. Whatever else had gone wrong with him, his love for Gideon's girl had been pure and complete. He lifted her away, and began a slow, slightly unsteady track towards Lee's car.

"I spy," Gideon began thoughtfully, sotto voce, as soon as he was out of earshot, "something beginning with... N."

"*Nutter*," Lee fired back instantly, and pressed his knuckles to his lips to silence a freaked-out snort of laughter. "Oh my God, Gid. Shut *up*. He's lost it, hasn't he?"

All kinds of things are getting lost today. I never take my wedding ring off; I just never do. "Yep. Whatever he had, it's lost."

"What are we gonna do with him?"

"I don't know. You're the one who invited him back for dinner."

"I just thought, maybe if he spent a few hours in a normal household..."

"By which you mean... *ours?*"

"Yeah. It was a long shot. But maybe you can call his counsellor while he's with us, and she can come out and sit with him, try and peel him back down from the ceiling of wherever the hell he's gone."

"Okay. Not the worst idea."

"And I don't want to manipulate the poor sod, but he loves his alone-time with Locryn and Tamsie. I'll probably have him calmed down by the time we get home."

"It *is* the worst idea."

Gideon spun round. There was his brother, right at his shoulder. "What is?"

"For Rufus to travel home with Lee. For you and Lee to be separated at all at this time. I can't explain this to you now, Gideon, and I don't want to waste time trying. I will drive Rufus. Lee and Tamsyn can go with you in the truck, and the two of you can come back and collect Lee's car some other time."

A pang of angry jealousy went through Gideon, and he stepped back, dismayed. What the fuck was the matter with him? He'd used to feel like this back in the bad old days of his relationship with James, when he'd spent half his time convinced—and had eventually been right—that someone else would come along, someone not afraid to hold James's hand in public and be *out* with him. Was Zeke suggesting Lee couldn't be trusted alone with Rufus?

Outrageous. Then, Gideon had never liked Zeke. Christ, how could he, with all the bad blood between them, Zeke's bigotry and resentment of his very existence? Gideon couldn't even remember when his brain had decided upon the familiarity, the fraternal sweetness, of *Zeke*. The starchy git's name was... "Back off, Ezekiel. Lee can do what he wants."

A flurry of movement in the church doorway made all three of them turn. A grim-faced paramedic had just backed out into the sunlight, at the head of a stretcher bearing a body so frail it barely disturbed the blanket tucked around it. How did it feel, Gideon wondered, to have to care for someone who'd burst human bodies like bags of cement, to wipe that person's mouth and tenderly lift them? The medic knocked the wheel framework into place with a blindly expert kick, and he and his colleague rolled the stretcher down the churchyard path between the nodding heads of the buttercups. Ezekiel would probably know. Like their father, he'd be enough of a hypocrite to bury her, spieling out some cookie-cutter elegy over her grave, even though he'd never known her.

Gideon had always hated that. Take the most bitter-hearted, backbiting old bigot in Dark village, the one who'd religiously spat on the ground after James had gone by on his way to school, and Pastor Frayne would stand there in the crematorium and call her a pillar of the community. And you couldn't tell Zeke and the pastor apart, could you? Not really.

Ezekiel. Zeke. Gideon swayed and rubbed his eyes. Alice vanished off through the lychgate, leaving only a single pale hair attached to the front of his vest and an echoing voice in his head: *I've been working on the pair of you. Haven't you felt things falling apart? I can do it in three words: you never met.*

He detached the hair. It seemed to tighten around his fingers with razor-wire power, a life of its own, and he rubbed it off on the rough lichen of the nearest gravestone, shuddering. These feelings about Zeke were the ones that had grown up with him, grown into him, until he'd met Lee. Lee, who'd taught him that even the least-loved of nature's children might be different after death, and a few kind words to send them on their way might not be hypocrisy but the opening notes of a cosmic symphony, a forgiveness beyond understanding. For some reason this comforting thought made Gideon's vision turn scarlet with sparkling rage. "Does *everyone* have to be forgiven?"

Zeke's eyebrows flew up. "*You* were."

"Oh, what—for my original sin? What kind of church comes up with that idea—little unborn babies with sin on them? I fucking hate that idea so much. If ever you breathe a word of it to Tamsie—"

"I've told you. I've lived a narrow life. I know I've been blind and a fool. And I *don't* mean that, no. I mean you were forgiven, back in... I don't remember. My head hurts."

"Sorry," Gideon said, turning to catch Lee's stricken glance. "Sorry, Zeke. I don't much mind who travels where, all right? As long as we get out of here. For God's sake let's just go."

***

Shade and sunlight flickered across the police Rover's windshield. Up ahead, Lee's indicator flashed as he pulled to the kerb to allow the ambulance to pass. Then he moved on, out through the last of the winding lanes and up to the junction with the main road. Gideon followed, leaving the careful two-second gap drummed into him from his driving lessons. Nothing worse than rear-ending your other half. Briefly lost in speculation about how the insurance would work, he almost did it, and he pulled himself sharply together.

The Rover was second in the motorcade, the hearse bringing up the rear. The travel arrangements had turned out exactly as his brother hadn't wanted them. Gideon wasn't sure how this had happened, except that Rufus had jumped into the front seat of Lee's Escort before Zeke had been able to get near him. Like Tamsie, Zeke at that point had appeared to give it all up, and had slumped wearily behind the wheel of the hearse, leaving Gid to clamber alone into the truck. It hardly mattered. They were all heading home, and just as well. Gideon had the clearest memory of offering Elowen a lift. "Oh, it's fine," Elowen had said. "Granny Ragwen says any broom will do, so she's off to the hardware store. I'll just hop on the back."

And that couldn't be right. Gideon was prone, he knew, to bouts of summer flu. They seemed to get worse around full moon, and he could see a beauty on the rise right now, a lacy ghost on the shining afternoon blue. None of this made sense either, so he in his turn surrendered, and just kept his eyes on the road.

The route back took them through Lamorna. Gideon loved this run. No banks of hawthorn blossom now, but the bushes towered and arched, a dense barricade full of birds and small creatures atop the drystone walls. Sunshine and shade, sunshine and shade...

A glare like a nuclear flash. Gid swerved, knocked his sun visor down and grabbed for his shades. Hitting his hazards to warn Zeke, he tried to discover the source of the light.

The fields to his left were filled with solar panels. The drystone and hawthorn hedges had been stripped away along the road's edge, replaced with raw pine posts and chicken wire. No care had gone into the installation's alignment: all afternoon all summer, the panels would blind drivers on the eastbound road. In the midst of this murderous silver sea, a single megalith shot skywards as if trying to escape. Lee was the man for ley lines and weird energies, but Gideon could almost hear the huge stone's ongoing whale-cry wail for help. So lonely, so lonely. Cut off from its network, severed, all alone...

Christ, it was one of the Spinner stones. The land on his left belonged to Mabel Pascoe, and last summer a body discovered in these fields had saved them, the delay caused by the investigation just enough to let a scheduling change go through. The Spinner stones were connected, and therefore the earth between them was sacred too. Mabel could farm but not build. Oh, the panels were a good thing in themselves, just like every wind turbine and green supply was good, but not here! Why here, for God's sake, on one of old Kernow's last stretches of unspoiled moor, when wasteland lots stood empty on brown-belt acres around half her villages and towns?

That question had been answered decisively last year. *Not here*, Historic England had said, and the JCBs and lorries with their loads of pine posts, wire and panel fittings had vanished from the Pascoe fields overnight. That hardly mattered, though. A battle waged all that time ago was nothing. Gideon had driven through here last week, and the fields had been green and intact.

He slewed into the nearest layby. Lee had done the same thing and once again Gideon just barely avoided him: hauled up the handbrake and sat gasping. The layby was a broad one, created for tourists who wanted to stare in wonder at the great standing stones strung out across the fields. Here DI Lawrence had gone to meet a lady known to Gid until then as her childminder, checked nervously up and down the road, and then pressed a passionate kiss to her mouth. The layby was right opposite the Pascoes' farm gates. Gideon could, he supposed, march through them and up to the house, find Mabel and demand to find out how she'd sold out her sacred trust for a gigantic, fully operational solar farm in the space of seven days.

Lee would most likely come with him. Ezekiel, too, pulling up behind the Rover. They'd all three been embroiled in the struggle for the land, and for Nate Pascoe's lonely soul. Maybe together they could make this travesty not be. God knew they'd done it before.

Lee unfolded from the driver's seat. He was white-faced and yelling, and not about the farm. Gideon had so seldom heard his voice raised in anger that he barely recognised the sound of it, and half-fell out of the truck onto the grassy verge that bordered the layby. Peripherally he was aware of his brother coming to join him. "What's going on here?" Zeke demanded. "Where did all those panels come from? Are they filming something around here? Is it a set?"

"What the hell for—Barn Wars?"

"None of it was here yesterday. I came out to visit Reg Penyar. You remember him—old codger who used to belong to the coven around here..."

Gideon tuned him out. Of course he remembered Penyar, old chicken-head, who'd have betrayed his coven-mates for nothing more than zealotry and vengeance. Still worthy of pastoral visits from Minister Frayne, apparently. Forgiveness as a concept was in the air today, flapping about like a flock of terrified doves. Gideon strode towards Lee's Escort. Rufus was out of the car too. An overhanging hawthorn twig had hooked his cap off and it was dangling there like an absurd fruit. He was backing off, face a perfect mix of defiance and defence. "Where did you go?" he choked out, staring at Lee across the hot metal roof of the car. "Who did you turn to, when he turned on *you*?"

Lee's hands were clenched on top of the open door. "Rufus, this is the last time I'm going to warn you. Shut *up*."

"No. No, I won't. I've lived with this, and all those memories, and he just got scot-free away with it, like he always does everything else. He nearly killed you in Kerdrolla, and where did you go? You came running to my house."

"Running? You *drove* me there. I needed shelter, Rufus, somewhere to be with Tamsie that wasn't..."

"Where? The House of Joy?" Rufus covered his face with his hands. "But that never happened, did it? Christ, I'm going mad."

Lee turned to face Gideon. "I think he is. Don't listen to him, Gid. Don't mind him."

"I don't. I'm just interested in... how *you* remember the thing that never happened, too."

"It's okay. I'm just playing along. Rufus, I swear to God, if you don't put a sock in it..."

"No. Not this time. What's the point? Everyone might as well know." Rufus unhooked his cap from the tree and jammed it on top of his spiky, lightning-struck skull. "I've tried to get over you, Locryn—but everything's over now, isn't it? Daisy's left me, and I don't blame her. I only really loved Amber—and you."

With an effort so intense that Gideon almost heard the creak of his knuckles, Lee let go of the door. He took a couple of unsteady steps in Gideon's direction. "Please don't listen to him."

Through static in his head, Gideon sought out the sweet, true new ways of perceiving the world which Lee had taught him. His jealousy over James had been a passive thing, sad and resigned, a waiting game. Every moment of his life with Lee blazed in his memory like fire. "You must know," he grated out, not caring that Zeke was right behind him, "that he could show me drone footage of the two of you having it off on top of Minions Hill, and I still wouldn't believe it."

Lee's smile shone out briefly. "Yeah. I know."

Rufus looked back and forth between the two of them. Some jealousies were of the active kind, Gideon knew from years of house calls to scenes of domestic affray, and would burn up their target rather than let go. "All right," Rufus said, like a man who'd set his house on fire and no longer cared to escape, so long as Lee and Gideon burned too. "All right. Here's something more for you, then. I've finished up all my research now. I've had all the time in the world, without a baby crying, and this is what I've found out. Your house isn't the house of joy, or even the house of the wolf. Chy Lowen means *House of the Wolves*."

Gideon sighed explosively. "For God's sake. Not this again."

"Right. Poor crazy Pendower, Sergeant Weird-Shit with his books and his obsessions. Well, now I know what it was all for.

You know who held a copy of the deeds to Chy Lowen? Baragwanath and Co, that's who. I walked in while the office was being searched and I just took them. And I found the names of everyone who's lived there in the last three hundred years, Gideon, and I chased back through old newspapers and police reports, and in every family there's always been one."

Lee spun to face him. "Rufus. No."

"Always one. So here's what you should know, Guardian Frayne. Chy Lowen, the House of the Wolves, is hereditary home to all the Bodmin beasts. Each one of them, nearing the end of his time, makes sure it goes to the next, just as Dev Bowe did for you. And this is all nonsense and moonshine, except that he has a watertight alibi for every moment of his escape from Lamshear Hall on the night when John Tregear was killed. It wasn't Dev Bowe. It was you."

"Is that what you call love?" Lee rasped, staring at Pendower hopelessly. "I thought you *did* love me, Rufus—far too much to say any of that!"

Lee needn't have worried. Gideon was distracted. "Lee," he said, holding out an unsteady hand. "Our wedding rings. I know they're at home somewhere, I know we just have to get there and find them, but... there's no mark from mine on my finger. No mark on yours."

"Oh, Gid. Don't look."

"I have to. What's happening? Why... Why are the solar panels here?"

"Some things are leaking through. I tried to seal the gate with Alice—to take the edge off her curse, have it all land on me, but..." Lee stopped, swallowed audibly, ran a hand over his hair. "If we'd never met, you wouldn't have gone out to the Pascoes' farm that night."

"I would. Why not?" This was insane, but the insanity had thorns like a wicked patch of brambles, snatching him, dragging him in. "I've known Nate for years. He'd still have asked for me."

"Not if you weren't around to be asked."

"Christ. Did I die without you? Because that's how it feels right now."

"Oh, darlin'. No. We never met in the first place. You probably just... went away."

"Lee, stop this. For God's sake."

"I can't. I'd give anything. But, look—what's happened here, with the farm and the solar panels, that's just something small. Maybe it doesn't get any worse."

Gideon broke paralysis. He strode to seize Lee's hand, grasped it tight and towed him over to Ezekiel, who was watching this unfolding scene with the same harrowed vigilance he'd displayed at the church. Well, Zeke watched over things. Like it or not, there he was, the stone eagle, deeply human now but still a witness, an arbiter among the unfolding chances of life and fate. He married people, sanctified their children, put them in the ground. "Zeke, *you* stop this," Gideon said helplessly. "I am not having any of this seventh-fairy bollocks where Lee throws himself under some kind of cosmic fucking bus to save the world. Make him stop."

But poor Zeke just stared. Gideon should have remembered that the pastor didn't decide about the hatches, the matches and dispatches: just dealt with them when they came his way, a kind of solemn midwife, a companion on journeys between the worlds. The only sounds disturbing the summer air now were Rufus Pendower's heartbroken sobs. "I didn't mean it," he cried, voice cracking up and down through its register. "I didn't mean to give up our secret, Locryn! But even now he doesn't hear it, even now he won't hear what he is. And you won't tell him, and so the whole world falls apart. How do you know he didn't die without you?"

"Because," Lee said distinctly, with a deep-laid rage Gideon had never heard before, "we never fucking *met*."

"But there's a thousand ways it could have happened. Think of all the things you saved him from. Maybe that's what the Beaumont Hall ghosts meant—when they said someone who loved you would die."

"Do something for me, Rufus."

"Oh, God, Locryn—anything!"

"Fuck *off*." Lee turned the full silver blaze of his attention back to Gideon and Zeke, as if Rufus had never existed. "Listen to me, both of you. I did cut a deal with Alice Rawle, and I don't have much time. I... I've done something stupid."

A thousand alarm bells went off in Gideon's head. Suddenly he was wide awake, gluing moment to moment, clue to clue across the last few weeks. He flew through inner data banks, every lost soul he'd encountered on his path through the wounded and desperate of the world. *I've done something stupid*—anything from bashing an errant spouse on the head with a pan to eating a month of prescription meds in one go. Lee had prescription meds for the headaches his visions sometimes brought on. "Shit. Something's wrong with you. Have you taken something, some drugs, or—"

"Jesus, no, you beautiful bloody idiot." Lee shook his head in disbelief: "Of *course* not. But I should never have driven, not when I'm like this."

"Like what?"

"I can't believe I did it. I drove Tamsie. It must be all part of... all part of what's wrong, like..." He swayed, put a hand to his brow. "I think it's coming. Like you not going to Trelowarren with me yesterday."

"Like... Oh, fuck. Yes. Why the hell didn't I go?"

"Alice, I think. At work on us, like she said—weaving her curse. But we let it in, Gid, just you and me. I should have talked to you, like bloody Sergeant Weird-Shit says. And you... Oh, God, my love, you wanted it. When some bad bastard does some evil thing on your turf, and the law can't touch him, you want... You want..."

He dropped to his knees. Gideon went down too, like a stone, in time to catch him and break his fall onto the gravel and daisy-starred turf. "Sweetheart? Sweetheart?" He drew him across his lap, propped him and cradled him. "Shit, his nose is bleeding again. What is it, love? A monster? Something I can unmask for you?"

Lee stared up at him. In the course of six loving years—even in front of the registrar's desk in Falmouth, clasped hand in hand while they said their vows—Gideon had never seen such a look as that, such a purity of devotion. He wanted to fall into it and drown. He'd been told by Zeke and Rufus Pendower that Lee was worth a hundred of him, that he didn't deserve to touch the hem of his robe. Yes, let him drop and drown and dissolve in that pure silver love before Lee himself worked it out. "Gid," Lee whispered. "My chain."

"What? Is it hurting you? Can't you breathe?"

"Just... take it off me."

Gid couldn't spare a hand. He glanced up at Zeke, who knelt awkwardly, reached beneath the back of Lee's neck and undid the catch. "There," Zeke said, with a deep, rough tenderness that was as new to Gideon as Lee's sudden rage at Pendower had been. "What do you want us to do with it, Lee?"

"Give it to Gid. Tell him to... Tell him to find me in the cave."

"I don't have to," Gideon broke in. "Christ, Lee, you're right here. I don't have to find you. Zeke, call an ambulance. He's sick."

"I will, but take the chain, Gideon. Let him see that you're doing as he says." Zeke eased the heavy silver links into the daylight, where they flashed and flared in the sun. He held the chain out to Gideon, who took it as if his brother had just laid Lee's soul in his hands, and then—a heartbeat before Gid could burst into tears of raw terror and frustration—pulled out his mobile and dialled.

Zeke's attention shifted to the verge by the Rover's tyre, where a sheet of folded A4 paper was fluttering, ready to dance off on the breeze. He put out a hand to secure it, shook it out and scanned it while he spoke to the emergency-services operator, dryly reeling off location and details. He was grey by the time he hung up. He held the letter out to Gideon. "They're on their way. This must have fallen out of Lee's pocket. You have to read it."

"What?" Gideon was too busy to attend. He was tucking away Lee's chain, making sure that Lee could see he was doing exactly as he asked, that he always would. He found a scrap of tissue and began to wipe away the blood from Lee's face. "Not now, Zeke."

"Yes. Now."

Gideon took the sheet from him. He left a bloody thumbprint on the letterhead of the Trelowarren hospital's radiography department. He read—carefully, in the circumstances—from start to finish.

Then he closed his eyes. "Oh, Christ. Oh, Lee, my own lad. No."

"They can save him, Gideon. If he goes to hospital now, he can be saved."

Gideon only heard the last part. His mind, in frantic recoil from all the things he should have known, should have seen, should have done, leapt barricades of time and swept him back to the burning church. The last mists vanished and he understood how it was that he'd stood in that firelight, blood on his hands, a world ending around him, and woken up next morning—no, *the morning before*—clean and forgiven, and everything newly begun.

His daughter could turn back time. He sat up, raising Lee in his arms. "Zeke? Get Tamsie."

His brother's face clouded. But he too understood the little girl's gifts, and when push came to shove was as much prey to human temptation as anyone. Had learned to love Lee just as much. He ran for the car.

He was back less than thirty seconds later: Gideon had counted each one in the jump of the pulse at Lee's throat. "She's asleep," Zeke said, and his words fell like stones down a well. "We can't make her do this. She's just a little girl."

"Oh, Zeke. Please."

"She saved Ma for us. She saved my sons on the moor. She's... wiped all the tears from our eyes, Gideon—changed the world twice. She killed someone for us today."

"No. No. Alice is alive."

"An empty shell." Zeke got down stiffly onto one knee, placed a hand on Lee's head. "Still," he said brokenly, "I will go and fetch her if you wish. We can try."

Gideon saw it, saw them trying. He wouldn't let Zeke bring her: it would have to be his own work, to open the Escort's back door and wake her up. For once she'd have cried herself to sleep. Her curls would be sticking to her brow, her fine skin flushed like Lee's in feverish dreams. He'd have to lift her out into the sunlight, carry her, turn her so that she could see her beloved Lee, one of the two souls appointed as her guardians and guides through this world, laid out flat on his back and bleeding. He'd have to hope the sight of that would trigger her gifts. "No. No. I don't even want her to see."

As if he'd finally done something right, Lee shifted in his arms. His lost gaze focussed. He raised one hand: placed it tenderly on

Gideon's cheek. "Find me," he whispered, and his smile dawned, the faintest reminder of the sweet light that had shone through all Gideon's days since they'd met. "Find me and love me again."

Chapter Thirteen
(Prologue to Volume Two)
The World According to Alice

The Kemps lived in a tiny mid-terrace house on the outskirts of Dark. Gideon had attended there every day since Lorna's disappearance. For his first few visits, the family had seized upon him like an angel. What he'd become to them now, he had no idea. He was pretty sure he wasn't helping any more. But he couldn't stop.

He knocked tentatively at Sarah Kemp's front door. After a few seconds Joe Kemp appeared behind the frosted glass. He looked very tired this morning, the waiting and watching beginning to take serious toll. He was one of the few in the village who could still find a smile for the visiting copper, and Gideon returned it gratefully.

"All right, Joe? How is she today?"

"Oh—about the same. Any fresh tidings?"

Always the same exchange. Gideon knew it could only alter now by a miracle, or the news that would end everything.

"Nothing yet. I just wanted to tell Sarah that Lorna's details are online now with the international missing-children's database."

"Thanks. International, though? She vanished while she was playing with the Prowse kids on the moor. She didn't hop on a plane to Marbella."

"I know, but..." Gideon hesitated. Joe had been fond of his brother for all his faults, and none of the leads to Alf had panned out. He was long gone. "Someone might have taken her out of the country. Anyway, it's worth a shot, isn't it?"

"I suppose so. Look, before you go through... Sarah's got someone with her."

"Okay. I can come back later."

"To be honest with you..." Joe scratched his head. "I'd rather you went in now. Sarah wants to try every avenue, but I'm not too happy—"

"Who's with her, Joe?"

"Somebody called Lee Tyack. A psychic. Now, Gid, don't be angry..."

Gideon wasn't angry. There was no point in spending out good rage on these sticky bits of fluff who attached themselves to the edges of a crime scene. Cornwall had plenty of them. The important thing was to detach them, send them blowing off on the breeze, before they could do any damage.

He strode through the narrow little passage. Sarah Kemp was sitting at the kitchen table, Lee Tyack opposite her. Yes, a fine example of the type—long skirts, gold bracelets chiming. Probably good-hearted: they usually were, and certainly she was gazing at Sarah with genuine concern. Organised, too. A file was spread out in front of her, and she was wearing unusually sensible shoes.

He planted himself by the table. He didn't often use his presence, his rugby-player bulk, to make an impression, but he wasn't sorry when the fall of his shadow made the psychic jump.

"Sarah," he said, gently as he could, unable to keep an ancient Bodmin rumble from his voice. "I know you're distraught. But I don't think you'll help anyone by listening to someone who's a well-meaning idiot at best and at worst a charlatan."

Oh, but he *was* angry, wasn't he? Beneath an aching shell of self-restraint, angry and betrayed that Sarah had chosen this path. The charlatan stared up at him, not visibly insulted. "Oh dear," she said. "I do seem to have come at an awkward time, Mrs Kemp. I tell you what—I'll go and make my other calls around the village, and I'll come back and see you later, eh?" With that she gathered up her folder and made for the kitchen door, nodding pleasantly to Gideon en route.

Sarah Kemp sprang to her feet. "What the bloody hell was that for, Gideon Frayne?"

He stared at her. Her eyes were raw from grief and sleeplessness. "I'm sorry. But I've got to protect you—"

"From my social worker? That was Sue Harley, you great plod!"

"Shit. Joe didn't say she was here."

"No, she came in the back way while Lee was talking to me. Oh, I see—it was him you meant to have a go at, was it? Why shouldn't I talk to a psychic, Gideon? What bloody good have *you* done, to try and stop me finding help elsewhere? It's been a fortnight—thirteen nights on that moor for my little girl, if she's even still alive. You've been useless. You've done nothing. You've..."

Gideon stared down at her. There was nothing—no friend, no kindly held-out hand, no salvation in the world, to stop him from vortexing down with her into the bottomless pool of her grief. "And did he?" he managed at last, over her sobs. "Did he... *Could* he help you?"

"No. He was totally honest. He said he sees..." She rocked herself, tangling her fingers into her hair in a spasm of fear and misery. "He says he sees monsters, but they're always wearing masks, and sometimes he can't take them off. He left when Sue Harley arrived. It's too late. You missed him. He's gone."

About the Author

Harper Fox has become a well-loved go-to author for fans of M/M romance. Here you'll find immersive tales of excitement, magic, drama, all underpinned by the ordinary processes of love, hope and loss in an imperfect world.

Harper has garnered critical acclaim for novels such as *Scrap Metal*, *Brothers of the Wild North Sea*, *Seven Summer Nights* and *The Salisbury Key*. She is also creator of the enduringly popular *Tyack & Frayne* mystery series. Many of her ebooks are also available in paperback and audio format. You can find news of her current projects and full backlist at her website, www.harperfox.net.

A northerner at heart, Harper has returned to her native Northumberland after a spell in Cornwall. She travels between the two as often as she can, and feels she has a home in both magical kingdoms. She is married to Jane, and owned by three cats.

Made in the USA
Coppell, TX
27 July 2020